The Nilwere

Tim Boiteau

Published 2024
ISBN: 978-1-960534-21-7 (Paperback)
ASIN: B0DKSYRCTM (eBook)

Written by Tim Boiteau
Interior illustrations from Depositphotos
Edited by Olivia Dean

Published by Grendel Press LLC
www.grendelpress.com

Contents

1. The Cinder — 3

2. Keep Out, Cinder — 23

3. Abbey Creek — 35

4. Deeper and Deeper — 51

5. The Thing in the Woods — 65

6. In Shining Armor — 81

7. Mistress Constance — 91

8. The Good Doctor — 109

9. A Charming Host — 123

10. The Library — 147

11. Love Games — 167

12. The Hour of the Mother — 179

13. The Smell of Blood — 193

14. Thingkley's Plaything — 203

15. The Next Mistress — 215

16. La Bavure — 229

17.   The Book of the Family   243

Epilogue   263

Acknowledgments   274

About the Author   275

Dedicated to Dongfang and Simon,
by my side through the journey from concept to book.

As I was in youth
Timeless as my trade,
Ne'er beyond death's door,
Born anew each day.
—an old spell

The Cinder

The thing in the woods found her.

She had heard fleeting whispers about the creature all her life, but it wasn't until Constance Dunn was twelve that she heard her first vivid description of the Nilwere.

"You got business in the city, you take Highland Road," advised Faith Sallyforth, a regular customer at Dunn's Fine Meats and Fancy Sausages. "Don't know why these witless couriers insist on riding down Forest—vanishing left and right. Why, the night of our wedding in Three Flocks, when Abe drove us back towards Canton, he took Forest Road against my protestations. Sure enough, a few miles out of town, I heard a faint rattle over the clop of hooves—*tick-a-tick-a-tick-a-tick*, it went, like an army of disciples striking their prayer drums—and this foul stench filled the air, and then, swear to the Father, I spotted it out there in the woods, massive as a mountain, wearing the fog like a cloak, and watching us with its hundred-odd milky-white eyes from deep in the darkness. I shoved Abe aside and took the reins and whipped our horse into a frenzy. The wardrobe my father carved for our betrothal gift tumbled out the back of the cart, but I refused to stop for it. Don't imagine I'd be telling you this now if I had. Either way, I can't pray at the temple anymore because of the sound of the drums. Whenever I hear them tapping, I smell that powerful swamp-gas stench again and break out all over in goosebumps."

"Quit spouting your tripe at the girl," Thurgood Dunn said, emerging from the backroom, apron smeared with gore. Her father's appearance having broken the spell of the story, Constance remembered to make change for their customer. "She's got enough of that to deal with being a Dunn."

"Oh, stuff!" Faith puffed with feigned indignation before proceeding to launch into a litany of complaints ranging from the cost of ice to the bullet hole in her parlor wall that no one would pay to repair since Sheriff Sykes shot dead the perpetrator.

Unable to get a word in edgewise, Thurgood retreated once more to the backroom. Having successfully driven him away, Faith lowered her voice, her apple-cheeked face leaning across the counter, giving Constance a whiff of licorice and stout. "You just go and pay Abe a visit at the Fairwater, Connie, and hear what he has to say on the matter of the Nilwere."

To the rhythm of hacking in the backroom: "Abe was purblind"—*whack*—"even back at the conception of time"—*whack*—"when you two exchanged vows. Yes"—*whack*—"I'm sure he's seen all manner of Nilweres"—*whack*—"through those binoculars he calls spectacles." A final, decisive *whack* served as an exclamation point—end of sentence, paragraph, and topic.

Faith gave Constance a look of warning and shake of the head as she accepted her change and wax-paper packet of chopped chicken, then offered both of them an obligatory "good day."

During a supper of mincemeat-stuffed squash that evening, Constance found her gaze wandering to the slit drum collecting dust on the hearth mantle, an innocuous bibelot no more.

Afterwards, Thurgood headed out to the Fairwater Saloon to bellow along to Abe Sallyforth's honky-tonk piano, and Constance, still skeptical but also eager to learn more, related to her mother the scene from earlier that day. Rachel Dunn was sitting at her workstation in the corner of the living room, carving a figurine of what appeared to be a rebel from the People's Uprising, its face masked with the vizard of a serene and beautiful woman.

"What do you know about the Nilwere, Mother?" Constance asked.

Rachel turned towards her daughter, the light of the hearth illuminating the marbled bloodstain birthmark on her face.

"I don't know about the Nilwere or the Rotbear or the Boondockie or the Monster of the Lakeland or the Ghoul of Abbey Creek or whatever folks want to call it, but woods that deep must conceal strange things, Connie. I've never been farther than Bowen's on Forest Road, and I wouldn't travel that way again. I had an uncanny feeling while I was out there, a sense that if I wasn't careful, if I took just one wrong step, I would be falling through the trees, helplessly plunging deeper and deeper into the woods, swallowed up and forgotten to the world."

"But loggers and couriers come and go that way all the time. It seems safe enough."

"Old Lady Yorin took Forest Road with her young beau many years ago." Rachel plucked up the wooden rebel and bench knife and continued to carve, pausing for dramatic effect. Even as they moved, her strong, lean hands gave off the impression of stillness, praying the figurines into existence with a mantra of knife blade whispers. "The story goes that they lost their way, and when she returned weeks later without her husband, she was a madwoman aged into the ancient thing she is now."

"Where did you hear that?"

"Mrs. Faith Sallyforth, admittedly." She smiled, turning back to her desk. The shelves above her were crowded with hundreds of minutely detailed wooden figurines—soldiers, bakers, farmers, hucksters, sailors, fishermen, bandits, harlots, heroes and deities from *The Book of the Family*—none of them yet complete, still waiting for the final touches to emerge fully into the world.

Constance watched her mother's hands work, bemused, trying to fit together Faith's account with what her mother just related to her, yet a coherent tale failed to emerge.

IN THE YEARS THAT followed, a recurring nightmare plagued Constance.

She was one of her mother's wooden figures, a painted cedar Constance Dunn that could be manipulated and propped up around the apartment, and a strange rattling sound haunted their home, a sound neither Rachel nor Thurgood could discover the source of. As the rattling grew louder, Constance realized that it was coming from inside her, from within her womb, and though she tried to tell her parents—to warn them that the Nilwere was coming to get them, crawling its way into the world through her insides—her panicky voice was muffled by wooden lips that would not part and a heavy, cold tongue that would not budge. In the apprehensive mornings following these nightmares, she would flex her hands and exhale with relief to find that the rattling inside her belly had ceased, her stiff flesh grown supple again, and she would whisper her warning into the darkness.

Two seasons after Constance's seventeenth birthday, the morning after one such nightmare, Faith Sallyforth entered the shop dazed and bereft of color, coils of gray hair escaping from the brim of her bonnet.

She blinked, looking around the small shop, then said, "Why, I can't remember what in the Family's name I came here for."

"Well, today is Dochday. Will you be wanting your brisket as usual?"

"Ah yes... brisket it is. Bless you, Fair Daughter. Bless you. Such a dear, dear, dear ..." she trailed off, losing her way to the noun at the end of the phrase and left to wander in a forest of adjectives. These were the last words Faith ever spoke to Constance—not even a distracted "thank you" when she accepted the wax paper parcel of meat with a scaly, ashen hand.

Several days later, Constance was returning from Lewiston's Knick-knackatory, her reticule fattened with a thick fold of dollar bills from her mother's figurine sales, when she discovered a clump of gray hair clinging to one of her brogans, growing out of its center a wizened finger as thin as a rodent's spine. She kicked it off, shuddering with revulsion, and sprinted back home, where she shut the door behind her, heart hammering, desperate to scrub her skin clean with a horsehair brush.

More and more Cantonites began showing signs of distraction and rotting gray skin, bits of themselves sloughing off as they roamed the streets, but it wasn't until the bodies began to pile up in alleyways and the sewage ditch in the center of Main Street that Mayor Increase Lancaster, proprietor of Lancaster Icehouses, assembled a town meeting. Ginger muttonchops and mustache glistening with wax, the mayor commanded the stage, towering over the hundred-odd restless souls in attendance, not a few gray-faced individuals among them concealing their hands in gloves and their hair in bonnets and bowlers. Though it was a chilly autumn evening, the mayor, a marine mammal of a man, wiped beads of sweat from his brow with a cambric handkerchief as he took matters in hand.

"Citizens of Canton, a plague has struck our dear town," he bellowed, his stentorian voice booming through the town hall, startling the nightingales that had taken roost in the shadowy rafters. "Doc Harwood suspects it to be a disease known as the Cinder, and rest assured we are doing everything in our power to put an end to this. I personally dispatched a rider to the University of Hemlock to obtain medical succor. In the meantime, Doc and I are appointing a team of Cinder Specialists to patrol the town, track and check the spread of the disease, and keep the streets of Canton clean!" The fatty folds of his neck quivering, he swept a beringed hand towards the left wing of the stage, where an unlikely assortment of Cantonites (not a few tipplers among them) shuffled into view, the sallow-faced and bushy-bearded Doc Harwood at their head.

Over the next few days, the Cinder Specialists, armed with buckets of paint and sable-hair brushes, stalked the streets of Canton, their beaked masks stuffed with nosegays to overpower the harmful miasmas that seeped out of the dead. Constance grew distracted from her book when she heard the plodding of hooves and the trundle of wheels outside the shop, and watched as a pair of stoop-shouldered buzzards appeared across the street from Dunn's Fine Meats and Fancy Sausages. The Specialists gathered up the anonymous gray corpse that lay on the stoop of the Grundwell residence, tossed it into the back of an ox cart already loaded down with a host of fly-enticing cadavers, and slathered the door with a thick red slash that seemed to drip blood onto the sill for the rest of that afternoon.

The following day, when she delivered plates of smoked sausage to Sheriff Sykes and Doc at the station, she found every other door of Main Street runny with red.

"Thank ye, Connie," the Sheriff said, the sparkle in his blue eyes gone that day. He took the plates from her and ushered her out before she took two steps inside the tiny, stuffy station. Despite his efforts to spare her the sight of what lay inside, Constance glimpsed the cots and moaning patients so gray and squamous they resembled charred logs. In the open jail cell, a harried Doc Harwood set aside a blood-spattered saw and wiped a spray of red from his face with a damp towel. "Be careful out there," Sheriff Sykes said, squeezing her hand, then shut the door.

As she returned to the shop, she couldn't help glancing towards the edge of town where the pile of bodies beneath Castle Hill reached nearly a quarter of the way up to the ruins that sprawled across the clifftop. What she saw transfixed her: the mound of bodies beside the gallows appeared to be moving. No, it wasn't the bodies, but the scores upon scores of rats scrabbling over the dead. She saw, too, that small feline forms crouched in the long grass of the baseball outfield near the cliff. One by one they glided up towards the mountain of cadavers, now disappearing, now reappearing in the rivers of wind-swept grass, before finally pouncing onto the putrescent flesh and coming away with juicy rodent specimens hanging limp from their jaws.

"They're not afraid," a garlicky voice rasped at Constance's shoulder.

She recoiled, turning to find Charity Hobbs breathing down her neck.

"G-good afternoon, Dear Mother."

"The cats have too many lives for the Cinder to do them any harm—yes, Fair Daughter, that's true." The old hunchback winked.

The butcher's daughter, ever agreeable, never contradicting, nodded her understanding. The beldame's face was caked with hearth ash, a crumbly dark-gray foundation that smoothed out the warty landscape of her face.

"But to outwit the Cinder one doesn't need as many lives as a cat—no, no, Fair Daughter—a snail-shell pendant would also do the trick," she said, her chicken claw of a hand pulling said charm conveniently from the pocket of her patched frock coat and dangling it before Constance's eyes. The snail shell in question was the size of a robin's egg, a brilliant topaz ringed with taupe bands, lustrous in the autumn light. "To trap and confuse the demon when it tries to invade the heart."

Reading the doubt in her mark's eyes, Charity sank her claw into Constance's arm and forced the pendant into her small hands. "Free of charge for this winsome girl, but the girl's parents will need protection, too—yes they will, yes they will—and Thurgood Dunn is too foolhardy and cantankerous a man to agree to wear a charm."

Before she knew what had happened, Constance had paid Charity seventy-five cents each for two straw poppets (two dollars total since Charity couldn't make change) and received instructions to stuff them with the hairs of her mother and father, cover them in hearth ash at night, then wash them clean in the light of dawn. There may have been too much of her father in Constance to feel these fetishes could work, but she slipped the pendant around her neck anyway, dropping the snail shell down her chemise so her father wouldn't spot it.

THAT EVENING, THERE CAME a banging at the backdoor downstairs (the entrance to the Dunn's home above the shop), and Thurgood stirred from his penny sheet and pipe, a dark expression falling across his brow. Constance had been absorbed in one of her Eton Brimley novels, and Rachel was in her workshop corner as usual, her knife blade unearthing the eyes of an impossibly minute babe. As the knocking continued below, shaking the house with its urgency, vibrating inside Constance and evoking her nightmare of the Nilwere, shivers ran up her spine, and both women looked towards Thurgood, the official answerer of after-hours callers. He rose, grumbling, and headed downstairs, shouting for them to cease their infernal rapping.

While her mother easily became reabsorbed with her work, Constance took the opportunity to dip into her parents' bedroom and, after a quick search of their pillows, found what she needed. As she brought the two strands of hair to her room, she heard heated talk coming from downstairs and crept to the landing, avoiding the creaky wood planks that she knew would betray her presence. There she hovered, peeking down towards the back stoop where several men wielding lamps and rifles were conferring with her father about a roundup of some sort. Thurgood spat at their feet, barked an obscenity, and slammed the door in their faces before he stomped back upstairs, too vexed to notice his daughter ducking into her room.

Late into the night, Constance startled at each report of the rifles, and though she tried to keep track of the shots, as she fell in and out of sleep, she soon lost count. Early the following morning, in the cold, dim light of predawn, Constance brought her ashy poppets outside to the Main Street pump, when she heard a commotion down the street and saw a small crowd gathered before the mayor's house. The poppets clean, Constance stuffed them into her apron pockets and hastened down the boardwalk to see what all the to-do was about.

There, strung upside-down from the picket fence surrounding the mayor's garden, were the carcasses of some fifty cats, their faces frozen in devilish grins, their blasted innards dripping onto the boardwalk.

Hours later, while the two women were preparing breakfast, Constance noticed an alarming streak of gray in her mother's dark copper hair. When she pointed this out, Rachel rushed to the looking glass, snipped it out calmly, then tossed it into the hearth fire. Breakfast preparations continued, but by the end of the meal, more gray had already crept in.

After finishing all the washing-up, Constance snuck off to inspect the poppets under her bed for ash and discovered with a flush of guilt that she had not completely cleansed them. But with dawn already past, she would have to wait to complete the ritual tomorrow.

A misty rain fell outside, pedestrians scuttling along the boardwalk, bundled against the cold. Only two customers came into the shop that day.

The first was wearing a checkered Harvest Dance eye mask. "If the Cinder can't recognize you," the easily recognizable Beth Otterham confided, "it can't take possession."

The other, Pious Kelly, had driven a delicate bow of bone through the pockmarked flesh around his third eye.

"Raven wing bone," he commented, noticing Constance's curiosity as he took his packet of ground beef from her hands, but then he felt a little more clarity was in order: *"Raven wing bone plucked at night, make the demons all take flight."*

Wiping her hands on her apron as she watched him go, she wondered if the mask and bone were more of Charity Hobbs's peddled fetishes or if others had taken to the dubious business of hawking charms.

At the end of the workday, she found her mother in the apartment, sitting stock-still at her woodcarving station, turned towards the window, and staring out at the rain, all those nascent figurines staring at their creator from the complex of narrow shelves. She was wearing her lavender wool gloves and matching bonnet.

"Mother?" Constance choked on the word, feeling a swell in her throat. "Are you well?"

Rachel turned stiffly towards her daughter and smiled, her shaded birthmark the color of eggplant, then went back to staring out at the street.

"Why are you wearing your gloves? Are you planning on going out?"

Rachel made no reply.

As she stood there watching her mother, she heard a small voice in the back of her mind.

"Do you have bloodstains on your rump from when your father spanks you?"

It was the voice of a snot-nosed Jacob Downing, from school years ago, asking her if it was true that her father didn't wash his hands after work, thus turning his wife all bloody-looking when he touched her. The comment had so dumbfounded Constance that she had just stared in brow-furrowed confusion as the boy went on. Then, out from the gaggle of children at recess, a girl with bouncy golden-red ringlets and canines as sharp as a fox's had slunk up behind Jacob and yanked down his knickerbockers, and with that swift move, the children began jeering at teeny-tiny Jacob Downing. Constance's mother's birthmark had been forgotten; Constance herself had likely avoided receiving a mean sobriquet, and she would forever feel a debt of gratitude towards Amity Lancaster, the mayor's daughter. Still, Jacob's taunts had awakened Constance to the cruel gossip that swirled around her mother's appearance.

Maybe that's what's wrong, she thought, going to her mother, kneeling down beside her, and petting her gloved hands.

She just overheard some snatch of baseness and took it to heart.

That's all.

It can't be the Cinder.

Not Mother.

T HOUGH CONSTANCE REPEATED CHARITY's charm and washed the poppets clean with a frightening intensity the next morning, the gloomy weather persisted all day, so Constance couldn't be sure if she had performed the rite effectively. All that day, the snail shell between her breasts burned as cold against her skin as the heart of a snow golem, and she thought of confessing to her father that she was to blame for her mother's illness, and indeed that she might be to blame for the destruction of Canton itself at the hands of the Cinder.

At midday, she tramped upstairs to rewarm their breakfast, but after lighting the stove fire and bringing the plates of food out of the icebox, she noticed the quiet in the apartment, and her skin began to crawl. She approached the living room, looking towards her mother's workstation, overcome with presentiment.

Her mother was not there.

Nor was she in her bedroom, nor down in the outhouse, nor in the smoking shed, nor kneeling in the vegetable garden, nor pumping water on Main Street.

Constance burst into the sausage-festooned backroom of the shop, fighting down the stirrings of panic, and reported the situation to her father, who contemplated a mound of bloody meat as his daughter worked her way through the list of places in which Rachel couldn't be found.

Without speaking a word, Thurgood set down his cleaver, wiped his hands, unstrung his apron, and was out the door. Constance returned to the shop counter, stared down at the account book she had been engaged in before seeing to dinner, but the figures on the page only swam before her eyes. In the distance, Thurgood's hollers of "Rachel! Rachel!" rang off the false front of every building along Main. Then, as if she were shocked back to life, Constance hastily shed her apron and green snood, rushed back upstairs, quenched the stove fire, and soon her voice had joined her father's.

The two of them ate a supper of breakfast leftovers that evening, the silence of the meal only heightened by the unnerving scrape of utensils on cutlery. Afterwards, she made a digestive mushroom tea for her father, which he downed in one gulp while it was still scalding hot.

"Damn the Son, what do you think you're doing?" he asked in a hoarse voice when he saw her slipping her chocolate-colored cloak over her shoulders.

"I'm going back out there with you to find Mother."

"One of us needs to be rested enough for the shop tomorrow morning."

"Please, Father, I don't want to be alone here. I can't. It's too horrible, this empty apartment."

"And what if your mother comes home while we're out looking?"

"You think she might?"

He tugged at his thinning tuft of dark hair. "Fine. Just till the Hour of the Father. If we haven't found her by then, you're to return home, and no argument from you either."

They had already scoured every inch of the town during the daylight hours, and while there remained the grim possibility that she had fallen into the Fairwater River or even the waterlogged sewage ditch of Main Street, Thurgood would not yet entertain such a thought. They redoubled their efforts, searching for many hours more every alley and side street, every barn and pigsty, even the dark nooks beneath the boardwalks, then circling out to the recently reaped farmland surrounding Canton, knocking on bloodied doors and receiving no answer from the people holed up inside, either because they had succumbed to the Cinder or because they were fearful that the ash demon, disguised in the skins of their neighbors, was seeking them out.

The moon was on its descent over the town when the tolling of the temple bell broke the quiet, its four solemn knells announcing the Hour of the Father. Without a word, Constance pulled her father's face down to hers and kissed him goodnight, then returned to an empty home.

Following a restive night, she rose hours before dawn, prepared the fire in the wood stove, made porridge and biscuits, buttered eggs and fried ham and tea, anxious for news and afraid to let a moment pass without filling it with movement and industry. She chopped wood; swept the stoop, stairs, and kitchen; emptied the icebox drip pan; stoked the hearth fire aflame, her eyes dry and swollen inside her skull, like they were not her own, like they were parasites gorging themselves on the visual minutiae of her life.

There came the crack of a gunshot outside, and Constance rushed to the window upstairs at the front of the apartment. Though it was still dark, she could just make out down the road the black rockaway carriage of Mayor Lancaster surrounded by a throng of masked citizens. Then—another salvo of gunfire, flashing bursts of smoke, a woman's shrill scream. Someone in the crowd slumped over and fell face-first into the mud, then several men pulled the corpulent mayor from his conveyance, swarmed over him, and battered his prodigious form with the butts of their rifles.

Constance suddenly remembered the clump of hair with the finger inside it from many days ago and began to fret that somewhere in the house or the shop below—in some dusty, forgotten cranny, behind a bed or beneath the couch, wedged between books on the bookshelf or secreted away between one of their pages—there rotted a piece of some Cinder victim. The idea of this would gnaw at her mind forever until she hunted it down and excised it from their home. So she began to clean again, this time with a vengeful hysteria, singing tavern songs to drown out the shouting from down the street and Amity Lancaster's pleas for the assailants to have mercy on her father.

The mist that had crept into town overnight began to curl away with the rising sun, revealing glimmers of sky for the first time in days, and with its exit, as if it had been made of creatures of vapor, the mob also disbursed. The temple bell marked the Hour of the Daughter, usually a bright and joyous sound, but this morning its tolls only underscored the eerie silence that had settled over the streets.

Then the front door burst open, slamming against the wall, and when Constance heard her father's boots thumping up the stairs, she rushed to the top, heart pounding, and saw in the dusky light Thurgood carrying his bride. The woman looked nothing like her former self—shrunken and bald, gray and wrinkled, her birthmark lightened to a mauve hue, and her nostrils leaking a powdery sludge—her clothes nothing more than tatters, soiled and reeking of excrement. "She was wandering Forest Road," her father explained as he stripped off her mother's filthy raiment. Constance averted her eyes more in horror than out of respect. Thurgood laid her down in bed and covered the shivering remains of his wife with a goose-down quilt she and Constance had stitched last winter.

Her father turned to Constance, who was wringing her hands, at a complete loss.

"Get a hold of yourself, Connie. Your mother needs you."

Nodding, she set to work. After preparing a bath, she made fresh tea, then set off to fetch Doc Harwood, navigating towards Riverside Road. Soon she was standing before the doctor's domicile, the door painted with three oozing red slashes, the windows dark. She and her father had knocked on this very door the previous evening, but Constance was in too distracted a state of mind to remember. So she banged on the door again, this time for several minutes, then circled around the alleyway to the back and knocked on the doctor's office door.

There came no answer.

As she turned to go, a scarecrow in a threadbare jacket appeared at the alleyway entrance, giving her a start. Hunched and gray, either from disease or benign old age, it staggered towards her.

"They carted Doc to Castle Hill yestereven," it drawled in a gravelly voice.

Constance approached warily, but as she neared the poor creature, recognition dawned on her. "Jacob!" she gasped.

Indeed, it was her old classmate Jacob Downing. Dinky Doodle Downing, as he'd become known after that day in the schoolyard so long ago.

"They carted Doc to Castle Hill yestereven." Jacob pawed at his face with a hand missing all but two of its fingers. His pimples had been buried beneath the flaky gray layers of his necrotic skin.

She felt the need to speak, to offer him some words of solace, but for the second time in the history of their interactions together, she simply stared dumbfounded as he limped past her, repeating the news about the doctor and his family now to the empty alleyway, or maybe to the mongrel snarfing up lumps of gray flesh from the muddy ground. Had he even been addressing her to begin with, or was he simply stuck in a loop of futility, a broken clock now telling the wrong time?

Constance hurried away, and upon reaching Main Street and the statue of Duke Guillemet Cantone, she saw down the road towards Castle Hill that the rain-slick dead comprised a veritable mountain, which now most definitely was moving, those still-living bodies that had been dumped on top of the deceased shifting like earthworms in a clod of moist, steaming earth. Even from this distance of a quarter mile, she could hear their plaintive moans and demented soliloquies bleeding together into a haunting chorus. Beyond, in the yellow woods and the distant mountains, autumn, the Season of the Mother, burned on with an aching, dispassionate beauty.

Back home, she delivered the news that Doc had succumbed to disease, and Thurgood studied his daughter with a novel, intense clarity burning in his eyes. He grabbed her hands and inspected the nails, then turned her around and loosened her bun, her long hair spilling down her back. He took these umber tresses in his hands, examining every inch, every strand, of them, and in doing so, the snail-shell charm was tugged up to Constance's neckline, though she was too alarmed at his behavior to realize it.

"Father, what are you doing? You're frightening me."

"No signs of the Cinder. You're still well, Connie." He placed his hands firmly on her shoulders and turned her around. "You're leaving Canton," he said, then noticed the charm and took it in his hands. "What's this?"

"Nothing," she said, attempting to pry it from his grip.

"You were messing with poppets too. I saw them under your bed when I went to fetch another quilt for your mother. Charms and fetishes and tommyrot. Oh Connie—"

"They're for our protection."

He yanked it from her neck and flung it to the floor, where it shattered, the shards of shell scattering across the kitchen. "You remember your history lessons? Remember the People's Uprising? You'd be hanged or worse if—Well, never mind that now. You're to pack a bag immediately."

"What? Why? Mother needs—"

"Your mother needs you safe. As do I. Pack some traveling clothes. Time is short. Fetch us a doctor from Hemlock. There's been no answer from the mayor's courier. I fear the man may have met with some unforeseen accident. You'll take the mule and my pepperbox and ride to Bowen's, then pay a courier to ride ahead if you like, stay there, and wait out the Cinder. But whatever you do, you're not to return to Canton until you hear word that it's safe here."

She downright refused, ordered her father to sit and eat the cold and lusterless breakfast she had prepared hours ago, tried to force him into his chair, and the two grappled with each other, which ended in Thurgood embracing his weeping daughter.

He finally got his way.

Constance was to leave at once: she would save two days' travel by taking Forest Road, and not the wending, sometimes treacherous path of Highland Road in the mountains. It was, he assured her, the right decision, one that could mean saving more lives—most importantly her mother's.

As she pulled out the carpetbag from beneath her bed, Faith Sallyforth's voice came to her again, admonishing her about the dangers of Forest Road, the Nilwere, its fog mantle and milky eyes and the tap-tap-tapping of its wooden fingers.

But it was a voice she easily dismissed, drowned out by the louder and more pressing cry of the Cinder.

It was no time for wives' tales.

She would be fine.

Except that the thing in the woods found her.

Keep Out, Cinder

A T THE EDGE OF town, beyond the circumference of the wheeling buzzards, a party of travelers passed the leaning sign "Canton, Pop. 2541" (a deceptive figure now), to which a less welcoming addition had been nailed—"KEEP OUT, CINDER"—the red letters running down the grainy face of the ashen-hued plank. Aside from warning wayfarers from entering Canton, the sign also seemed to address the disease itself, pleading with the creeping spread of ash to release the town from its grip.

The party consisted of the black rockaway (Mayor Increase Lancaster's carriage minus the man himself) drawn by a vigorous white-and-brown roan. The soberly attired driver, Mr. Emmanuel Solemn, cut a narrow figure, with a nose like a parrot's beak and his lack of a chin concealed by a wispy, white billy-goat beard. But with its curtains pulled all morning, Constance did not catch even the briefest glimpse of the carriage's passengers. Behind the conveyance sauntered the Dunn family mule, Lento, whose normal duty consisted of pulling the un-sprung cart from farmhouse to farmhouse during Thurgood's slaughtering rounds, but he was equally content to spirit an unwilling Constance from the plague town.

The first nightfall would find them lodging at Bowen's, where Constance would hire a courier to gallop ahead of them, according to her father's suggestion; the second night would pass beneath the low-slung inn known as the Steelhead, built over the rapids of the Fairwater River; and before sundown of the third day, they would be clip-clopping down the gaslit cobblestone avenues of Hemlock.

That is, if all went according to plan.

Several miles into the journey, Constance breathed free of the foul air of Canton with its fly swarms and vermin-clogged alleyways. The forest was a riot of colors, leaves jeweled with sunshine, the muddy road mottled with stained-glass shadow. The ground sloped downward, rounding a rocky, heavily wooded elbow of the Fairwater River, and the booming of the rapids reached the riders of Forest Road out of the steep gully, commingling with the honking of geese overhead and the twittering of finches. But Constance found little pleasure in the beauty surrounding her. She was forever brushing gray human hairs and slivers of nail from her dress, real and imagined—and as the distance between her and her family increased, and with it her guilt, the words appended to the town sign clung to her lips like a plea, like a prayer, like a promise.

She had fallen into the meditative daze that Lento was capable of inducing, the mule unable to trot for more than a few minutes at a time, preferring his easy saunter. Any attempt to eke out a quicker gait from him was met with head jerking and side-stepping, fits of champing and braying. The carriage, swaying and bouncing along the ever-worsening conditions of the road, grew more and more distant over the course of the morning, and not once did a curtain part or a pair of eyes blink out at her. Constance assured herself that tiring the beast out would be advantageous to no one, so she allowed Lento to mark his own time.

She ate in the saddle, picking a few items from the sack her father had packed. There were biscuits and ham from breakfast, a circle of black bread purchased from the baker, a wedge of cheese, two onions, three apples, oats, and strips of sweet lamb jerky, a skin of wine and one of water—plus grain and carrots for Lento. Enough for three days. She kept her dinner frugal, for she wasn't sure how welcome migrants from a plague town would be at Bowen's or the Steelhead, and suspected they might have to make do with their own vittles and spend the night in the stables or camped out in the yard like gypsies. In any case, she wasn't very hungry, every bite soured by the horrific images she'd witnessed around Canton over the past two weeks.

Around midday, she spotted a lake far in the distance and was soon passing through a broken land of brooks and streams, which puzzled through the forest and rendezvoused with the river. Its steps lowered, the rockaway had parked against the backdrop of the sparkling lakeshore, and Constance spotted Amity picnicking with her governess on a blanket down by the water. The roan was feeding out of a bag; Mr. Solemn, beneath a big straw hat, his bolt-action rifle slung over his shoulder, stood watching the road and ruminating on a bit of tack.

As Constance approached, he seemed to stare through her, beyond her and into the forest.

"Good afternoon, Kind Father," she said.

He stirred out of his reverie, his eyes focusing on her at last, then swallowed the tack with a grotesque thrust of his Adam's apple. The parts of his face seemed misaligned, as if different sections were under the control of different people, pulling him apart in opposing directions. The mellow, white brow did not belong to his light-brown eyes with their suspicious crinkle of crow's feet. His beard did not coordinate its motions with the fat lips of his lopsided mouth.

"I think I will ride on ahead, Mr. Solemn. I imagine you should catch up and outstrip me in no time, and this way we shall arrive at Bowen's closer together."

Mumbling his understanding, he bid her adieu. She spurred Lento on but only advanced a few yards before Amity sang out her name: "*Con*stance! *Connn*stance!" The voice was much changed, musical and light, as if sung by a different bird entirely than the one that had been screaming earlier that morning.

Constance returned the wave.

"Well, come here, you goose," Amity laughed. Constance could see the governess quietly admonishing her ward, though Amity seemed to dismiss the woman with the toss of her hair.

Constance left Lento to graze and water along the shore, then walked along the pebbly beach towards the ladies. The air was fresh and invigorating, and the sunlight here fell soft and warm on the skin, as opposed to the cold damp of the woods.

Amity moved aside her green bonnet, which she had set down beside her on their tartan wool blanket, and patted the spot where it had once rested. "Sit, sit, do," she said. Amity had been a beautiful girl, with blue eyes that seemed half-submerged in the waters of a dreamland, a small upturned nose, delicate features, and lissome figure. In the passing years, every mote of those girlish charms had become amplified with that intensity of early womanhood, turning her into an alluring creature. In her dark-green dress, the ringlets of her shining red hair spilling down and framing her face, she looked more fairylike than human.

Constance complied, conscious of every way they contrasted—with her worn clothes and work-roughened hands, Constance looked more the part of Amity's servant than her friend.

"Temperance, Constance; Constance, Temperance," Amity said by way of introduction. "Goodness, this sounds like the tedious beginnings of a moralistic poem."

"Pleased to make your acquaintance, Fair Daughter," Constance said.

"Likewise," said Temperance with a reserved nod of the head and a tightening of the lips. She was very tall and very pale, her features pinched but not uncomely, her raven curls meticulously tucked inside a pale-yellow, ruffled bonnet.

But Amity was not prepared to give up on her joke yet. "*With Temperance and Constance, the little ant doth toil, carrying crumbs and ... stones of plums, to a queen that he doth spoil.*" She laughed at her own cleverness, and it was an infectious laugh, so Constance laughed too, a hollow sound, for she felt there was nothing worth laughing about. She had not laughed for many days, come to think of it, and it struck her as unnatural that Amity could. Temperance, perhaps from all their time spent together, must have worked up an immunity to Amity's laughter, for her small mouth only smiled. "Well, Ms. Jones, what do you think? Not too terrible for an extemporaneous quatrain, am I right?"

"Yes, although I'm not sure that moral entirely meets with my approbation."

"Oh, you try one, then. A moralistic about Constance's mule! What do you think, Connie?"

"My breath is bated," she said.

"Please don't try my patience, Amity. My apologies, Constance."

Constance began to say, "Not at all," but Amity interrupted.

"Oh, never mind, you old bore. Have you eaten, Connie? Have a slice of the bread." Among a picnic of cold chicken and pickled eggs, pastries and wine, there was a glazed pumpkin bread of which Amity handed a slice to Constance. "Try a bite, have a munch." She smiled, and

Constance remembered the girl's vulpine teeth and the air of mischief they lent her.

Constance nibbled at a corner. It was moist and richly spiced with nutmeg, ginger, and cloves. Even so, she struggled to eat it, recalling the sight of the cur ravening the bits of diseased flesh in the alleyway beside Doc's.

"Isn't it glorious? Thank the Father that Beatrice's Pastries was still open, but dear me, it is rather dull riding in the carriage. I wanted Temperance to read to me during the journey, but she developed a headache doing so, what with all the jostling, and for the past hour she's been doing nothing but massaging her temples."

"Are you feeling well now?" Constance asked the governess, who at this moment, at any rate, was not massaging her temples.

"The fresh air has assuaged my condition somewhat." The pain denied her attempt to smile.

"I say an amble down the lakeshore would do you good, don't you think, Temperance? And loosen that bonnet of yours; it's squeezing your visage bloodless."

"She can be so tiresome and timorous, always cultivating some new phantom ailment," Amity confided once her governess had been dismissed but was still not quite out of earshot, crunching down the shore beneath her parasol (bonnet unadvisedly still in place). "We've practically been hermits these past two weeks. She's so frightened of the Gray Demon. I suggested cramming you in with us in the carriage, but she wouldn't hear of it. 'Oh Amity, you know what your father said'"—here Amity tightened her mouth and put on a fusty accent—"'he said you don't know who is afflicted with the disease until it's too late. Now recite to me the pluperfect passive conjugations of *fara*.' Stuff and nonsense! She'll still be summoning out of me the verbs of dead tongues while all the rest of the world is dead from Cinder!" She gave Constance a playful shove to punctuate the punchline of her joke.

Constance covered her mouth to hide her feigned giggle.

Amity tore off a shard of skin and white meat, and her whiter teeth made quick work of it. "Well, in any case, I've come to a decision: I don't fear the Gray Demon, and I officially"—here she made an overelaborate mock bow towards Constance—"invite you, Mistress Constance Dunn of Canton, Daughter of Mr. Thurgood Dunn Butcher, Heiress of Dunn's Fine Meats and Fancy Sausages, to join me and my insufferable governess in the bounciest gig trip you ever will experience."

After more polite laughter Constance declined as graciously as she could manage. "I really couldn't. Lento won't be able to keep pace with your roan."

"Lento? What, from the Eton Brimley novel? Ha, what a spiffing appellation for a mule! The unhurried Count Lento Daring plotting revenge against the ass that sired him! Well, send the good count trotting back home posthaste. Just think what high jinks we'd have, how easily the hours would pass if we were only to wile them away in each other's splendiferous company." Here, there was much arm tugging and eyelash batting.

"I'm afraid we've come too far. Lento might lose the way."

A mischievous smile appeared on Amity's lips, one canine pricking at its plump corner. "I know... we'll have the staid Ms. Temperance, speaker of four useless tongues and master of watercolors and the pianoforte, on muleback! Oh, pleeease, Dear Constance. Please, please, please! It would be the subject of a thousand whimsical paintings. I can see it now: *The Bumpy Courtship of Ms. Temperance Margaritte Jones by Count Lento Daring.*"

Constance pressed Amity's green-gloved hand, sorry to spoil her fun. "No, Amity. I wouldn't put the poor creature out."

"Do you mean Ms. Temperance or the mule?"

"Amity, be nice."

"Killjoy." With a roll of her eyes, Amity pouted, then rebounded in a trice. "Then you'll leave him at Bowen's and ride on with us from there."

Constance relented at last.

"You must think me callous—no, no, no, don't protest—trying to seek enjoyment and distraction for myself on our journey, and I—" Her tongue flicked across one of her little fangs, as if to stop itself from running on. Her eyes strayed to the form of Temperance, who had made much progress down the shore, resembling a sheared swath of autumn forest in her amber dress, russet shawl, and yellow bonnet. When Amity did continue speaking, her mind seemed to have shifted onto a different tack: "Well, well, what else can one do? Sit there in the carriage fretting about every old townsman that's come down with the Cinder? They're all mad for staying, that's what I've been telling Temperance." She laughed again, though her good humor was waning, and it now required a sip of wine to rally her spirits. "Ah, pretty Connie, you and I are the clever ones." Here she petted Constance's shiny umber hair, which had been shaken loose from her bun during the ride and now fell down the front of her cloak (in her haste to leave, she had forgotten her own bonnet). Perhaps Mayor Lancaster had spoken similar words to her daughter last night, convincing her that abandoning the town was the sensible choice, the only choice for them to make.

They ate in silence for a moment, and Constance noticed how the rough, grimy fabric of her red dress brushed up against the lustrous dark-green taffeta of Amity's. She tucked her skirt hem under her leg, reminded of similar little moments of embarrassment she had experienced when faced with the contrast in their circumstances.

"Tell me, do: Where will you stay in Hemlock?" Amity's questions usually came in the form of orders.

"With my father's cousin, a cartwright, and his family. I've never met them, well, not since before I could speak." Thurgood had scribbled out a letter of introduction for the purpose in his slanted, hasty scrawl, and with this and a pouch of money for expenses, she was to make do until the situation in Canton had improved.

"Won't it be capital! Mother has been in Hemlock since spring caring for my grandfather. I took a trip there last summer, and when I visited, we all had a ride on a locomotive called *The Silver Spirit*! It only carried us half a mile and spat scalding-hot steam every which way and was terrifically noisy, and there was a huge commotion when a woman's terrier scampered onto the tracks and was crushed to death, but you wouldn't believe what a thrill it was. And with you being so near once we're settled down, it will be like old times, like when we were children, and we can ride *The Silver Spirit* together!"

"That sounds very exciting," Constance said sincerely.

"The Hemlock balls are like scenes from the Courts of Lagdon in a Brimley novel, Mother says, everyone dressed immaculately, theatrically, sensationally, as furbelowed as wedding cakes! I will probably have to burn these rags and begin anew—and the gentlemen, oh the gentle-men"—she fanned her face with the requisite flair of drama—"dashing and mysterious and heart-stirring, they wear these shockingly tight pants known as gaspipes and imposingly tall hats called stovepipes and these skinny bow ties called piston rods. It's utterly droll, like they're half machine, half human. I tell you it's another world, Constance, *another world*."

Her spirits rebounded from that brief moment of darkness earlier, Amity prattled on about the exciting fashions and inner workings of Hemlock society, about her own upcoming debutante ball planned for the spring (the Season of the Daughter, naturally enough). It was said that Hemlock had been built for young lovers—never mind its strategic position at the mouth of the Fairwater River where it emptied into the Shamrock Sea—ideal waters for one such as Amity, who possessed beauty and confidence and means. On and on she talked, and Constance gazed out at the glinting water of the lake, so massive you could not make out the other shore.

Strange. She was not aware of a lake of this size so close to town.

She took another bite of bread while Amity continued to proselytize on the gospel of Hemlock and its primary pillars of faith: Drama and Romance, Balls and Fashion.

And everyone I know is dying.

Maybe Mr. Solemn is dying.

Maybe Ms. Jones is dying.

And Amity.

And me.

She closed her eyes, shutting out Amity's voice and the sound of the waves and the rustle of leaves in the wind, her mind growing dark and quiet. There was what felt to be a long moment of peace and tranquility, but then in the darkness something started to take shape. Little specks, one beside the other in rows, gray and amorphous at first, but as the light grew in a slow dawn, she found herself staring at the figurines her mother carved. The funny little things that had over the course of her life found their way into her dreams and nightmares, inspired pride and evoked joy and sadness. The oblongs of wood that had told her more about her mother than anything else could have, more than the bloodstain could or her comforting silence at supper or the fairy tales she told to her as a child. The figures stared back at her, their tiny eyes glistening and human and pleading with her, and all of them were changed, no longer creatures pulled from fiction or history books: they were the citizens of Canton, the victims of the plague, immortalized in cedar. They were Faith Sallyforth and Jacob Downing and Doc Harwood and all the rest, but there was a gap in their ranks, a gap that only Constance would fit into.

KEEP OUT, CINDER.

Her eyes snapped open, reality flooding back in. How long she had been distracted Constance could not say, but Amity was still gabbing, unaware of the quiet epiphany that had just occurred, and Temperance Jones was still ambling along the pebbled shore.

"I've made a grave error," Constance blurted out, unable to contain herself. "I'm sorry, Amity," she said, standing, placing the guiltily nibbled bit of pumpkin cake back down amidst the spread of food. "I must go."

"Go? Go where? What are you saying, silly Connie? Sit, talk with me."

Constance shook her head. "My family needs me. Here"—she reached into her inner cloak pocket, pulled out her reticule, and took several dollars from it, placing them in Amity's hands—"when you reach Bowen's, hire a rider to go on ahead to Hemlock. Fetch doctors back to town. I must return. Indeed, I should never have left."

"Connie, I don't need your money. Connie! Are you listening to me?"

Feet crunching over the beach, blood drumming in her ears, Constance hastened over to Lento, then tugged him back towards the road, Amity calling after her all the while, in her sweet, singsong alto.

Abbey Creek

T HE GIG FAR BEHIND her, Constance was overcome with relief now that she was moving in the right direction, the *dutiful* direction, back towards her family, to be with her father and mother in these dire times. With an uncanny intelligence, Lento seemed sympathetic to her emotions, for he managed to maintain a canter for a mile or so before slowing to a trot and then at last back to his leisurely saunter, braying and shaking his head when she attempted to goad him on any faster.

During the trip to the lake, they had not passed any forks or deviations from Forest Road, so finding her way back to Canton should have been a simple task. Besides, Constance had memorized all the noteworthy sights they had passed that morning—the broken land of streams, the craggy ridge over the river, the misty spray of the falls; however, as the miles crept past, all of these landmarks failed to reappear. Even more disturbing was that the sun hung in the wrong position in the sky, hiding up in the dazzling canopy to her left—the same relative position it had held all morning.

Confronted by these two worrisome points, Constance pulled out her compass to mark their heading, but the needle spun out of control like a whirligig in a gale.

As she looked down at the dizzying instrument, the light washed away beneath a passing cloud, and just as suddenly the crickets and birds quieted, the only sound the dry crackle of leaves under hoof. She pulled on the reins and listened to the uncanny quiet of the woods, her nerves on edge.

Tick-a-tick-a-tick-a-tick.

She started at the din coming from somewhere far off in the woods, so blurred and quick it was more of a chirr than a rattle. Frozen in her saddle, she scanned the thick brush, which crowded the road so oppressively that the branches clawed at her clothes, but she could discern nothing beyond a few yards away. Then the noise died away just as quickly as it had lived, and was lost altogether when the breeze stirred again.

Her nose wrinkled, the unmistakable stench of rot—which had haunted the town of Canton over past weeks—stealing past her on the wind, but that odor was also very faint, and with the shifting of the wind, she also lost the phantom smell. The clouds above scudded on past, and daylight washed back in, cleansing the woods and repopulating it with woodland sounds, bird by bird, insect by insect.

Is it the Nilwere, she wondered, *or am I being followed by the Cinder itself?*

She looked down at her hands, mustering the bravery to scrutinize her nails. Was that a new ridge on the cuticle of her pinky? And what was that discoloration on her right thumbnail? Had that always been there?

She spurred Lento on, wanting to, needing to, exit these woods as soon as possible. And yet the forest landscape, crowding in closer and closer, yellowing maple saplings springing up in her path, dead wood lying pell-mell across the way, continued to dishearten her.

It's all wrong. How is this possible?

She again went over her father's description of the journey, reciting it to herself, for she had memorized it word for word. There should have been forks in the road, well marked with mile signs, and come to think of it, she had not seen one sign all morning since the ambiguously worded warning posted outside of Canton. Besides, Thurgood had failed to mention anything about the road passing near a massive lake, a puzzling omission in an otherwise thorough description of the journey. He had also mentioned a logging settlement close to Three Flocks that they should have passed before midday, but she had seen nothing of the sort.

"Just one wrong step," her mother had said.

If doubt suddenly flooded into her heart, Lento paid no notice, keeping to his steady and leisurely clip, unbothered by the bare limbs that ran their fingers along his flanks, shaking his head and flicking his tail to disburse the unwelcome and prolific flies. Paying close attention now to the sounds of the forest, the birds sounded bizarre to her ears—more like the automated machinery of a cuckoo clock than the true thing.

She told herself that any moment the condition of the road would improve, she would pass a sign, would spot the sawmill through a clearing in the trees, would smell the smoke of a welcoming hearth fire, would make out the merry song of the lumberjacks, or would recognize some detail of the morning's journey. At this point, she didn't care if she came upon Bowen's or Canton or stumbled through the Royal Gates of the Palace of Hemlock. She just needed some unmistakable landmark to help her figure out where she was.

Another hour passed in this mixed state of denial and doubt and uneasy vigilance, the sun now well on its descent. The light, muted by an ominous, rumbling thunderhead, was dying fast in the woods, and having but pecked at scraps of food all that day's ride, Constance was famished. Uncertain and fatigued, she began considering making camp for the evening, when she saw around the bend that a wall of trees had practically exploded across the road, creating a brambly, splintered barrier. She goaded Lento forward and dismounted, then sought out a potential path through the skein of snapped limbs and trunks.

The crushed trees extended well beyond this one spot, creating a path of destruction that swerved off deep into the woods, but right near the edge of this wave of felled trees where it covered the road, she saw the black spokes and cracked felloe of a smashed wheel.

Leaving Lento on the edge of the chaos, she waded inside this horizontal-grown wood, ducking beneath thick boles of oak and slipping over thatches of pine and red maple, and here again came that reek of rot commingling with the fresh scent of split wood.

This was... no, it couldn't be... the wheel of the Lancaster rockaway. But how?

The question was eclipsed by a more alarming discovery: a form lying beneath the narrow trunk of a young chestnut tree, the taffeta dress torn and muddied, sullied red hair splayed out across a puddle.

"Amity!" she cried, stumbling over the precarious knot of limbs and squeezing down through a window of branches, till she was standing in the mud and could, though with some difficulty, slide the inert form out from underneath the trunk. Constance sat Amity up, manipulating her loose, mud-slick limbs with difficulty, but finally she had her head resting against a fir bough pillow and could examine her face and body. Despite being pinned beneath the tree, there were no outward signs of damage on her body, no broken limbs. The dress, though muddied, miraculously was not torn. There was, however, a nasty bruise marbling the side of her face, another darkening her eye, and dark blood was leaking out of her nostrils.

Flies permeated the air, buzzing in her ear, caroming off her flesh, searching out juicy orifices. Try as she did to shoo away the frenzied swarm from her and Amity's faces, the insects would not be denied, nipping at lips and the corners of eyes. Constance called out her friend's name repeatedly, but the young lady slumped there, unresponsive. Still, she was breathing, her face warm, her heartbeat steady.

Constance smacked her lightly a few times, shook her, and at last Amity's eyelashes fluttered. Her eyes opened, then suddenly she was in her rescuer's arms, face buried in her breast, eerily silent, shivering.

Scattered about the ground through the thatch, Constance could see more evidence of the rockaway, which had been completely torn asunder—here a swath of flayed leather, there a jagged tooth of glass—but signs of Temperance Jones or Emmanuel Solemn there were none, at least not that she could see from this limited vantage point.

A wind whisked up the leaves of fallen branches, sending them dancing and dervishing, and helping to assuage the festering swarm. A breath of cold stole through the wind, an icy tongue that probed its way inside Constance's cloak and dress. She helped Amity stand, then guided her out of the tumble of wood, a lengthy proceeding ending in torn garments and stinging cuts on both sides.

When they reached the mule, Constance pulled a spare woolen shawl from her carpetbag and wrapped it around the compliant, still-trembling Amity, then she helped the girl up and onto Lento's back. Amity, with wide-staring and unblinking eyes, sat the mule she had formerly mocked. *I suppose after all it's "The Bumpy Courtship of Amity Lancaster" instead,* Constance thought but quashed the ill-timed joke.

Constance retied her own kerchief and pulled her cloak tight about her body. When she started to return to the mass of felled trees, a hand grabbed hold of her shoulder. She turned back towards Amity, whose lips were trembling.

"I need to search for the others," Constance said.

Amity shook her head, her pallid face twisted with fear.

"I'll be quick about it," Constance assured her.

It was impossible to make a full search of the tangled maze of flattened forest, but she did what she could, making brief excursions over and into the pile, calling out the names of the driver and governess. When she noticed a peculiar thickness in the cloud of flies, she descended through the branches only to find the startled hazel eye of the dead roan staring up at her from within the twining of its sylvan tumulus.

THE TWO GIRLS WERE playing graces on the lawn in front of the Lancaster household, and Amity had just flung the wooden hoop into the air. An eight-year-old Constance caught it on the end of her feathered wand and bowed extravagantly according to rules of their own invention, when the mayor, announcing his appearance on the front porch with a tremendous groaning of the wooden planks, shouted to his daughter to "Mind your comportment," and Amity, blushing, had reflexively held her head higher, squared her shoulders, and pushed out her narrow chest.

Now, her lectures on ladylike comportment forgotten, Amity slouched in the saddle, making herself as small as possible, almost disappearing beneath the rough wool shawl. Constance kept a comforting hand on her lap, which Amity clung to fiercely, as if with talons, and they progressed in silence. Constance felt a sudden urge to ask after her father, to probe Amity's feelings about the events of that morning. Yet she held her tongue, and another mile or so passed in silence with no end to the darkening woods in sight.

Constance kept a wary eye on the sky through the broken canopy. She needed to get her bearings, but the compass was still acting mercurial and now the sun had sunk too low, the coming sunset obscured by the depths of the woods and the gathering storm, that she had trouble discerning north (homeward) from south-west (Hemlock-ward). She assumed that if they kept their heading they would either reach Bowen's or home, at which point she could report the attack and organize a search party for the missing travelers.

Lightning flashed, thunder drummed, a few thick drops of rain plopped onto them.

Missing travelers.

The phrase chilled her. After all these years hearing about people going missing on Forest Road, she was now caught up in that same reality.

C ONSTANCE FELT A GLIMMER of hope when signs of a village at long last appeared, but these hopes were soon dashed.

They crossed a covered bridge in bad need of repair and so veiled with spider webs that she doubted anyone could have traversed it in the past few months. Through the gaping holes in the planking, they saw a river rushing beneath them as they crossed, but whether this was the Fairwater or not, Constance could not say.

While the woods never ended, their character regressed, the towering ancients giving way to mature trees and stands of saplings and even the occasional glen full of wild grass. Skeletal farmhouses and drooping, broken-armed windmills peered at them from the distance in these sparse woods like undead giants. Here, only remnants of fencing stood, the fragmented memories of enclosures over which families of deer casually leaped. The westering sun appeared from behind the overcast sky, imbuing the land with a golden and ochre glow and long, fleeing shadows.

At the sun's entrance, Constance at last got their bearings; they'd been heading north. For what it was worth.

Amity sat upright in the saddle when they passed a sign on the almost-vanished road that read "Abbey Creek"—a name vaguely familiar to Constance. The community near Bowen's was, of course, called Three Flocks, but Abbey Creek...

Then, she remembered. "The Ghoul of Abbey Creek." This was the phrase her mother had uttered in passing during their conversation about the Nilwere—one of the many designations ascribed to the thing in the woods. However they had managed to stumble upon this place, Constance could not fool herself into believing it was happenstance.

The cluster of houses and buildings at the center of this village looked as ailing and decrepit as the bridge—their signs rotted off, every pane of glass shattered, doors fallen off their hinges, collapsed roofs, trees stretching out their crooked limbs where walls had once stood. The silence of the place was a separate presence. It seemed to have cold eyes that followed them as they progressed past the wilderness-gutted buildings.

Though it was doubtful anyone had passed this way recently, judging by the ambitious construction of the bridge spiders she had hacked their way through, as well as the lack of shoeprints in the muddy path, the image in her mind of a wounded governess or coachman curled up and dying in pain somewhere in this tumbledown town was too poignant to ignore. So she called out to Temperance and Mr. Solemn repeatedly, waiting between shouts for a response, pricking her ears for the sound of a faint whimper or groan, but she heard nothing beyond the scampering of squirrels and the cawing of crows.

It took them only a few minutes to pass through the abandoned town, beyond which the woods petered out, yielding to a rocky countryside. Lightning danced across the horizon, which was now a purple so deep as to be nearly black. Layers of grayness advanced towards them out of the darkness, blurring the land, the roar of the wind advancing with it. But the approach of the storm was slow, as if the elements were toying with them.

Ahead, atop a steep, grassy hill, perched the titular abbey of Abbey Creek, a plain building of stone and mortar tethered to the main road by a winding, narrow dirt path. From the road at the base of the hill, Constance searched for any sign of life for a moment before deciding that this abbey, like every other structure dotting this decaying country, was also abandoned. But even if the Brothers and Sisters had abandoned the abbey, the Holy Family never would, and it was the presence of the Family (not their earthbound devotees) that mattered, that would protect them in their time of need. They could wait out the rain there, spend the night, and she could light a candle, strike a drum (well, perhaps not), and say a prayer for the people of Canton—and for Amity and herself

She led Lento off the main road. Up the path they trudged, and Constance was soon out of breath, finding the slope dangerously steep and punishingly stony, jabbing and prodding the soles of her feet through her well-worn brogans. Lento, eyes wide with concern, had just as much difficulty and twice refused to move until goaded with a juicy beet.

Amity, emerging further from her traumatized stupor, dismounted to help ease the burden. Traces of concern had crept back into the once pallid mask of her face, as she glanced back at the approaching waves of rain. And though her eyes were still wide staring, there was at least intelligence in them; they were once again connected to the world.

The party zigzagged up the hillside, which grew rockier and more broken and slippery, the pale stone pulverized into a loose, sandy gravel. At one point Constance slipped and found herself clambering on all fours, when she noticed thin prongs of bone jutting out of the ground. Here was a finger and the hollow shaft of a cracked femur, there was a curved knife of jawbone, a few broken teeth jutting out. Casting her eyes over the surrounding area, she found that these crushed remains blanketed the entire slope leading up to the abbey.

She glanced over towards Amity, but the mud-begrimed girl was climbing through a patch of thin grass, oblivious to the ossuary beneath her feet. The grass began to shiver beneath the first touches of rain, and the whining bluster of the wind careened through the abbey's empty hallways, open windows, and arches above.

Standing, Constance continued up without a word to Amity, and as they reached the abbey, the downpour finally swallowed them up.

There was no door—such barriers to entry were forbidden by the Brothers and Sisters for symbolic reasons, for it was said that after death, when a pure soul returned to the House of the Family, no door would bar their way. The girls led the mule inside, then unloaded and unsaddled and fed him. Once Lento was happy, they huddled by the entrance, and Constance, ravenous and exhausted after the long day, brought out her sack of provender and the wine skin.

As they ate, she pulled out her father's pepperbox pistol, checked that each one of its six cylinders was loaded, and set it on the ground beside her.

She found Amity had been watching her. "Thank you, Connie," she said in a broken voice.

"The white swan trumpets and spreads her wings. She ruffles her feathers, a frightening thing. Fending off predators for Amity's sake, she leads the flock safely back to the lake."

Amity smiled, flashing her mischievous fang. "You had half a day, and that's all you could come up with?" she said in a broken whisper rediscovering its music.

Constance rolled her eyes, and they both laughed.

C ONSTANCE WAS TRANSMOGRIFIED INTO wood once again. So too were Amity and Temperance, the three girls arranged around the tartan wool blanket by the lakeshore. Or was it an island? Yes, and beneath the surface of the sparkling water surrounding them, the boughs of a darkling forest waved and swayed. The wind gusted around the picnic of female figurines, but the tendrils of their filigreed hair did not budge.

Tick-a-tick-a-tick-a-tick.

The sound filled Constance's heart with dread. Trying to warn her friends, she rocked her unyielding body back and forth, back and forth, till she fell forward with a *knock* into Amity's lap.

Her ear pressed up against Amity's body, she could hear the girl's muffled voice as she attempted to improvise more poetry for everyone's entertainment, and from this vantage, the sound of the rattling was much louder, for it was not coming from within Constance this time, but from within Amity's womb.

Tick-a-tick-a-tick-a-tick.

As she watched, from within the rigid folds of Amity's taffeta dress, a pale-white peg of wood appeared.

No, not wood... bone.

It was a skeletal finger emerging into the world, worming its way out, twitching this way and that like the feeler of a grasshopper. Constance tried to scream through her paralyzed lips and tongue, but the vibrations of her muted voice only drew the sawdust-caked finger nearer to the wooden mask of her face. It hooked onto the corner of her mouth and began to bore its way inside.

Constance's eyes suddenly opened to the darkness, and her voice ripped through the silence with a short dying scream. She was brandishing the pistol, threatening the empty night air, but when it dawned on her that she had been having another nightmare, she released the firearm, letting it clatter onto the broken stone of the ruined hallway. Amity's arms were around her in an instant, and she kissed her forehead and whispered, "Shh, Connie. We're safe."

Constance lay back beside her friend and stared up at the blazing tapestry of stars suspended above them, the weavework of an unfathomably clever hand.

They were quiet for some time before Amity finally spoke: "It was me."

Constance turned to her.

"I was ashamed. And tired. And ready to be free of him. We were leaving Canton for good, and yet the worst part of it was following me. I just couldn't take anymore of it. Long ago—when he took you, I should have said something, but I was craven. And furious. Because I knew he was stealing my friend from me. There were others, you know—scullery maids and other bosom friends of mine and even Temperance—but you... It was the first time I woke up to what was happening in our household, though I did nothing about it for many years, not until yesterday, when I saw my chance. I simply couldn't stand the prospect of it continuing on in Hemlock, and so I sent word to Sheriff Sykes about my father's intentions to flee the town. He swore an oath punishable by death as mayor to see the town of Canton through all of its trials and tribulations. You can just taste the linger of the People's Uprising in that oath, that royal bloodlust. Well, he was fleeing, and I wanted him to be seized. I wanted to see him pulled from the carriage, struggling and screaming about the injustice of it. Injustice—"

Amity had been gazing up at the stars, but now she turned to Constance, a pleading look in her misty eyes, then grabbed Constance's wrist, and the latter winced.

"I've committed unforgivable sins, Constance. The sin of looking the other way when so many were suffering, and now the sin of betraying one's father."

As she said this, she laid her head against Constance's shoulder, the vibration of Amity's voice a quick, fleeting thing that recalled the nightmare from which Constance had just woken. She searched for the right thing to say. "You're not to blame for what the mayor did to me. We were just children—"

"But say you forgive me!"

"It is not you who needs to be forgiven."

"But I need to hear you say that you do anyway, Connie."

For some reason, Constance couldn't bring herself to say the words, no matter how much Amity pleaded to hear them. There was a power in those words, power that she would keep as long as she never spoke them. "Hush, hush now, Amity. What matters is that we are safe and have each other once again. We'll find our way out of these barrens, don't you worry. Why, you'll be having your hand kissed in Hemlock before you know it."

Deeper and Deeper

Constance awoke in the chilly morning to find the abbey lying in complete ruin beyond the entrance hall where they'd hunkered down for the night. Collapsed walls and rusted religious relics were obscured by a mist that glowed in the sunshine, parting like white flickering flames. Amity still slept, and Constance smiled sadly as she looked down at her friend's purple, swollen face. She remembered with some bitterness the last day they had truly enjoyed together before a wedge had been driven between them.

She and Amity had been playing a game of checkers in the parlor of the Lancaster household one afternoon years ago, when the mayor had appeared and asked Amity to run a letter down to the courier's office. It was the last Houseday of Spring, so the servant girl was on holiday. When Constance volunteered to accompany her friend, the mayor suggested instead that she could tidy up the parlor, as there were guests expected soon.

She obeyed, Amity left, and Mayor Lancaster wandered off into another corner of the large household. But several minutes later, when she was putting the board game back into the cupboard, she heard the floorboards groan behind her and knew that it was not Amity returning. In an instant she was struggling with the mayor, kicking and slashing at him, but he was much too big for her—a walrus in a waistcoat—and had her turned around, her dress hiked up, pinned against a table decorated with various bibelots, among them a few of her mother's carvings, which watched her with sad blue eyes before being knocked over in the ensuing violence.

His hand clenched over her mouth, his jiggly belly crushing her buttocks, the edge of the desk digging into her stomach, she felt a sudden shock of pain as he jabbed into her what she thought must be his other hand. Her eyes darted wildly around, looking for something, anything that could help her. Then, in the looking glass over the table, she spotted Amity's pale, shocked face for a brief moment before her friend closed the parlor door, leaving her to her fate. Constance experienced a moment of confusion, seeming to be looking through Amity's eyes, staring at the mayor assaulting her friend; then the door shut, and so did all sensation in Constance's body. No sound, no pain, no motion, just a frozen, colorless image.

That had been the last time Constance had set foot in her friend's home—she even stopped attending the Winter Solstice Party, to her parents' surprise, since this had always been one of her favorite holiday fetes. But even though a dark stain had marred their relationship, and Constance was consumed with fury for the mayor and his daughter and even Mrs. Lancaster, she and Amity continued to see one another for another year or so. The friendship, their interactions, it had all changed, as if everywhere they went, everything they did, every word they spoke, was in the presence of some third unseen person, perhaps the ghost of a wronged girl. Eventually, the first graces of womanhood lured them away from childhood attachments, and they became as familiar as strangers. But now, the rage that had burned inside Constance had finally burned out, and something like the old affection she felt for Amity remained in her heart. Even if she could not say the words, she did forgive Amity; she understood her friend's pain, the difficulty of her position.

Constance carefully groomed her, scratching mud from her dress and pulling bits of leaf and twig from her hair. That was when she noticed a few coils of silver hair.

Amity's eyes fluttered open, and they said good morning.

They ate hard biscuits and blue cheese and jerky, Constance barely tasting the food, distracted by those silver hairs in Amity's grimy hair.

I should say something, she thought. *No, I won't. Doing so would only frighten the poor thing.*

After packing, they led Lento back down the slope of bones and to the road. Beyond Abbey Creek, the road stretched across wild fields and was swallowed by a wall of forest, which was more cheerful this morning with its warm, vibrant colors and thick carpet of leaves. The cold morning fog lifted, the sun now shining through a shifting patchwork of clouds, the air fresh and crisp as a sip from a mountain brook.

Amity's mood had rebounded since the trauma of yesterday and the unburdening of her guilt, so much so that she was back to prattling and poetizing as the two girls walked on either side of Lento. Finally, Constance could take the cheery talk no more and brought up the matter she had been meaning to once Amity's mood had recovered.

"Amity, I don't wish to dampen your spirits, but do you remember what occurred yesterday?"

Amity's smile faltered. "I remember, I do, it sounded like a rattlesnake. Even from within the rockaway we could hear it out there. A rattlesnake—no, hundreds of agitated rattlesnakes. Then all at once the rattling died down, and there came a sudden crash.

"Mr. Solemn reined in the horse.

"'Downed tree,' he said and hopped down to see if he could shift it out of the road.

"'Did you hear that sound before the crash?' I asked Temperance. 'Do you think that was the Nilwere?'

"'Oh, Ms. Lancaster, I expect more from you,' she clicked her teeth while massaging those sensitive temples of hers. 'The Nilwere is nothing more than schoolgirl nonsense, a bugaboo meant to keep children walking the righteous path through the deterrent of fear. I read an enlightening essay on the subject that proposes that the "forest" the creature is said to inhabit is nothing more than an amalgam of our collective fears and base natures, and by extension, a child that wanders off track in the woods, is actually a metaphor for straying off the Way of the Family, the straight and narrow, however you want to put it. Thus, the child that loses its way in the woods, is becoming wild, barbaric; indeed, they are becoming the very bugaboo they were meant to fear. No, don't put any stock in tales of Nilweres, but rather attend to the very real dangers of longclaws or highwaymen.'

"I merely sighed during her wearisome lecture and was trying to get a look through the window, when I noticed the thick stand of trees along the roadside was practically heaving, as if all those trees were being throttled by giant invisible hands. Presently, Mr. Solemn's rifle went off, the both of us jumped, and when I turned back toward Temperance, her lecture cut short, there came another surprise. After so many years together, I thought nothing in the prudish, staid reservoir that was Ms. Temperance Jones remained that could surprise me, and here she was pulling a brilliantly polished derringer out of the ruffled sleeve of her dress. It was an act I could fathom you performing, Connie, but not her, not my Ms. Jones.

"She saw my look of astonishment and said, 'What? No need to be so shocked. We'll call this a lesson in sensibility, Ms. Lancaster. Even a lady must rely on herself for protection from time to time.'

"Then she shooed me aside and took my place by the window, studying the bending and snapping trees around us, her little pistol gleaming. After that one report from Mr. Solemn's rifle, there had been nothing more, and the woods suddenly grew still.

"I asked Temperance if she could spy anything, but she just shook her head.

"Then—but oh, it was horrible—Mr. Solemn began to scream, and that rattling ratcheted up again, so close to us now that the sound seemed to drum against the windowpanes. Temperance could stand it no longer. She threw open the door and leaned out, aiming her pistol, but before she could get off one shot, the forest seemed to collapse around us, crushing the carriage with me inside of it and Temperance thrown aside.

"Everything became confused and jumbled. Even now I can't be sure what happened next. It felt to me as if I were a nut inside a shell, for the carriage was stripped away around me, and I was frantically scrambling on hands and knees through this maze of limbs, squirming along in the mud. Though Mr. Solemn had grown quiet, Temperance had taken up his torch and was screaming, 'The Name of the Father, the Name of the Father, the Name of the Father!'

"That was the last I remember of it. I must have knocked my head against a tree, for the next thing I knew, I was in your arms."

In the sudden quiet following Amity's tale, a noise caught their attention—wheels splashing through the mud—and they exchanged glances. Leading Lento to the side of the road, Constance reached her hand into the carpetbag and drew the hatchet her father had tucked away there. This she handed to Amity, who nodded, testing its balance. Then she reached into her cloak pocket with her left hand and slipped her finger around the trigger of the pepperbox.

First to appear around the bend were a pair of mangy buckskin horses with milky, dull eyes. Behind them creaked a covered wagon, and at the reins beneath its bonnet sat two men. Both were very stout, clearly father and son, the grizzle-bearded elder clutching the reins, while the youth was busy rolling a cigarette.

Impossible to tell the contents of the wagon, given the cover and the angle of its approach, Constance slid the pistol from her pocket and gripped it at her side, keeping it hidden from view.

The younger man tucked the finished cigarette behind his ear and rose, calling out to them. "Good morning, Fair Daughters!"

His accent, pleasant and musical and drawn out, was unfamiliar to Constance.

"Good morning, sirs," she said uncertainly, watching their approach with a wary eye. Beads of sweat collected under her arms. Her palm was slick with sweat, and she adjusted her grip on the hatchet.

"Are you familiar with these parts?" the man continued when they were much closer, smiling a gap-toothed smile. "We seem to have lost our way."

They had halted right alongside Lento, and the young man, with the cigarette behind the ear and revolver on the hip, was only a few feet away. Close enough, she thought for him to make a lunge towards them—

Then she noticed the child poking her head out from behind the two men, her hair wavy and blond, face plump and smudged with dirt.

Meanwhile, the man must have noticed the pepperbox at Constance's side, for he cocked his head and grinned all the wider. "Be not afraid, Fair Daughters, for I will not draw on you. We are peaceable folk—farmers lacking a field, is all. Isn't that so, Father?"

The older one nodded without smiling, scrutinizing them beneath the brim of his straw hat. By now, another face had squeezed in behind the father—a boy a few years older than the girl.

"If you'll excuse my saying so, it's clear to see you've had your troubles. As have we. Whither are you bound?"

"To Canton, sirs."

"Or Hemlock," Amity inserted.

"Indeed, or anywhere in between, really. We've only been two days on Forest Road, but already it seems we have lost our way. My friend was attacked and lost her companions."

"Attacked by what?"

"A creature of some sort," Amity said, her ladylike comportment fully restored in the presence of these travelers, "but I didn't get a good look at it. Even so, from what I heard during the assault, I suspect it may be an entity known in Canton as the Nilwere."

"And what manner of entity is the Nilwere?"

"Unfortunately, there's not much agreement on that. Few have seen it and lived to tell the tale."

The young man grew quiet, looking back and forth between Constance and Amity, then at last towards his silent father. "And Hemlock, that's what you said?" He exhaled noisily. "Then one or both of our parties is indeed well and truly lost. We departed Glassdale on Houseday week last."

"Glassdale?"

"It's nothing more than a little hamlet in northern Blackwood. We were westward bound, making for the River Highgate, but have known for a couple days now that we must have strayed, but certainly not all the way into the State of Clairmont. You're welcome to accompany us till we can sort out our cart from our horse, then we carry on our separate ways."

"Your offer is most kind," Constance said, "but I must warn you we have been exposed to a grave pestilence known as the Cinder. It is too early to tell if we were infected, but it would be advisable to keep a distance for now."

The man nodded grimly, glanced again towards his father, whose expression revealed nothing. "I wish I could say we were strangers to the Cinder, but not so, not so. I reckon it'd be fine if you hang back in the wake of our schooner. We'll keep in sight, see that you're safe."

Constance and Amity fell in behind the wagon, which continued on as before with the young man now walking at its side, rifle slung over his shoulder. From the rear, they had a better view of the interior, which was crammed full of barrels and crates and sacks, two chickens and a cock (all caged), and one old dog with slime in its eyes who never so much as glanced up the entire duration of the journey. From the wooden arches beneath the canvas, a number of hammocks were suspended, and the two children lazed in these at times or clambered over the boxes, fitting themselves in where they could. Amity played peekaboo with the girl. As for the boy, ruddy-faced and long-haired, he had a slingshot and an endless supply of stones, which he aimed at squirrels and rabbits and a weasel-like creature that Constance had no name for. He would fire from his perch atop a box at the back of the schooner jouncing over the uneven road, then would hop down and dash into the woods to collect his game. In this manner, he bagged several animals throughout the day and always looked to Amity and Constance for approval, both of whom provided him with little patters of applause and exclamations of "Spiffing good shot!"

It was, of course, reassuring to be in the presence of others, even if the story of how these migrants had gotten lost was so disconcerting. The young man checked on them every now and again—just a turn of the head and a gap-toothed smile, enough to satisfy him that they were safe, a small gesture that nevertheless warmed Constance's heart. He was not as handsome as Sheriff Sykes, to be sure, but he was friendly and looked strong and capable.

Meanwhile, the woods grew deeper and grander, and Constance recalled her mother's words about the unsettling, unknown depths of the forest. Constance had never before seen trees so massive, with boles as big around as houses at their base and towering hundreds of feet above them. Everything here was novel—the birds, the critters, the insects—even if things did look vaguely recognizable at times, like a familiar tune played in the wrong key.

The entire day was spent watching the towering trees, listening to the tentative sounds of creatures she could not name, and crossing unknown rivers on creaking or crumbling platforms. Sometime well after midday it grew prematurely dark, and the first drop of rain struck Constance on her left hand. She glanced down and blanched, transfixed by her fingertips, then with teeth clenched she quickly sheathed it in a gray leather glove. When she looked up at the sky, every leaf was shaking as if in the throes of ague. Soon it was a roaring cascade, a wall of water beyond which the wagon and the rest of the world vanished.

Constance gloved her right hand too, then pulled the chocolate-brown hood of her cloak more securely over her head. Amity, who had grown tired long ago and mounted the mule, was huddled, shivering, beneath the shawl. Constance hastened to pull an umbrella free of the tightly packed bundle atop Lento's croup and handed it up to Amity, who extended it over both of them as best she could manage.

Though they plodded onward for some time, the road quickly grew water-logged and impassable, filling her brogans and soaking her stockings, and they had to face the prospect of passing the night in these woods. Constance led them off the road, where the ground rose and impressive cataracts of runoff gushed down. She helped Amity dismount, and the two of them unburdened Lento of the supplies, leaving him to wander and whicker while they set up a tarp between two trees.

After they hunkered down on a blanket, Constance kicked out of her waterlogged brogans, slipped off her stockings, and wrung them out.

"Thank the Father," she muttered, thinking more of Thurgood Dunn's thorough packing job than the deity who'd sent this rain.

T HE DARK OF THE storm slid seamlessly into night.

The temperature had dropped since the start of the downpour, and now they were both freezing in addition to being wet.

They spent the time singing tavern songs in low voices; Amity recited a few of the hundreds of poems Temperance had made her commit to memory, and of course they gossiped about Canton, even if it felt wrong to do so, for over half the names that slipped over their tongues had already passed into the House of the Dead.

"I tell you what I would like, Connie: cinnamon donuts and hot apple cider with a dash of whiskey!"

Constance licked her lips. "How about lamb stew with fat juicy turnips."

"Oh, I abhor turnips, Connie! No, no, simple, listen: hot bread fresh from the oven with a huge slab of butter melting over it. Oh, it's such torture. I must have it. I must."

"Bacon and eggs."

"Quotidian, but still, with a well-deserved reputation. Ahh, I know, I have it. A link of spicy pork sausage from none other than Dunn's Fine Meats and Fancy Sausages, pan-fried with pickles and sauerkraut, and served with a frothing pint of beer." She clasped her hands together in complete rapture.

"Why, I think I might have one of those. A boiled one, at any rate. Let's take a look." She opened her pack, sorting through various bits. It all looked purplish black and indistinct, so (with trouble in the damp) she lit the oil lamp and made a more proper study of things. Brightening, Amity peered over Constance's shoulder. "Ah yes, pumpernickel, and all this damp has kept it from hardening too much, and, yes, I thought so, one link of spicy sausage—"

Something popped out in the woods.

Amity tensed and Constance shut up, shielding the light of their lantern. She scanned the woods with her light-ruined eyes, waiting for something to make itself known to her. But she could see nothing ...

Another *pop*.

After a moment's hesitation, Constance unshielded the lantern, for if there was something out there, it had already seen them, and hiding from it would only prolong the inevitable. She uncorked the wine skin and took a sip to fortify her nerves, then passed it to Amity.

Another sound came to her ears, closer than before. *CRACK.*

She turned towards the sound and had to stifle a gasp. A dark, billowy form stood not ten feet from them, near the umbrella, which Constance had left leaning and outspread on the ground.

"Fair Daughters, I didn't mean to startle you." It was the voice of the young man from the covered wagon. "But we were concerned for your welfare."

He approached the umbrella, set down a small white bundle beneath it, then retreated a few paces.

"I would join you this evening and make merry, if not for this pestiferous season. The Cinder touched our village as well, you see. Took my mother and sister, and took the parents of the little ones we brought along—and practically everyone else. The land is poisoned, my father said, and so we departed. They need me now, but in a few days' time, when we can be sure that you're not ill, you can ride with us if you so choose. Goodnight."

He turned and the darkness soon swallowed him up. Hood up, Constance scuttled out of the tent and unfolded the linen package, discovering inside two green apples and a cold, charred, spatchcocked pheasant, perhaps a day old.

"Thank you, Good Son!" she called after him. "I hope someday to repay you for your kindness! Bless the Family!"

She rewrapped the food using the rote method she learned at the shop, then under the protection of the umbrella returned to Amity.

They laid out their supper and Constance spoke the Prayer of Gratitude:

"For this air we breathe,

And this heart that beats,

For this wine that slakes,

And this food that sates,

For these hands that build—"

She looked up as she heard Amity's voice joining hers:

"And this earth we tilled,

For this blood that flows,

And this mind that knows;

We give thanks to the Family."

Then they bit into the cold, tough flesh.

Unspiced, unsalted, unmarinated, singed, it still ranked among the best pieces of meat Constance had ever eaten. She stripped the bones clean from the thigh and sucked off every stray bit of gristle and cartilage, then tossed the bones out into the darkness and cleaned her gloves and greasy mouth on a small portion of the linen. They ate the apples—stems, core, and all. Then some cheese and bread, and finally the spicy sausage, washing everything down with swigs of wine.

Nearby, Lento huffed and snorted, calmly rummaging and at ease in the shimmering, lamplit rain.

Meal finished, they sat back, leaning against each other beneath the tarp, their gloved hands in their laps.

"Connie?"

"Yes, little swan?"

"Are your hands cold?"

She hesitated a moment—a needless question, they were freezing, of course—but she understood. "No."

"Neither are mine."

The Thing in the Woods

CONSTANCE WOKE LATE IN the night.

The rain must have ceased hours ago, leaving the woods dripping and wilted and fragrant with the disintegrating leaves. She shivered, rewrapping herself in her cloak. One of the knots holding up the tarp had come loose, and it now sagged over her legs, soaking her fresh pair of stockings. She shifted closer to Amity, their bodies pressed together, and lay there for a few minutes, watching the woods, her breath smoking. The moon was swollen and bright, close to setting, and its light colored the night quicksilver. Nothing moved out there, too cold and wet for the nocturnal world to go about its routine. Amity slept restively, murmuring for her governess, clutching at her shawl.

Constance closed her eyes, trying to return to sleep, but the details of Amity's story from the day before kept replaying in her mind, and she couldn't help but wonder just what Temperance and Emmanuel Solemn had seen before they died. Her thoughts were growing more and more muddled, bleeding together and swirling down into the dusky maelstrom of sleep—when she heard the distant boom.

Her eyes popped open, the fuzziness of her mind clearing in an instant, flushing out the murky waters. Amity's eyes were open too—orbs of gray and black staring back. Constance pressed a silencing finger to her own lips and continued to listen, head raised slightly off the ground to free up both ears. Her heart beating fast, she pressed her gloved hands against Amity's, and they huddled close together.

"It's nothing, I'm sure," Constance whispered. "Sleep."

Wide-eyed, breathing in short, shallow breaths as if she'd been flung back into her former state of shock from two days ago, Amity could barely even nod. But minutes slipped past, and she at last managed to shut her eyes. Her heart rate evening back out, Constance also closed her eyes, but they darted busily and pointlessly behind their lids, dancing to the frantic rhythm of her disordered thoughts. Amity's hands squeezed her own, and she returned the pressure, an echo of solace.

Moments later the sound repeated, and both Constance and Amity's eyes opened simultaneously. Then she understood that she was not only hearing it; she was *feeling* it. The rumble came again after a ponderous interval, louder this time. And again, the intervals growing shorter and shorter, her heart beating jackrabbit-quick all the while.

A bizarre fear suddenly seized her—the source of this thudding could *feel her* as well, could feel the insect fluttering of her tiny heart in the empty, oceanic night. Releasing her clutch on one of Amity's delicate hands, Constance laid one hand across her breast, as if by doing so she could pet her heart, could console and calm it—*be still, be still, be still*—but instead she became aware of how the pounding channeled down the length of her arm, through her elbow and into the moist earth.

Father, I'm driving myself mad. It's nothing. It's a moose, a longclaw, perhaps some madman is felling trees in the wee hours.

As she thought this, she heard the distant but unmistakable groan of wood splintering, the rushing of leaves, and the boom of a tree trunk crashing into the earth.

Finally, she sat up and pulled her cloak tight about her, concealing the paleness of her face and neck. She tucked her feet, in their damp gray wool stockings, beneath the hem of her dress, whose deep red was almost black in the darkness. She listened as the felling of trees grew closer and closer ...

Lento startled and brayed but stood fast. Constance crept over and touched the spooked animal, Amity following close behind. The mule was stamping and huffing, rotating his ears outward, nostrils dilating, eyes wide, shaking his head, tail swishing. Constance whispered comforting words into his ears, stroking his mane. "Beautiful, brave thing. Protect your Constance and Amity, and we'll give you a treat. We need you to be brave for us. What would you fancy? A beet? Some oat bread and molasses?"

The mule resisted her at first, backing away, but as soon as he escaped her touch, he seemed to decide that, yes, consolation was preferable, so he let Constance pet and bolster him up, still resisting and fussing with indecision. Amity helped steady him, but the way she shook, eyes darting here and there, suggested she needed just as much support.

Constance smiled despite her fear, brushing his forelock, and pressing her face against his muzzle. However, her smile faltered as she realized the impacts of falling trees had ceased. The woods had grown darker too, and it took Constance a moment to realize why.

Something had just now eclipsed the light of the setting moon.

She could see at some distance a lumpy, massive outline, a hillock sprouting out of the ground and engulfing the road. It was too dark to make out any of the details, but whatever it was, it did not breathe but only emitted a rotten stench, thick tendrils of it reaching out to them like a spreading fog.

From farther down the road came the whinny of a horse and the cries of the migrants.

"Amity," she whispered, "we're too close to the road. We must flee deeper into the woods."

Amity's eyes were wide, and she was blubbering silently, frozen to the spot, so Constance guided her up onto Lento's back, quickly untied him, her panicky hands fumbling with the rope.

She dashed back for the pepperbox which had been lying beside her on the tarp, when the creature began to move, dragging its bulk along the road with a rumble Constance felt in her bones. Moonlight flooded the shadowy woods, for the thing had slithered away, shaking the forest as it moved, uprooting trees, toppling them in a wave along the road. Lento snorted and, uncharacteristically both for him and his namesake, dashed off, Amity clinging to his neck. Constance tried to grab his reins, but she was too slow.

"No, no, no," she called—too loud, too loud—fleeing after them.

In her mad haste she stumbled and slid down an embankment of slimy leaves, colliding with the wet bole of an oak tree, and by the time she regained her footing, the mule had vanished into the night.

Then the screams began.

S HE WOULD LATER LOOK back on that night, overcome with shame and regret.

There were the reports of gunfire, the wails of the children, a screaming horse silenced by the wet tear of flesh and the crack of bone. And she could hear *it* dragging itself across the ground, could hear the quivering and flapping of its flesh and that omnipresent percussive rattling.

She had not made it far before stopping, burrowing beneath the thick layer of wet leaves in a bower underneath the weeping limbs of a twisted, old camperdown tree.

There, trying to shut out the sounds of carnage, she soon felt the hot bloom of piss spread through her drawers. Trembling, she repeated silently the opening line of one of the Mother's prayers: "Merciful Mother, Merciful Mother, Merciful Mother, Merciful Mother."

The rest would not come to her, leaving her mind stuck in this spasmodic loop.

Someone was gasping, calling for help for the longest time. It was the young man with the gap-toothed smile, who had given them the pheasant and apples.

Yes, I'll move and go to his aid, she thought, her feet like stone, her body frozen in place.

I'll move now. I will.

At the end, when the echoes of the screams and gunshots had died, she could sense that the creature wanted more, that the massacre had not sated its taste for blood. All told, only a few minutes (which felt like hours) had passed between the first and last of the screams, the moon still hanging on the horizon, as if stitched in place and unable to bow its way offstage. *The Book of the Family* was replete with such tales—when traumas so great occurred that the Heavens altered course, that souls became detached from their bodies and wandered freely. And maybe Constance had actually escaped with Amity but left behind this small, craven fragment of her soul to experience more poignantly the guilt of flight and survival.

The creature, the thing in the woods, lingered there for a long time. She heard pops and explosions of gas, the obscene sound of flesh rubbing together excitedly. It never once grunted or moaned or spoke, but every now and then she heard that clacking or rattling sound. A chorus of clacking—not twigs or prayer drums or rattles—no, it was like hundreds of little bones knocking together.

A pale gray mist floated over the ground, and before long stray bits of golden morning shone through the trees, gilding the sodden earth and the carpet of fiery leaves. The creature had finally departed, she knew, from the tentative ratcheting up of birdsong, the freshness of the air, and from the unseen weight lifted from the woods. Constance crawled out from her bower, parting the camperdown's tendril-like branches. Her long, dark hair had completely spilled out of its bun, spangled with twigs and leaves—like a sylvan sprite—her dark-red dress begrimed with rotten leaves.

She scanned the woods for any sign of Amity or Lento—a flash of golden-red hair or a pale muzzle, a soiled green dress or a muddied fetlock—but saw only the wet trees and a scrim of mist that withheld much of the forest from her. She worked up the courage to call out for her friend and her mule in a loud whisper, but to no avail.

Then she climbed the embankment she had tumbled down hours ago. At the top she continued her search for the mule's trail, but there was no sign of freshly trodden leaves or snapped saplings or torn swaths of garment or any of those other convenient tracks she could remember from the adventure stories she had read as a child.

At last she came upon her campsite and found her cloak and Amity's shawl, and there was the pepperbox she had gone for then dropped again in the confusion. She donned her own cloak and neatly folded the garment she had lent to her friend. Then she plucked up her hatchet and pistol and crept as quietly as possible towards the road, vigilant for signs of life or movement.

When she reached the road, she was struck by the malodorous, blossom-wilting stench lingering behind—fecal and rotten—but also the perfume of splintered wood and sap. She noticed the trail veering away from the road—a narrow clearing that stretched a hundred yards or so into the distance before turning away, from which pine and spruce trees had been battered aside, some uprooted and lying flat or bent at pathetic angles.

In the other direction, toward where the migrants had camped, Constance squelched through the mud, ears pricked, turning over every sound near and far. The clatter of branches sounded like long, yellow claws knocking together. The rushing of the wind could have been air puffed out of giant nostrils. From a distance, she could see that the wagon was no more—ripped and pulverized, its components scattered. Foodstuffs ruined, equipment destroyed and unidentifiable, barrels of grain exploded. She scanned the woods again, consumed with paranoia, sure she would find some giant eye blinking at her from behind the file of swaying trees. Her line of sight was so limited, the tapestry of the woods so intricate and impenetrable, the mist still so thick, that she could see nothing.

As she got closer to the clearing, she found gobbets of horse—a hoof, a pulpy mass of mane and skull shards. Here was a rifle snapped like a twig, the wooden stock splintered, but the steel not completely separated, just enough so that if Constance had wanted she could have looked down both lengths of the barrel from its center.

Then there was a child's arm.

Her stomach twisted at the sight of the small, slender limb lying gray and blood-spattered in the mud, so delicate. There was a boot with a gory spear of bone sticking out of its opening.

Hard leather, dark.

It was the young man's foot and shin inside there. She remembered the taste of pheasant and retched, dropping to her knees.

When she rose, wiping her mouth, her knees were shaking, threatening to buckle. She felt the blood draining from her face and thought she might pass out, but she continued on, finding more and more pieces, everything mixed together, telling an incomprehensible tale.

No sign of Amity.

Turning stupidly in small circles at the center of the campsite, Constance noticed a curious detail: everything was ruined, and yet, from what she could tell, the beast had not consumed anything, not even the chickens, whose crushed bodies she found squashed into the mud—the attacker had not been motivated by hunger. Bills of the unfamiliar currency from the State of Blackwood could be found scattered about the site of the attack, like the leaves shed from an exotic tree—the attacker had not been motivated by greed.

Another puzzling point was the presence of rotten flesh among the fresher pieces. There were entire limbs thick with flaps of livid skin stretched across them, yellowed bone that might have been years old, and a skull veiled with a putrefying slime, its jawbone shattered from buckshot.

Constance was at a loss as to what she should do. She left the scene of violence and found her way back to her own strangely small and tidy campsite. It had a guilty tidiness. She sat down on the tarp and listened to the honking and chirping and twittering of birds, sounds which had an unsettling and false cheeriness to them. It was as if the woods themselves were trying to deceive her, to lure her into a sense of safety before thrusting the horror upon her once more.

Eventually, she washed out the taste of vomit in her mouth and changed her drawers. She drank a little water, then ate a bite of the sharp and crumbly cheese. Her hunger grew keener as she ate, her bites less mechanical. She craved tea and oatmeal with honey and butter—better yet, a quotidian plate of bacon and eggs.

The numbness and idiot paralysis that had overtaken her in the night was beginning to thaw out. She felt a curious gaping emptiness in her chest when she remembered Amity playing peekaboo with the child, the clever boy with the slingshot, the green apples, the roasted pheasant. Her body felt as if it had been carved out.

But what could I have done? she asked herself. Had she attempted to intervene, she would have ended up another piece in the confused smorgasbord of corpse parts.

She pulled out the pepperbox revolver and examined it. Each of its six rotating barrels contained a round, but then again, a shotgun hadn't stopped the thing. A fresh wave of guilt washed over her. *Why did I let go of Lento's reins? If I hadn't, Amity would still be here with me, I wouldn't be alone in this wilderness. Why was I so fatuous? Why?*

She looked up toward the sky, as if expecting an answer to these silent questions. By now, the clouds had dispersed, giving way to a clear blue. The colors were vibrant, the air growing warm, and the moisture dissolved into great curtains that scintillated as they rose through the shafts of sunlight.

She tucked the gun into her gray ribbon belt and began pacing around her campsite, gathering up her belongings, rolling them up or nesting them inside one another, and packing her carpetbag and the sack of camping equipment and victuals her father had prepared for her.

This was the third day since their departure from Canton. There was little hope for Constance's mother at this point, unless the courier that had been sent earlier to Hemlock had at last returned with medicine and a doctor. Not an impossibility. Either way, lost as Constance was, she could only continue down this road and hope to stumble upon some bastion of civilization, from which she could get her bearings and find her way home.

In the remote chance that Amity would find her way back to their campsite, with a knife and the blunt end of the hatchet Constance carved an arrow in the bole of a maple tree, pointing the way she intended to travel. Beneath it, a C.

As she passed the massacre once again, Constance took the time to move bodies out of the wreckage, bury them beneath a mound of leaves, and mark the spot with a circle of stones. She may have accidentally included some horse or dog along with the humans, but no one would blame her for it. Then she gathered up some of the unspoiled provender—a hard loaf of black barley bread, a wedge of cheddar cheese, various dried fruits and roots, and filled one of the extra skins with beer from the unbroken cask.

It would be enough to keep her.

THE TERRAIN GREW ROCKIER by degrees and soon giant shards of stone thrust up through the forest floor. The road wound up the side of a cliff face fuzzed with lichen and disgorged her from the forest and into a breezy, sun-kissed meadow teeming with goldenrod, which swept up to a jagged rocky ridge. To the left, the forest of stunted, gnarly trees dropped away to a collection of lakes and ponds (she counted at least twenty before losing track) like the burrowed holes of some colossal serpent. Beyond all of this rose snow-capped mountains standing like the serrated edge of a frosty blade on the horizon. The mountains near Canton were nowhere near as grandiose as these. Like the lake they had encountered on the first day of their journey towards Hemlock, these mountains should not exist.

Looking back down the winding road she'd traveled, a flash of red made her catch her breath, but a gust of wind revealed it to be the waving branches of a sumac tree, the hue of its leaves mimicking Amity's fiery curls.

Disappointed, the illusion had reminded her of her duty, and she arranged in the center of the road an arrow of stones with another C, then continued on.

She ate her dinner on a table of rock, taking beer and dried cinnamon apples and salted carrot slices. Then she peeled all the golden skin off her onion and ate the sweet, pungent flesh in layers, her eyes stinging and watery by the end. Her fingertips were tingling; she wiped her lachrymose eyes before examining her fingers in the sunlight, discovering that one of the spots had grown since yesterday. Even now, she prayed it was campfire ash—campfire ash that would not rub off no matter how vigorously she tried. She slipped her gloves back on and gazed out at the landscape, mind a blank.

KEEP OUT, CINDER.

A coldness washed over her as a down of clouds eclipsed the sun, fleecing the land of its warmth, the line of shadow racing off into the distance as quick as a falcon. It was one of the most beautiful places she had ever seen, with the light split up by the clouds, creating an umbrous patchwork. She seemed to be witnessing many countries, many worlds, many days, many lives all at one time, and all of them clipped and spread out before her, for her sampling pleasure, like the buffet at the Winter Solstice Party.

And this year?

Who will remain to attend?

She continued to eat, tasting nothing.

There were signs of civilization: here and there cottages dotted the meadow, with stone fences lacking sheep, no smoke puffing out of the chimneys, the walls in disrepair; the broken, barely visible road had been marked with obelisk milestones carved in a foreign script that was so faded the compact orthography seemed to have been submerged in the stone; far off, she even spotted the remains of a castle spread across an island and spilling out into the water.

Nearby, a small tollhouse sat at the juncture of the main road and a small, dry riverbed, the structure itself nothing more than three remaining walls—the fourth wall and roof having been smashed or caved in with time. Beyond it was a collapsed bridge, its gray planks scattered among the rocks.

Her meal finished, she packed her belongings and traversed the uneven ground towards the tollhouse—the closest of all the ruins dotting the countryside. Peering inside, she found it just as wild within as without, the sunlight filtering down through the sagging skeleton of the ceiling. Then, a surprise. Covered in moss and crawling with insects, a flattened metal boot was poking out of the rubble where the stone wall and ceiling had caved in.

A soloret, she reminded herself, recalling her fairy tales.

She stepped inside, startling out a few yellow snakes, and recovering from the mild shock of them slithering over her brogans, she shifted a couple of ceiling beams and then stone after stone. There were maybe fifty of them, none of them too heavy.

Once she had moved everything off to the other side of the tollhouse, she saw beneath all that rubble exactly what she had suspected to find: an old suit of armor lying tangled and crushed in the weeds, still relatively intact, but rusted and weather-eaten and flattened in places. She saw no evidence of a body inside, no tunnel of ribs papered in desiccated flesh, for through the seams and chinks of the armor, there was nothing but space, cobwebbed and weed-choked and insect-busy.

Perhaps it had been some decoration of an eccentric tollhouse keeper. Indeed, the style of armor was that of one of the southern kingdoms, she guessed, based on the intricate arabesque patterns and pictographs etched into the tarnished and rusted metal. Still, Constance was no expert and could not say exactly which kingdom it was. Suits of armor were taboo—the sorts of decorations you would have found lining the halls of nobility, before those halls had been ransacked and burned—and the only one she had encountered before now (outside of fairy tales) was the curiously small one in the front hall of Mayor Lancaster's home, which had always given her goosebumps as she fought to stifle the image of the puck scrawny enough to squeeze inside. This one, though bigger, was just as useless, crushed as it was, but even so, she could tell it had once been a thing of beauty.

As she wandered back to the road, the groan of metal came to her ears, and she turned back, watching the skeleton of the tollhouse, listening for more, but all was quiet, just the whispering flux of wind in the grass and her hair and all that it touched.

The meadows had descended gradually, almost begrudgingly, into more woodland. And for hours now she had been plunged back into that oppressive and repetitive world: like the jerky animation of a young woman in a zoetrope, forever walking through a forest. She had preferred the open air, had breathed easier out there, where the promise of escape lay in every direction, where the approach of a monster could be spotted from miles away.

At times, her nostrils would twitch as her nose caught some phantom scent in the damp air. She paused at every freshly fallen tree, studying it for traces of the Nilwere. At one moment when the breeze shifted just right, she thought she could hear over the rustle of leaves that curious clattering sound from early this morning, but her ears had been playing tricks on her all day, and she was having trouble discerning phantoms from facts.

When she did at last come across its tracks, wide as a locomotive's, snaking out of the woods and over the road, there was no mistaking it. The crushed trees, the snapped branches, the lingering stench. She also noticed a sludge glazing the ground and the trunks of the trees it had rubbed up against, within which she found evidence of its victims: fingers and teeth, chunks of greenish flesh and fragments of bone.

Using some broken sticks, she left another arrow and C in the road, and it was at this moment that she noticed the darkening of the sky and heard the distant rumble of thunder.

Another Son-accursed storm.

She drew the revolver, readied it for firing, stuffed it back into her ribbon belt, and continued on. An hour or more passed, the sky growing darker and darker, but the rain still withholding.

Then she heard a faint braying, and she at once grew alert, for distant though it was, she recognized the timbre and pitch of it, even the frightful wobble of the creature.

Lento.

She set forth with a newfound sense of determination, as if by recovering the poor, dumb beast she could amend the wrongs of the previous evening, could bring back the dead migrants, retrieve the pistol *before* untying the mule—unravel the shawl of time and re-darn it in a new design, a better, less-bungled version

She sprinted, calling out Amity's name, calling out Lento's name, and the braying ceased momentarily.

When she rounded the bend in the woods, there was the mule, bedraggled and scrawny, a ways down the road, but no sign of her friend. Lento brayed again when his master appeared—he brayed plaintively, accusingly—and as she approached, he continued to do so in what struck her more and more as dismay. When he turned, she saw that the poor beast had been wounded, a gash torn open along its side, coating its underbelly black with blood.

She had made it only a few steps towards him when suddenly an old elm tree crashed down on the road between them, and an immense, foul mass spilled out on top of the tree, as if the forest had vomited up something too unpleasant to stomach.

The thing in the woods had found her.

In Shining Armor

ONCE THE CREATURE SPILLED out of the woods, it damaged something in Constance—a veil that separated the real from the unreal, a veil that, once torn, no matter what else would follow, left her ever after doubtful, wondering if she were still in fact wandering Forest Road.

In all the years she had heard about the Nilwere, Constance Dunn had envisioned some species of horrible beast, something between a bear and a longclaw—a shadowy, elephantine wolf with glistening teeth as big as arms and shaggy black fur that obscured its shape, which loped about on two legs and had a taste for careless children that didn't listen to their parents. But as with so many things, the horror turned out to be human, or, in this case, *humans*, for the mass seething before her was a composite of flesh and bone corded and knotted and fused abhorrently together, not of a single dead person but of hundreds of human cadavers.

Many now were threadbare skeletons twisting around and worming through fresher flaps of blue-black corpse, and still others were dripping with putrefaction, skin bubbling and bursting with gas. As the blob before her writhed, a trunk of tangled bodies separated from it with the tearing of flesh and craned upwards, causing a wave of maggots to slosh out onto the ground. Its great mouth was twenty or more hands splayed out in a circle, the wriggly fingers like the eyelash feelers of a Venus flytrap. Countless milky gray orbs pimpled this mound of rot, out of which the deformed faces of its component pieces stared out in glazed-eyed death.

As she stood there frozen with horror and repulsion, the torrent began. She was soaked through in no time, skin cold, clothes heavy and clinging, the umbrella poking out of her carpetbag forgotten, and still, neither she nor the thing nor Lento moved. Lightning crackled down somewhere nearby, momentarily coloring the creature in novel ways, before the washed-out blues and grays of the storm flooded back over everything.

The revolver, like a piece of timber floating to the surface of a pond, rose before Constance's eyes, her hands attached to it so lightly there was almost no connection at all between them and the instrument of death. She became aware of the smooth feel of the metal and wood and the gun's heft, and as her focus shifted, she fixed her grip, set her mouth, squinting in preparation of the blast, and fired. The thing exploded in her hands with a plume of smoke, the crack like a new voice in the choir of thunder, then slipped from her grip and dropped into the brown puddle swilling around her feet, vanishing with a plop unheard above the ringing in her ears and the thrash of rain. The bullet sank into the mass of bodies, and it quivered, shedding off a negligible chunk of itself.

Constance dropped down into the muck, dug into the puddle, mud sloshing down into her gloves and sucking them off. Panicked sounds escaped a mouth that didn't seem to be hers. She felt as if she had slipped inside the body of another person, squeezing their arms on like snakeskin and their face over hers like a mask centimeters too thick. Coming to her from some faraway world, she heard Lento's mad brays and hoofbeats as he dashed off.

The ground rumbled as the Nilwere began its slither and tumble towards her, but she would not look up—could not bring herself to see more of it.

Her fingers grazed against something solid, then it slipped away.

A shadow loomed over her, and the limb of some long-dead human ripped free of the creature and splashed into the mud beside her, still clawing and moving in its curious parody of life.

The reek of death impregnated the air, overpowering the notes of burnt powder and the mineral scent of rain. Her fingers, clawing through the mud, landed on the revolver at last, and she lifted it, her eyes following with reluctance. Its massive appendage, like a flower stalk of rotten limbs, blossomed and struck down, pinning her to the flooding earth. The gun went off, muddy as it was, firing by some miracle, but the bullet shot out into the forest.

The ground shook as the Nilwere churned and lurched, jerking her face-down through the mud, the dead limbs coiling about her, split black fingernails clawing at her skin. She wriggled and fought against it, desperate for a breath, waiting for the moment when she could blow the slop from her lips and nose and snatch a gulp of fetid air.

Suddenly, she was airborne, dangling upside down, her hair dragging through the mud, and at last she breathed—breathed in the full effluvium of the corpses. Rain washed down the sludge of decay, down her legs, soaking her clothes, down her chin, across her lips, up her nose. She imagined the center ditch of Main Street after a storm, having washed in its share of rotten vegetables from the vendor's trash stalls, a drowned a rat or two; she imagined her own face plunged into the filth, the slimy wash of it—and was violently sick, relieved to rid her body of whatever poison was running up her nose, trying to find its way inside her.

Then, her head struck against a stone with a crack, and all was dark.

H ER BODY HAD GROWN numb.

For a moment the world moved away from her, scrolling out towards some starless darkness. In a sudden panic, she remembered the creature that had found and abducted her, and she realized she was being carried upside down, rocked and jerked this way and that by the uneven surging motions of the creature, suspended in the air by its sole tendril of decaying flesh.

The words of Faith Sallyforth came to her mockingly: "You got business in the city, take Highland Road." Constance wanted to cry and beg Faith's forgiveness for not believing her. But no. Faith was dead. She'd been one of the first to have her hair fall out and limbs rot off. Constance would never again see Faith Sallyforth's friendly, apple-cheeked face, would never hand her those two pounds of ground pork on Maydays or the one pound of brisket on Dochdays or any of it. Only in memory would she see the woman's pleasant, ruddy face come through the shop door and hear her cheery greeting and engage in a little chat. Faith Sallyforth, her parents, Amity, all of Canton.

"I'm sorry," Constance whispered to the upside-down world that scrolled away from her. "I'm sorry, I'm sorry."

As her mind cleared, she became aware of the world beyond the shifting squelch and heaving slog of the Nilwere, beyond the thunder and roar of the rain, a sound...

Tucka-tuck, tucka-tuck, tucka-tuck.

Hoofbeats.

At a gallop.

The sound grew sharper, clearer by the second.

Her heart leapt, and she turned her head, scanning the upside-down woods to her left and right. Lightning struck, and in that instant she glimpsed a dark form, rain-thrashed and flitting through the shadows at the top of an embankment—like some gargantuan raven flapping and stirring up the wet, dead leaves. A tree was cleaved in two by the blast and crashed onto the road behind them, its other half erupting in flames along the edges of the jagged splinter, sizzling and hissing in the downpour.

The darkness deepened anew following the white brilliance of the lightning, and Constance's dazzled eyes lost track of the form. Perhaps it was just some forest beast fleeing in terror from the Nilwere after all.

But then the drum of hoofbeats returned to her ears, the cloaked figure reemerging, now riding swiftly along the rocky edge over the road. The rider was aiming a rifle two-handed, the reins looped around the crook of one elbow. The next moment another boom thundered through the woods, a bright flash bursting forth from the barrel.

The effect was instantaneous. The thing's grip loosened on Constance, and she tumbled down the slope of bone and decay, splashing into the mud, then scrambling away as the living mausoleum began to shake and convulse, the only sound the disparate clicking of its hundreds of sets of teeth in the percussive, macabre concert that had haunted these lands for so long.

She crawled through the puddle, gasping for help. Every detail of the scene suddenly became magnified: the pummeling of the rain, the blessed fragrance of the mud, and the look of her slate-colored fingertips, cracked and splintered.

I have it. I do. Father, save me. Mother, comfort me. The gray demon has possessed me.

Behind her came a great slopping crash as the Nilwere's integrity gave way, and the assemblage of melded-together body parts now spilled across the ground, no longer as a giant atrocity, but a hazard of rotting pieces. A thick, high stench that had built up inside the creature rolled across the ground, washing over Constance anew. She gagged and pulled the hood of her wet cloak over her mouth and nose.

A voice was calling out to her. "Are you injured?" It was raspy, harsh, and deep.

Woozy, her head throbbing, she struggled to her feet as the horse and rider ambled down the slope. She glimpsed the rider's face beneath the shadow of his hood, making out little but the shape of an aquiline nose and thin lips set in a grim expression. The rifle, which he had slung behind his back, still smoked, making him seem as if he were a creature formed from the mist.

"I... I don't believe I am." The image of flaking, flinty gray skin inserted itself into her mind's eye. "I thank you, sir. You saved me. I owe you more than I could ever repay." She glanced warily back at the pile of bodies, half expecting them to reassemble right in front of her eyes. Before Constance had even the time to resign herself to her fate, the creature had been slain, the sudden shift in circumstances as unreal as the procession of events in a dream.

He studied her for a moment, then said, "What are you doing out here alone?"

"It's a long story. I hail from Canton. Do you know it?"

He nodded, and she took his familiarity with the name of the small town, his lack of surprise upon hearing it, as a positive sign; perhaps she and Amity had not traveled too far afield after all.

"I was with another young woman and a wagon of four others who hailed from ..." The name did not come readily to her mind, and panic fluttered in her chest, as if by losing the name of their hometown she was effacing their memory in some way. "Glassdale. *Glassdale*. In Blackwood. We were attacked."

"You held your own admirably. Such an atrocity might very well drive some mad. Few would fight back the way I saw you do."

"You saw me attacking it?"

"I have been tracking this beast through the wilderness for some time now. Are you ill?" he asked in his gruff way.

"Yes... but how did you know?"

"Approach."

Constance obeyed but only took several steps, not wanting to endanger her savior. "We were traveling to Hemlock to seek a doctor. You see, the only physician in Canton, Doc Harwood, had fallen prey to a disease known as the Cinder—it has consumed nearly everyone." She wondered how, if at all, this stranger was managing to piece together the fragments of her story.

"You don't look ill."

Constance clenched her fists and exhaled heavily, holding out her left hand for him to see. The mud had washed away, and the gray spoiling two of the fingertips on her left hand was unmistakable. Maybe some of her hair had begun to gray like Amity's had, but if so, she didn't want to know. "The first signs of infection have begun to show. You're familiar with the disease?"

"Come closer, Fair Daughter."

About ten feet away already, Constance shook her head. "The party I was traveling with, they kept a distance from me and the other young woman. I do not wish to risk your life."

"I'm not frightened of Cinder infection."

"Why not?"

"I have worked up an immunity to it. Come. I will take you to my manor, and we will see how far the disease has progressed."

"I cannot, sir. I must return to Canton. Many more are infected, and with the Nilwere destroyed, the road is once again safe—"

"At my manor there is refreshment: a bath, a bed, rest."

She shook her head.

"There is a doctor, as well," he continued, "skilled as any one you will find in Hemlock."

"A doctor?" She took a step closer. "One that can cure the Cinder?"

"Yes," he nodded. "A man with considerable experience treating the disease."

She licked her lips.

"Give me your hand. Ride with me. I will see to your safety."

"But my village—"

"I understand the predicament you are in, but you can accompany me without compunction. I will send a rider to travel to Hemlock through the night. By morning, succor will be obtained. Within days, a doctor and a wagonload of supplies will have arrived at Canton. By the time you yourself are healed and returned safely to your people, the plague should be under control. Rejoice, Fair Daughter, for your ordeals have come to an end."

The rain was slackening, but still he kept his head hooded, face concealed but for the tip of his nose and his frowning, wrinkled mouth with its thin, slack lips.

"Thank the Father," she said but wondered why the benediction sounded so uncertain on her lips.

She took his large, gloved hand, and he helped her up onto his piebald stallion. Strapped to the mount behind the saddle she was surprised to find her carpetbag.

"How did you—" she started.

"Put these on," he said, interrupting her, and handed over his own black riding gloves. She slipped them on, her fingers barely reaching past the base of the fourchettes, the soft silken lining warmed by his hands; it was a relief to cover up her cracking, discolored fingers. "Not too far a ride, we will arrive before midnight," he said.

And they galloped off.

Mistress Constance

"Connie, come look," Amity whispered.

She was kneeling on the window seat, dressed in her nightgown, a candle in her hand. Constance slipped out of bed, her stockinged feet buffering out the cold in the floorboards as she crossed the room. It was the eve of the Winter Solstice, and the mayor's house was full of the warm, comforting odors of spices and sweets and roast meat as the servants cooked on through the night in preparation for the banquet the next day. For several years straight, Amity had invited Constance to sleep over on Winter Solstice Eve, so she had someone to make mischief with. That evening, they had skulked down to the kitchen and filched a plate of currant rolls and had just finished gorging themselves, licking their fingers clean of the creamy frosting. Then Smidgen, the Lancaster dog, had begun yipping downstairs, and Amity had crawled out of bed and over to the window to see what was the matter.

Constance joined her, and kneeling side by side they peered down on the snow-covered streets of Canton. There stood a figure in the center of the road, spoiling the fresh white mantle. For a fleeting moment, Constance thought it was a tree sprouting out of the ground, pale at the bottom, its top limb blackened.

Then, she noticed the footprints leading out from a nearby alley, and she realized it was a naked woman, old and wrinkled, everything exposed on her frail, sagging body. Her frazzled, icy hair grew out in a great white fan all the way down to her thighs. And her left arm, barely thicker than Mr. Prisewick's schoolhouse switch, stuck straight up past her head, twisted around, its skin black and covered with frost, except for the unnaturally white hand, which appeared to be porcelain.

"She'll freeze to death out there," Constance whispered.

"Father says it would be a mercy," Amity responded as she snuffed out the candle.

"Why?"

"That's Old Lady Yorin," Amity said, eyes still fixed on the tiny figure below.

Finding that no further explanation was forthcoming, Constance asked, "Who?"

The woman did not move an inch, just stood swaying in the wintry wind.

"You haven't heard the rhyme?"

"S-sure I have."

"Oh, Connie, you're so transparent. You must learn to dissemble."

Constance ignored her. "Let's go get her. It's the Winter Solstice after all. We'll have good luck next year if we help someone tonight."

"No, Connie. She's dangerous, a madwoman, don't you know? Thinks she lost her arm—that black thing hanging over her head. Supposedly, she comes from a farm near Tree-on-the-Hill. Everyone died there of some pestilence years and years ago when she was my mother's age, and she's been wandering from town to town ever since." Her voice lowered even more. "They think she's cursed."

Constance would later hear a different story about Old Lady Yorin from her mother, and Pious Kelly had his own variation. Ultimately, no one seemed to know the truth, but at this moment, Constance did not doubt a word of her friend's story.

As they watched, Sheriff Karst and Deputy Sykes appeared on the scene, the two men bearing blankets, which they wrapped around the woman, then led her back along her tracks and vanished into the alley. After they had gone, all that remained were sets of footprints meeting in the center of the road.

Smidgen had long since quit his yapping, and Amity, bored and yawning, climbed down and returned to bed, Constance at her heels.

"Knock, knock, knock, what's at the door?" Amity sang as they climbed back into the big bed piled with quilts.

"What's that?" Constance asked.

"Yorin's black arm wriggling on the floor."

Constance tittered uncomfortably. "You're going to give me nightmares."

This, of course, was the wrong thing to say to Amity, who flashed her fang with delight. Once they had burrowed down into the little, dark cave they had been lying in before Amity went to go investigate the disturbance, she began again:

"Knock, knock, knock, what's at the door?
Yorin's black arm wriggling on the floor.
Clump, clump, clump, who's down there?
Yorin's black arm slinking up the stairs.
Scratch, scratch, scratch, nothing to dread.
Yorin's black arm waiting under the bed."

"That's horrid," Constance said and reached out to grasp hold of Amity's hand, but the touch of their fingers together felt odd. "Amity?"

Her friend had gone suddenly quiet.

She could feel the cold seeping up through the mattress and shivered. It was too dark to see anything down here in their quilt burrow, but holding onto Amity's hand, she batted one of the quilts aside, letting in a wash of bright moonlight.

She saw the hand she was holding and gasped. Amity's fingers were mere stumps, hacked off just before the knuckle, except for her thumb and pinky, which alone fit along the contours of Constance's hand. Old surgical wounds, flawlessly healed, their tips dimpled like worm mouths. What's more, Constance's ring and pinky fingers had also been severed, the one at the first joint and the other at the knuckle. When she looked up at Amity, she found the shiny red hair shriveled into the dry white kinks of Old Lady Yorin and the sylph-like face wrinkled and melting off—

Constance's eyes opened, and she stifled a scream, instinctively clenching her left hand into a fist, feeling that all of her digits were intact. She sighed with relief, but then recalled the Cinder, the first signs of the disease, and understood the significance of the dream—the portent. Her face was pressed against the sturdy back of the stranger, their bodies moving in tandem to the rhythm of the galloping horse, her arms encircling his strong, narrow waist. The presence of another was an instant comfort, and the fact that he was handy with a rifle and rode a healthy steed added to that relief. She was safe. Thank the Father, she was safe.

She could hear the horseshoes striking stone and saw that they had left the muddy road and were crossing a bridge over the narrow finger of a moonlight-glazed lake. Above them the sky was a graveyard of shattered clouds, disintegrating before her eyes. Frigid and wet, much of the mud washed off from her body, she sat up, teeth chattering, wrapped her sodden cloak tighter around her person, and managed a distance with a tad more propriety, difficult as that was to achieve given the circumstances.

On the opposite end of the bridge, they trotted along a cobblestone avenue flanked with perfectly conical hedges and lamp posts, their flames flickering horizontally in the wind, conjuring huge, sweeping shadows. Beyond stretched out a beautiful moonlit parkland that glistened with the rain.

They were approaching a three-story great house of stone and mortar, larger than the Lancaster household and the Fairwater Saloon combined, certainly the largest building she had ever seen before—probably as large as the Palace of Hemlock itself. Its face was lined with tall windows, a few of which were illuminated by candles, but many more standing dark and shuttered.

"I'm afraid I have a few matters to attend to," the rider said as he reined in his horse at the end of the drive. He dismounted and helped her down. "However, my servants will tend to your needs. I will wake the doctor and have him pay you a visit before you sleep tonight. Be well, Fair Daughter." At that he seemed to seize up with pain, grimacing and bracing himself against his steed.

Constance reached out with concern and put a comforting hand on his shoulder, but he shook it off and mounted (not very nimbly). Then, taking Constance's carpetbag and all her meager effects with him, he rode off through a raised portcullis between the split flights of an imperial staircase that ascended to the entrance.

Constance stood there a moment, wringing out her wet hair and staring after him as he and his horse disappeared into a dark tunnel beyond the portcullis, utterly bewildered by the man's strange behavior. Once the volley of hoofbeats faded and her hair was a modicum more dry, she looked back down that avenue of gas lamps and hedges and caught movement in the shadows.

A figure was watching her from behind one of the hedges.

She reached instinctively for her pepperbox, but either she had dropped it during the fight or had tucked it into her carpetbag afterwards. In all the confusion, she couldn't remember which.

Thanks to this gentleman savior of mine, I am now completely defenseless, she thought as she backed towards the stairs.

The figure advanced, lurching out of the shadows and into the lamplight, one foot of its horrendously bent legs dragging, making a disturbing squeal against stone, and the other foot clanking down. Covered in moss and clumps of sod, out of which sad wilting wildflowers sprouted, the deformed earthen creature leaned on a halberd as a crutch. In between all the mud, she caught glints of metal reflected in the flickering, shifting light.

The creature was wearing a suit of damaged armor.

Not just any suit of armor, but the same one she had discovered in the ruins earlier that day.

Constance turned and dashed up the stairs as the knight in sullied armor hastened after her. By the time she reached the top of the stairs, the figure had also reached the bottom step of the left flight and was struggling to mount it. As Constance watched, the knight lost its balance, fell with a clatter, sending pieces of armor tumbling away.

Everything was still once again.

Constance approached the balustrade and looked down at the scattered mess of muddy armor, but she saw no sign of whatever creature it was that had been holding together and animating the various pieces of armor. Then she noticed the helmet begin to vibrate, tilt backwards, then roll slowly over the cobblestones until it bumped into the breastplate and twisted into place on the gorget. At the same time, all the leg and arm pieces began to reassemble into limbs—the sollerets fitting into the greaves, the gauntlets tucking into vambraces—and these limbs were soon flopping and clanging across the stones, seeking out the torso.

Her nerves numbed from the shock of earlier that evening, Constance watched all of this in a cool, detached way before she realized that this armored apparition intended to try and climb the stairs again. A month ago, if she had come across such a thing as a haunted suit of armor, she would have fled, terrified. But after all that had happened to her, the only scintilla of emotion she felt was pity for this ancient spirit.

She descended the stairs and extended one of her gloved hands. Even through the thick fabric, she could feel an intense cold radiating out of the gauntlet, but this far from frightened her; her empathy only deepened. Ignoring the beetles scurrying out of the dark recesses of metal and onto her arm, she helped the assemblage of armor stand, and together, with some difficulty, girl and knight mounted the stairs.

"There," she said, smiling, when they reached the top and removed his gauntlet from her hand. "You're welcome. Again."

An earwig scuttled out of the visor and dropped onto the ground, but aside from that, the hunched spirit stood there, leaning on its halberd, stock-still, without showing the least signs of exhaustion from having made the climb.

"Well, if that's all, I'll be heading inside now."

When she entered through the massive double doors of the manor, which glided open easily as she approached, she could feel a prickle on the back of her neck as if the knight's invisible eyes were following her every move.

H ANGING FROM A POST in the marble-tiled front hall was an ornate lantern, its smoky fire casting the only light in the great room. All around her, fluted white columns rose and vanished in the darkness above.

Taking the lantern with her, she walked a few steps and turned back towards the door, but already she could see no sign of it. Nor was there any sign of all those windows she had seen lining the exterior of the building. It was as if she had been dropped into the center of this room as opposed to entering it through a door. Though this manor had seemed large from outside, she must have misjudged the exact scale of the place, for she could not make out a ceiling or walls in any direction, the columns seeming to stretch on forever.

It's like a forest, she thought, a chill running through her. Plucked out of one forest and transplanted into another.

As she wandered among these imposing columns, searching for an exit, she thought once that she heard someone whispering, but when she stopped to listen, there was nothing but the echo of her footsteps on the tile. At another point, she was certain she heard the faint rustle of a skirt nearby, which elicited in her a sense of déjà vu.

When at last she noticed a shaft of light in the distance, she sighed with relief and hastened towards it. The light in question was streaming out of a hearth fire in a sumptuous dining room. The chimneys of this hearth curved out and up like massive horns, and between them was a central window—though *window* was too quotidian a word for this intricate crystal world, which duplicated everything many times over like some great insect eye. She set down the lantern on a small alabaster pedestal near the doorway and strode over to the fire, where she stood warming herself for a few minutes.

A cough came from behind her.

She whirled around and found a gaunt old man in worn livery standing by the door through which Constance had entered. He bowed towards her, giving her a chance to see his bald, liver-spotted pate and dandruff-dusted shoulders. The decrepit creature spent a long time straightening up, and when he did at last crick his spine into its full upright posture, he stepped towards a small table in the center of the room covered with a lacy white fabric and lit by a silver candelabra with freshly lit white tallow candles. Constance hadn't noticed the table when she'd entered the room, but then she had been more concerned about warming herself than appreciating the decor.

The man pulled out the table's one chair, before which dinnerware had been set out.

"Welcome, Fair Daughter. We have been expecting you."

Exhausted and filthy and feeling very out of place, she walked towards the invitation and sat down while the manservant pushed in the chair to accommodate her.

"A supper has been prepared at the master's behest. We hope very much, very much indeed, that you find it to your liking."

"It's too kind of you. I ..."

"Yes, Fair Daughter?"

"I'm not sure exactly what's happening. This whole night has been one of confusion. I wonder when I'll wake up. I feel as if I'm still wandering Forest Road."

"As you say. Surely and truly I can sympathize with your disorientation upon arriving at such a gigantic and gloomy place as Erlwine Manor during the deep of night, but for the sake of your alacritous ushering into the dining chambers, it was necessary for you to pass through the Great Room, which is a cozy hallway during daylight hours but expands to unknown and befuddling dimensions at nightfall. In general, you will find this house much more to your liking come the Hour of the Daughter—of that I can most assuredly guarantee."

There was a knowing glint in his eye that Constance found as off-putting as his strange description of the room she had just now passed through. Her smile faltered, but then she recovered herself, managing to look very charming in the candlelight, bedraggled though she was. The rain at least had cleansed her of most of the Nilwere filth—or at least she thankfully couldn't smell any of it on her.

"I see," she replied simply.

A grim little man no taller than a child materialized without the sound of a door opening or any approaching footsteps. As he approached, Constance could not fail to notice the peculiar contours of his face: a pointed chin that swept upward and a pointed nose that curved down, together creating an effect like the horns of a crescent moon threatening to touch. His cheeks, too, were unusually protuberant and of an unhealthy pallor, the thin lips of his frog mouth liver-colored, same as the many folds of his eyelids. He carried a crystal bowl of water in which several rose petals shivered, plus finely stitched towels folded on a pewter tray.

The taller of the menservants retreated from the table to allow the child-sized one to set the bowl before Constance, and she removed the master's gloves and plunged her hands into the cold water. It instantly transformed from clear and sparkling to an opaque sienna. When she removed her hands and dried them, she saw clearly that the two fingers of her left hand (ring and small) had lost their nails. Indeed, the withered things had fallen out of the glove and lay now on the beautiful tablecloth, curled up like slivers of desiccated ginger root. The insensible flesh had turned the color of an overcast day, and she could just make out thin blood vessels branching out beneath the surface like black lightning. Recovering from this shock, she handed the towel and the master's gloves back to the little man, who then used a pair of tongs to transfer a hot steaming towel from the pewter dish and onto a porcelain side plate. Constance cleaned her face, then passed it back onto the little man's tray. Then he left the two of them, grunting as he waddled out.

Next up in the parade of peculiar persons was a scullion with an unusually elegant and willowy shape and a powdered wig at least a century out of fashion that contrasted with her drab apron and dress. Constance watched as the woman transferred the aromatic dishes from the service cart to the table: a creamy river snake stew; a dish of pickled tomatoes, cucumbers, and turnips; a cube of goat cheese infused with dried numbing peppers; fresh-baked bread; a rare, cold lamb loin seasoned with rosemary and nutmeg, bleeding at its core; and a decanter of wine. When Constance thanked her, and the scullion turned towards her with a bow, the butcher's daughter gasped—the woman had no face. There was only a smooth porcelain mask without eye or mouth holes, which looked nearly liquid in the candlelight, like molten pearl. In fact, Constance realized, as she watched the servant wheeling the service cart out of the dining room, her legs and arms also appeared to be made of porcelain.

The manservant watched Constance expectantly, and the latter, recovering from her shock, turned back towards the table and helped herself to the supper. Her mother had read her enough cautionary fairy tales to know that food was often employed to poison or charm or bewitch or transform careless children, but Constance was too starved to care at this point, managing a quick blessing before tucking in.

Her head and bruises throbbed with each bite of the meal and swallow of wine, but everything was so delicious, she easily ignored the pain. After a few minutes of eating and imbibing in quiet, her thirst slaked, hunger curbed, she slowed, growing mindful of the manservant's gaze from the shadows of the room.

"Kind Father?" she said, stifling a belch and placing her fork and knife down on the edges of her plate.

"Yes, Mistress?"

Mistress?

"Who is the master of this great house?"

"Why, Count Litney Erlwine the Twenty Thousand Five Hundredth, of course," he said with a wry smile.

Twenty Thousand Five Hundredth? What absurdity! she thought, imaging a man whose family line was older than all of Creation itself, for according to *The Book of the Family*, the number of generations of all of humankind only numbered in the low hundreds, but she made no comment as to the implausibility of such a title, assuming there must be a reasonable explanation for it.

"Where is the Count? Will he not be joining us for his repast after such a ride?"

"No, Mistress. Count Erlwine never dines this late," the manservant said, "for he finds it disagrees with his digestion."

She noted a slight elevation in his manner of pronunciation of this word, though she had no idea what to make of it. Either way, the term of address made her squirm a little; all her life it had been hammered into her to use the Designations of the Family: Father, Mother, Son, and Daughter. Sire, master, mistress, lord, your highness—all those terms of address had been done away with during the time of the People's Uprising. Indeed, to her knowledge, practically everyone of royal or noble lineage in the Northern Confederacy had been beheaded at the end of the Great War, hundreds upon hundreds of heads preserved, labeled, and displayed in an immense glass case in the Chamber of History in the Palace of Hemlock, like the morbid work of some ogrish naturalist. The closest she had ever come to dealing with royalty was in her relationship with Amity and the Lancasters—certainly Increase Lancaster comported himself as Canton royalty and cultivated such a demeanor in his daughter.

"When will I see the Count again?" she asked.

"You won't, Mistress." He cleared his throat, and another one of those smirks appeared on his face. "That is to say, not until morning, perhaps late morning. He will need to fully recover before presenting himself to you."

"Naturally." She smiled. "Could you tell me about him? It's just that he saved my life, and caught up in the moment and with everything that's happened, I don't feel that I adequately expressed my gratitude."

"I can and shall, can and shall, indeed, Mistress, for I have known the Count all of his life, having cared for him even as a vigorous and lusty babe. He is an exuberant man, fond of the hunt, overly fond, some might say, though I wouldn't hear of it. He never sleeps, but as a result he does require many hours of rest and recuperation, for one cannot continue on at his pace continuously, as I'm sure you must realize."

"Um, of course. How... fascinating."

He cleared his throat, nodding in appreciation of her remark. "Count Erlwine is a quite accomplished and remarkable individual; on the battlefield his sword is armipotent, his armor resplendent, his bravery highly commended; he is a musical prodigy, with perfect pitch and flawless memory of pieces, able to perform anything he has previously heard; he is an expert rider and athlete, having been known to swim the length of

Erlwine Lake on mild winter mornings; is also a marksman of some note, having taken the prize at the Longdale"—the name meant nothing to Constance—"Annual Fox Hunt on ten separate occasions."

"He is also a slayer of monsters," Constance added, "an achievement few others that I know can claim."

The manservant, who had also failed to introduce himself to her (a custom in these parts, Constance decided generously), nodded again with deep appreciation. "Indeed, how amiss of me to omissively omit and neglectfully neglect to add that most magnificent and monumental of achievements to my encomium of the Count. Thank you, Mistress."

She sliced off a bit of cheese and let it melt in her mouth, relishing the tingle of the numbing peppers on her tongue and wondering if Count Erlwine were wed. She decided on a less direct tack: "What about his family?"

"It is certainly a complicated family history, the Erlwines', but"—he checked his pocket watch—"momentarily he is the only one of his line."

When she offered a polite laugh at his joke, he did not nod his satisfaction the way he had with other comments or inputs of hers, and she decided that she must have committed a faux pas here: laughing at Count Litney Erlwine being the last living member of his family. Still, the manservant did not appear to have taken any offense. Rather, he stood in his obsequious pose in the shadows with only the tips of his nose and his smooth pate illuminated, awaiting to dispense more information like the exhumed corpse of a town crier.

"And what of the staff, other inhabitants of this... grand estate?"

"We are short-staffed for such grounds as these. Just myself, Mr. Thingkley (the diminutive fellow), Dr. Daybleed, and ..." He seemed to rack his brain, rocking back and forth on his toes as he did so. "In all the space of this great house, I might have overlooked one or two others, but yes, I believe that is all at the moment."

"And what of the serving woman?"

"Ah yes. Helwise, she's called. A most industrious and indefatigable specimen of the fairer sex."

She wanted to pry into the reason why Helwise appeared to be clad in porcelain armor but thought better of it.

"And Mr. Thingkley... he is a most... singular individual."

"I am sure, Mistress," he said, "that we are of the same mind and on the same page and stand in full accord with one another when it comes to our opinion of the singularity of Mr. Thingkley's person. "—Constance failed to understand a word of this, but nodded along encouragingly—"Abandoned, you see, was our dear Mr. Thingkley, as a babe of indeterminate age in the wilds (I presume on account of his deformities, but one never knows) and never quite picked up our common parlance with as great a fluency as you and I have done. It is difficult on account of his size and stunted intellectual development to hazard a guess at how old he was when abandoned or even how long he was left out in the wilds, swaddled and bound. The Helwises cared for him, suckled and raised him."

The Helwise*s*? Constance noticed how the one serving woman had duplicated over the course of a couple of exchanges, but again she remembered her place as guest in this household and thought not to probe further. Perhaps, after all, Helwise was one of a pair of twins.

As she pondered this, the chattering manservant's small, white eyes never left her. "In the meantime, might I be so bold as to recommend a digestive tea to serve as postlude and postscript to your meal?" He smiled fully now, which brought out a shocking amount of wrinkles from the corners of his mouth all the way up to the wiry brush encircling his skull. "It will be ready posthaste."

"I think not, sir. I'm terribly exhausted." Constance reinforced her point with an unintentional yawn.

"Perhaps you would care to retire to your rooms?"

"Shall I help with the cleaning?"

He chuckled. "No, no, dear me, what a question. As our most honored guest, you must not bother yourself with such trifles and trivialities. The Helwises are more than equal and better equipped to handle that task. Besides, as you might have anticipated, I say, as you might have prophesied and prognosticated, it is a bit of an adventure reaching your rooms"—*Marvelous*, Constance thought—"and thus it is best we set out as soon as possible and without delay."

"I see. No, that does not surprise me. Sir—I'm sorry I didn't catch your name."

"Smugrove, Mistress. At your disposal and service, of course." He bowed, concealing his simpering smile.

The Good Doctor

L IGHTING THE WAY WITH a candelabra, Smugrove led her through
a set of thick double doors that creaked open into a dim hallway.
The musty odor of wilted flowers pervaded this corridor, the scuffed
crimson carpet stretching on into the dark like an infinitely long tongue,
beneath which the warped wood of the floor spoke to them in squeaks
and groans. Every door they passed was shut, and through the keyholes
of some of these, there glowed faint firelight. The straight hall soon grew
into a crooked puzzle of a path: up and down a couple of stairs here,
turning at curious angles there—angles that seemed to turn back upon
themselves.

Mr. Smugrove led her on and up, on and up, and soon they entered
a gallery of windows looking out onto the wilds. The passageway extended across an expanse of roof quite unlike any she had seen before,
an ill-fitting puzzle of slanted planes and tiled domes and crenelated
walls that shifted before her eyes like ocean waves. This condensed city
of structures seemed to bear no relation to the stately manor she had
seen during her and the Count's approach on horseback. Overcome with
vertigo, she averted her eyes and focused on Smugrove's candle instead,
which was reflected in every one of those windowpanes like a gallery of
scintillated gemstones.

"This is Sunflower Tower," he said with a whiff of peppermint. They stood in a circular room with narrow embrasure windows overlooking a landscape of lakes and star-smeared sky. A narrow, stone stairway wound along the wall, fitting itself neatly between the windows. At the top, they reached a wooden landing with a dizzying view to the tower's base. Smugrove unlocked a door, bowed, and gestured towards the interior.

Constance thanked him for his attentiveness and stepped inside, suddenly desperate to be alone and tucked inside a cozier space.

Smugrove coughed.

She turned back towards him, and the old manservant looked embarrassed. "Mistress, may I inquire as to the state of your health?"

"My h-hea—" she stammered. "Yes, of course. How could I have forgotten?" She had been walking in a stupor, nearly insensible, but now felt the scrim of dreamlike unreality dissolve around her, leaving the horror of the Cinder in its place.

I am ill, I am dying, how could I have forgotten indeed?

She displayed her hand, seeing that the disease had progressed well beyond her fingertips, eating down close to the knuckles—she felt nothing in them at this point, and they barely responded when she tried to flex them.

"Ah, yes, yes, yes. I will inform the doctor that you are ready to receive him, but as he may be a few minutes, I would suggest taking advantage of the hot bath that has been prepared for you and, if I may be so bold, a change of habiliments may be found in yonder wardrobe." He pointed towards the far corner of the room.

As he droned on about the decor and amenities like a lonely hosteler, Constance swore that beneath the sound of his monotonous voice she could hear the sound of screaming, very distant, that of a babe.

"Did you hear that?" she said, interrupting the manservant's description of the oral hygiene sundries at her disposal.

"Beg your pardon?"

"A babe crying, screaming. But no, it's gone quiet now." She listened. "No, I can't hear it anymore."

"No doubt, Mistress Constance, you've been in large, old houses before this one, I imagine."

Constance nodded.

"And you will be familiar with the peculiar sounds and noises and disturbances that can sometimes be heard inside—wailing, whispering, creaking, et cetera, et cetera."

"Of course." She remembered the mayor's house especially, sleeping over with Amity, and hearing the entire structure groan beneath the pressure of wind, as if phantoms were holding a fete in the middle of the night, dancing and cavorting all about the house.

"Erlwine Manor is no different, save in the fact of its unusually ponderous dimensions."

"How do you mean?"

"Well, the larger the house, the more grandiose, the more room there is for mental trickery: the eccentric noises are transmogrified into full phantasms, tricks of the eye turn altogether into full people, traces of a ghost scent blossom into overwhelming bouquets. It is nothing, however, to fear—just the way the mind magnifies bits to scale up with the immensity of this place, with its thousands upon thousands of chambers."

"I see. Most unusual."

"Quite. I leave you now, Mistress. Wish you good health and goodnight."

Bᴇғᴏʀᴇ ʜᴇʀ ᴡᴀѕ ᴀ four-poster bed with gold-trimmed yellow curtains suspended from a golden rail, a color scheme that complemented the thousands of sunflowers and bumblebees that populated the wallpaper in a design of such chaotic complexity that Constance had trouble detecting any pattern to it. The woodwork of the bed was of an opulent design, knots of ebony vines and stalks woven together and displaying frozen black blooms. Beside it stood a wardrobe of a similar dark wood etched in the same motif, inside of which hung a dazzling array of feminine garb. A vanity screen matching the wallpaper concealed a cabinet with a basin and other essentials, and a great brass griffin tub, already brimming with chrysanthemum-perfumed water, steamed and filled the air with a fresh aroma. She selected a simple cotton nightgown from the wardrobe and carried it across the room and behind the vanity. She stepped out of her brogans and shed her hardened, muddy stockings, then with some reticence examined her toes.

No evidence of diseased flesh.

She peeled off the rest of her filthy, damp clothes, then placed everything in a laundry tub on the floor. At last, she eased herself into the scalding water. It was a deep tub, and the instant she lowered herself in, the water turned opaque and discolored. With a brass ladle and the supplied bar of soap, she cleaned every bit of her body, washing all the mud and leaves out of her hair, and feeling relaxed for the first time in days. She was aware that chrysanthemums possessed medicinal powers of some sort or another, though in her current state she could not recall what those might have been. Perhaps this was a step in the doctor's prescription.

Leaning back and closing her eyes, she took in deep breaths of the fragrant steam...

The next thing she knew, she startled awake, only aware that she had nodded off by the sudden change in the room's humidity and drop in water temperature. She shook the heavy torpor from her mind and limbs, pinched the flesh between her underarm and breast, then removed herself from the griffin, dried off, and slipped into the nightgown.

Presently, she heard a light rapping on the door, and a voice announced the arrival of Dr. Daybleed.

"A moment!" she called.

Constance completed her outfit with stockings and slippers, wrapped a yellow wool shawl about her shoulders, and tied back her wet hair into a small bun, examining her bruised face in the looking glass as she did so. There was a purple, swollen welt at her hairline and a thin streak of gray in her hair, but nothing as worrisome as her fingers.

The knocking repeated, as did the voice: "Mistress?" A quiet, timid thing flavored with a lisp unlike any Constance had heard before.

Constance sat down at the vanity arranged with powders and brushes. She neatened the skirt of the nightgown and faced the door. "Come in," she said.

A tall stick insect of a man entered the apartment, dressed in a tattered black suit and white frilled shirt front and top hat, which added to his unusual height. A swath of painted canvas hung down from the brim of his hat, veiling his face and most of his neck. She could see nothing of him, not even the skin of his hands, for one hand was gloved and the other was inserted into the aperture of a small box made from black canvas and wood, which he held at chest level with the support of his other hand. The canvas mask was painted very intricately into a gentleman's likeness, a gentleman with a cleft chin and mutton chops, a serene expression and kind brown eyes that shifted in size as the canvas rippled.

He nodded. Or was it a curt bow? Constance could not decide which, but she rose to return the same ambiguous gesture. He then moved mechanically to the writing table and seated himself, resting the small box on his lap and his free hand on top of this. The fingers of the gloved hand, she noted, were of an atypical length, like harvestman legs.

"I am Dr. Daybleed," issued a voice, not from the good doctor's face or veil, but from the box. "It is my pleasure to be of service."

The box vibrated with every word, the source of the voice being a small hole patched over with a sheer fabric, buzzing with sibilants and rattling with plosives, creating an effect that Constance had originally taken to be the man's lisp.

"I-I... the pleasure is all mine." Constance seated herself again, feeling rude for staring at the grotesque physician but feeling it would be impolite to look anywhere else.

"You will forgive the unusual appearance of my ferent box," Dr. Daybleed said, his superincumbent hand drumming its fingers against the device in question. "I suffered an injury during the Great War, a piece of shrapnel from a cannonball explosion, which cleanly sliced off and seared the majority of my face and throat, robbing me of my voice and senses of vision, olfaction, and gustation, but with the aid of this crutch"—he briefly lifted the box—"I am able to approximate normal functioning."

"Please. Speak no more of it. It is clearly a most ingenious contraption. Moreover, I-I-I am not at all disturbed by it."

"You are most gracious—and as to its ingeniousness, you are correct, Mistress. Now, I am here to give you a full inspection and to alleviate the Cinder symptoms that have been reported to me."

"Will your physic for the Cinder be painful?"

The box vibrated. "I don't imagine that undergoing the Cinder cure is something you would elect as part of your normal daily routine."

"I see." She looked down at the slippers she had chosen from the wardrobe, white with clever gold filigree, then back at the doctor. "And what, then, does it involve?"

"A special solution"—he depressed a button on the side of his ferent box, causing a set of small doors to spring open and reveal a miniature medicine cabinet from which he plucked up a delicate vial of citrine-colored fluid—"applied to a wound from which the pestiferous flesh has been excised."

Constance swallowed with difficulty. "Excised?"

"I'm afraid so, Mistress. I can show you the excision tools if you care to, though many prefer to obviate doing so."

"Count Erlwine said there was a cure for the Cinder. He said that his doctor had worked out a cure. That cure, then, is… is amputation?"

Dr. Daybleed nodded as his ferent box buzzed and popped. Every time he moved his head, the canvas veil shook and rippled slightly, and the painted face seemed to shift its expression, as if in worry. She felt, deliriously, as if she were speaking to two people at once: the man and some tiny creature concealed within the box.

"I can't. I couldn't let you. This"—she looked down at her hand, which she had foolishly gloved in one of the lacy things hanging in the cupboard; a single sob escaped her trembling lips—"my hand." She stripped off the glove and saw now the two fingers of her left hand were entirely gray, the last flakes of nail gone, leaving behind what appeared to be sculpting clay.

"Most distressing, we concur. The Cinder is an insidious plague, and we have made it our calling to eradicate it from the world."

"But you, all of you, I've infected you, haven't I? I warned Count Erlwine, but—"

The doctor made a dismissive gesture with his unboxed hand. "The staff of Erlwine Manor have worked up a resilience to the disease over time."

She nodded her understanding and looked down again at her hands. Her right hand had involuntarily covered up the infected fingers. Voice dropped to a whisper, she said, "I can't let you do it."

"No. I completely understand, and in my role as physician I can only advise, not coerce, you into making one decision over another. Consider, however, that if we act now, excision will be limited to, from what I can see, the distal and middle-phalanges of the left small and ring fingers. If you forgo excision at the present time and then change your mind tomorrow, it is likely the entire hand will need to be amputated. Or if you change your mind two days from now, the entire arm must be sacrificed, and by that time, due to the transfer of infected humors across the body, we might have to operate on the other hand or the feet. So you see: time is of the essence. The Cinder has entered and begun its work, and it is a relentless monster, never sleeping."

A relentless monster, never sleeping. Her mind clutched at the phrase, holding onto it for some inexplicable reason. Never sleeping. Just what Mr. Smugrove said about Count Erlwine.

"But is there no other way, Doctor?"

"I have worked with infected patients for many more years than I care to say—I was a seasoned surgeon even before the Great War."

That would make him close to one hundred years old, an age unheard of beyond the great heroes from *The Book of the Family,* who were said to have lived for many hundreds of years.

"Are you in correspondence with the surgeons at the University of Hemlock?" she asked.

"I have regular correspondence with several physicians in the Department of Cinder Studies and am familiar with their opinions on the matter. We are, in truth, at loggerheads regarding treatment, a disagreement ultimately about the nature of the disease—whether it is natural or magical in nature."

Her brow furrowed. "Magical? What is your opinion?"

A burst of static came from the ferent box, then: "You should not trouble yourself, Mistress, with such a question. It may have ill effects on the nerves."

"But if the disease is magical in nature—"

"It is not, I can assure you of that."

"But if it *is*—"

"Mistress Constance, magic was eradicated during the People's Uprising along with all of the court magicians, and I cannot allow you to entertain any alternative possibilities. In my lifetime I have seen people beheaded for less."

"But, Dr. Daybleed, if the physicians at the Department of Cinder Studies discuss the matter openly—"

"They're lucky they still have their necks, believe you me. Besides, even if the Cinder were magical in nature, there exist no magic healers, no one to dispel the magic. It leads us back to the same conclusion: only my method will suffice."

For the tiniest fraction of a moment, she had felt a glimmer of hope, same as she had felt when Charity Hobbs had offered her the snail shell pendant and the poppets. Besides, just this evening she had witnessed an animated mound of necrotic flesh, a suit of armor reassembling itself, and had ventured through the immense maze of Erlwine Manor folded inside the neat, relatively smaller frame of the great house—if magic couldn't account for these miracles, what could?—but she found she had no strength to argue with the doctor about such matters.

She felt she was dreaming.

Yes, I'm still trudging through the wild wood, pursued by a monster of many names.

She examined her left hand, then the other.

"Mistress Constance?" The box sounded patient, polite, almost content. It sounded as if it had nowhere else it would rather be than in this room, serving as translator between her and the doctor. "I can, of course, offer you prosthetics post-amputation. Something ivory or jeweled could be quite becoming on such a lovely young maiden as yourself."

She looked up at Dr. Daybleed, took a deep breath, and nodded.

CONSTANCE LAY DOWN ON the bed, the curtains drawn to her right and at the foot, leaving only a window at the left for the doctor's operating theater. His ferent box was a veritable magician's hat from which he produced all manner of strange devices. The first was a tray that unfolded into a wheeled table, upon which he draped a sheet of clean white linen. Then he plucked from various compartments with his spidery hand a number of steel implements. As the doctor made his preparations, she noticed his medicinal smell, which up close was overpowering. The doctor's breath was strangely labored, whistling through the unseen cavities of his carved-out face.

Trying not to glimpse the mutilated visage beyond the painted canvas, Constance stared up at the gorgeous, scandent woodwork of the bed—at the flowering vines that seemed to sprout up from the carpet.

Ropes, she found herself thinking. *For tying, for knotting, for connecting.*

She listened to the whine of the wind as it coiled around Sunflower Tower, she heard the twenty-four glass panes of the window rattling individually in the constant battle of pressure between inside and out. And yet again, she thought she heard the wailing of a small child. Not a babe, she decided, for she had the impression that the child was crying for something particular, approximating words—not the confused plaints of some purple-faced newborn.

Ropes. For tethering, for lassoing, for anchoring.

Dr. Daybleed presented with his right hand a cloth reeking of chemicals. "Mistress, please breathe deeply the fumes of this chloroform. It will let the operation pass in a much more pleasant manner for you."

For binding, for hanging, for drawing and quartering.

Constance glanced over at him, and in that instant, she thought she could glimpse around the edge of the canvas veil a sliver of the doctor's face. It was like some desolate, melted moonscape with its stark contrast between shadow black and bone white. She turned her eyes immediately back to the vinework of the bed canopy and allowed Dr. Daybleed to press the cloth firmly over her mouth and nose. "Do not be afraid," the ferent box crackled. "The surgery will proceed smoothly. You will be completely insensible, will not remember any of it. You will inhale deeply and you will fall very, very, very far down into the depths of the earth where you will be safe and locked away, where you will be comfortable and content, where you will be warm, where time and memory do not exist, a perfect place, a placid and peaceful place." She breathed deeply, trying to remain calm, though her heart was hammering just as it had when she had faced the monster hours earlier.

The black vines coiled above her as Dr. Daybleed pressed the cloth tighter and tighter over her mouth and nose. All the while, the voice of the box unspooled its soothing, lulling, mesmerizing speech, though the words had grown incomprehensible to her now, leaving only the crackles and percussive music behind. The woodwork began to transform, growing shinier, scalier, and she found herself surrounded by a great tangle of asps, winding in and out, headless and tailless, completely senseless things forever chasing and being chased by nothing. They were rattling, or was it the ferent box? She could spy no rattles, but she heard them, heard hundreds of them, just how Amity had described the Nilwere to her.

She watched the waves of asps for seconds or minutes or an eternity, then floated up and dove into them and swam with them and swallowed them and was consumed by them, the rattling growing louder and louder. She felt the cold, leathery scales brushing across her skin, felt them sliding into her mouth and across her tongue and down the length of her throat. They pushed into her vagina and rectum, squirmed into her nostrils and ear holes and eyes, squeezing into the bottomless depths of her being. Her belly heaved with their movements, her skin rippled as they wormed inside her, her head pulsed, her breasts and stomach swelled into impossible sizes, and she was filled up completely with the vibrating rattle of thousands of little, chattering, toothy mouths. Across this sea of snakes that she had melded with, that existed at once inside her and without her, the diminutive Mr. Thingkley crawled out of the wall, carrying several paper sunflowers taller than him. He crept towards her, wading through the snakes that were no longer scaly but fleshy with her own pink skin, and when he reached its center and found her hand, he licked the diseased fingers with his purplish tongue.

A Charming Host

When she came to, sunlight was streaming in through the seams of the bed curtain. Her head muddled and cottony, for many minutes Constance stared vacantly at the exquisite, gentle play of dust motes in the shaft of light.

She licked her dry lips. Her mouth felt sticky and tasted bitter, unpleasant. Then, she noticed her hand. It was throbbing, and as she became aware of it, the intensity grew into a pain like nothing she had ever known before. She tried to lift it, but the quilt was too heavy. With great effort, she propped herself up and lifted the covers. Despite the thick bandages wrapped around her hand, she could tell that the size of her hand was reduced from what it had been. It would have been painful to squeeze a whole hand inside such a shape. As she rotated it back and forth, her heart lurched and tears welled in her eyes. She cried for many minutes, first for the loss of her fingers, then for her mother and father, and for Amity and the dead migrants, and her poor mule Lento, and for Temperance Jones and Emmanuel Solemn, and for Jacob Downing and Faith Sallyforth and Doc Harwood, and for everyone she knew—for all of Canton. The focus of her tears grew less and less clear until they were just tears for the sake of tears.

Several minutes later, her mind clearer, eyes red and moist, she stood at the window. Yesterday's clouds had dispersed, leaving an empty sky above the countryside. The gorgeous spread of mountains in the distance were mauve and indistinct in the dewy haze.

She turned back towards the room and was surprised to see her carpetbag and umbrella set on the writing desk. Beside it were her clothes, cleaned and neatly folded, and on the floor by the door were her brogans, scrubbed and dried. She walked over and got dressed, mindful of the bandaged hand, which sent agonizing flares up her arm whenever it brushed against anything. Every time she looked down at her hand, that poor thing, she was shocked anew by its peculiar deflated appearance, as though it were some cruel illusion, a prank her eyes had played on her for far too long. She opted to wear her own clothes instead of the ones provided to her in the wardrobe, which were finer and more sumptuous than what she was used to.

Dressed and feeling more herself, she rummaged through the carpetbag. The hatchet, knife, and pepperbox were missing, but again, she must have dropped them in the mud last night when the Nilwere seized her.

And you're safe now, Constance. What need do you have for a weapon?

Behind the vanity, she found a basin of still-warm water; someone must have entered her chambers just before she had awoken. She washed her face awkwardly, using only her right hand, then wet and folded a rag before she rolled it in a bowl of salt, scrubbing her teeth thoroughly thereafter.

When at last she had finished, she stepped towards the exit—only to find the door locked.

Panic stirred in her chest.

Sure that she had simply made some error, she tried the handle again, straining and failing to turn it. There was a brass keyhole, through which she spied the landing at the top of the tower, cheerily sunlit.

She tried again more forcefully. Squeezed it. Jiggled it. Rammed her shoulder into the black door—

"Anything you require, Mistress?" a voice came from behind her. She turned, confused, sure that the room had been unoccupied before. Tentatively, she stepped towards the room's center, a chill running down her spine. Getting to her knees, she glanced under the bed. No one there. She peered behind the vanity, looked behind the wardrobe, but could find no one. Constance sat down on the mattress, brow wrinkled, scrutinizing the room.

The voice came again. "Mistress Constance, is there anything that you require?"

She rushed towards the sound, the far wall, then stopped. She swore it was coming from here, the impeccably polite voice of Mr. Smugrove (no mistaking that). Her eyes scanned the tiny portraits and lithographs of flowers of black and marigold, then by some trick of the eye, the images on the wallpaper appeared to extend outward from the wall, and she realized she was staring at a brass bell (the florets of the flower) jutting out of the wall beneath a crystal, which was set on the end of a brass lever (the compound eye of a bumblebee).

"Mr. Smugrove?" she said, feeling more than a little foolish, bending forward and directing her voice into the bell. "Mr. Smugrove, is that you?"

"None other. At your service, Mistress," came the prompt reply.

"The door is locked. I would like to leave my room."

"Ah yes. I'm afraid that at the present time, the door must remain locked and securely fastened as a safety precaution. You see, several years past, a somnambulist stayed with us and left her quarters in the middle of the night under the hypnotic spell of slumber and, presumably, lost her way—a true danger in Erlwine Manor, as I'm sure you can fully appreciate and apprehend. In either case, the young woman in question was neither heard from nor seen again."

"How horrible."

"*Most* horrible, to be sure, most horrible and tragic, indeed. Ever since that unfortunate occurrence took place, we have taken the necessary precautions and countermeasures and what have you to assure that we would never again lose one of our honored guests."

"I see. In that case, when *may* I leave my room, please?"

"One of the Helwises will arrive presently and promptly to escort you down to breakfast with Count Erlwine."

"Okay. Thank you, Mr. Smugrove."

"Happily at your service and disposal, of course. If you need anything more, simply call me through our bell system, which you will find to be quite convenient. I am seeing to the accounts in my office, doing the numbers as I say, and will not be out of range of hearing but will be perfectly within earshot, even for one of my advanced age."

"Excellent. Goodbye, then."

"Good morning to you, Mistress Constance."

T HE BELLS, BRIGHT AND distant, tolled the Hour of the Daughter, and soon Constance heard the turning of the key in the lock; then the door creaked open without a knock, permitting the entry of the same elegant porcelain figure from the previous evening, accoutered in a clean white apron and stiff black dress, which, tight-fitting as it was, still seemed voluminous for her gracile proportions. The taciturn woman shifted to the side of the entrance, her ivory arms hanging at her sides, poofy wig floating about her head like a cumulus cloud.

Though it was in no way lovely, Constance offered her a "Lovely morning," to which the woman tilted her head towards the door, as if she were trying to imagine Constance leaving the room.

Pleasantries concluded, Constance passed out of the chamber, and Helwise shut the door behind them, locked it, and slipped the key into her apron. As she did this, Constance noticed a small marking on the woman's mask, where the seam between the jawline and the cheek met: the numbers *612*, written in tiny cursive figures.

After a short trek through the manor, Helwise deposited Constance in a different dining room than the extraordinary glass one of the night before. Full of inviting, rich smells, the room in question was spacious, dominated by a long and narrow table, with a view that overlooked rolling hills spiny with stone and a procession of clouds scudding across a deep cerulean sky.

Constance approached the unoccupied table and seated herself near its head, then turned to inquire about the Count, only to find that Helwise had vanished through some hidden panel, for she thought she spotted the door just as it swung shut and blended seamlessly into the corner of an immense painting. Dramatic, violent, full of exploding cannons and fallen soldiers and ranks upon ranks of glinting bayonets, in the painting's background was the burning city of Hemlock and the Shamrock Sea, whose surface was wrinkled by the scores of ships assailing the fortified city walls with cannon fire. She recognized the blue-and-white labyrinth flags of the Clairmont Revolutionaries (later the flag of the State of Clairmont) as well as the golden-eagle banners of the King. For Clairmont, this, the Battle of Hemlock, was the decisive battle of the Great War, which consumed many kingdoms in the north. Modern history books were brief in school, beginning with the People's Uprising and proceeding through a short list of presidents. These plus *The Book of the Family* were all the history one needed, Mr. Prisewick had often told her class with a flick of his switch, and if a student were foolish enough to ask about the period of time after the accounts of the holy book and before the inception of the war, they could count on going home with smarting, red knuckles that day. In any case, she had seen smaller illustrations of this battle in her history book, but never anything on this impressive a scale.

Constance turned her attention back to the table, to the inviting aromas of breakfast. She waited politely for a few moments, but then surrendered to her hunger, plucking a soft, yeasty roll from a great pyramid. She searched around the many small jars and found the strawberry jam, scooped a generous amount onto it, and wolfed down the toothsome thing in seconds. She waited a few more minutes, then grew bored, ate another roll, waited a bit more, then poured some coffee and stirred in a modest spoonful of sugar and a dash of cream, sipped it, then caved completely, stood and opened tray after tray to fill her plate.

There were fried spicy potatoes still glistening with oil; soft-boiled eggs and buttered eggs and poached eggs jiggling in a rich, creamy sauce; links of sausages of various shapes and colors and potency; rashers of thick bacon; blood pudding and tiny quiches topped with sliced mushroom arranged to resemble flower blossoms; seared tomatoes, their skins crinkled like tissue paper; smoked kippers resting on beds of pickled onions and capers; stacks of hot cakes; flaky pastries of all sorts and shapes, overstuffed with cream and chocolate, beaded with currants, glazed with frosting; and interspersed throughout the spread of food an abundance of side pots and garnishes of jams and butters and cream and gravy and glass shakers of curious spices and peppers.

In her excitement to fill her plate, Constance did not notice the addition of two individuals into the room, who stood watching her from the grand entrance.

One was Smugrove, and the other was strikingly dressed in an open, rumple-collared white shirt, loose gray trousers, black vest, and maroon scarf. He was tall, his hair dark and wavy, clean-shaven, young, perhaps only a couple years older than Constance herself, lean and well-muscled.

Finally noticing them, Constance startled.

The man strode over to the table, smiling. "Welcome to Erlwine Manor. I'm glad you took the liberty to begin without me. You must be famished after yesterday's adventure."

He was strikingly handsome and robust, as formidable a presence as Constance would have expected from someone of his status. Yet, given the surroundings and the ghoulish individuals inhabiting the great house, that a man of such good bearing and finely chiseled features should live here amongst them struck her as more grotesque than all of the peculiarities she had encountered since her arrival.

This notion passed in a flash in Constance's mind before she remembered her manners and curtsied and seated herself so that Count Erlwine could do the same. While doing so she recalled her impressions of him from last night, comparing these to the real, breathing gentleman who was seating himself before her, eyes alive with hunger and passion and curiosity. Foremost of all was the fact of his age. She had assumed that her rescuer had been old—how old exactly she could not say, but certainly many decades senior to this young man. Nor did their bearings match very well: Count Erlwine this morning sat proud and straight, while the Count Erlwine of yestereven possessed more of a stoop, not very pronounced, but noticeable all the same. Regarding what she had seen of his face, the match was nearly perfect—a strong jaw and sharp nose. His lips today seemed fuller than they had before. Then there was the timbre of his voice, which had been rough and gravelly last night but now pierced into her directly. It was musical, moving.

Perhaps, after all, he had simply been fatigued after the hunt.

Constance took a polite, sensible bite from the unladylike mountain of food heaped onto her plate while Count Erlwine gathered up his own breakfast feast.

They began to eat in concert. The master of this vast estate's presence quelled her appetite, and she became all too conscious of the worn, rough fabrics of her clothes and the indelicacy with which she handled the assortment of utensils flanking her dishes, whose various purposes escaped her.

"How have you found your accommodations? To your liking, I pray." He ate an entire fried egg in one bite, yet the feat did not come across as boorish. Spirited, merely, and befitting a man of his physical stature. She couldn't help recalling what Smugrove had said last night: *"Count Erlwine never dines this late, for he finds it disagrees with his digestion."* She smiled, having difficulty imagining Count Erlwine ever suffering indigestion.

"Very comfortable, and the staff have been of the utmost help," she replied. "Last night's supper, and now this feast—" she started to reach for the coffee with her left hand but then remembered the injury and reached awkwardly across with her right.

Count Erlwine noticed, of course, and he must have read the ensuing silence for what it was—a passing cloud of melancholy, of mourning for the lost fingers. He cleared his throat. "Constance, I am at a loss about exactly how to express this, but I owe you my sincerest apologies."

Constance looked over at her host in surprise.

"By now, my deception to lure you here must be clear, and you would be right to feel aggrieved from such treatment. What I hope to defend, and what you must understand, is the necessity of said deception. The only chance I had of saving you was to bring you to Erlwine Manor and place you in the care of Dr. Daybleed, for I fear that otherwise you yourself would have perished from the disease." He stood and bowed deeply, holding the pose, and said, "I only pray that you can find it in your heart to forgive me."

Constance was at a loss. Before coming to breakfast, her feelings towards him had been conflicted, yet now, when examined in its true light, she understood better what had happened last night: Count Erlwine's silence, his terseness, subtle lies, and haste, they had all been signs of his concern for *her*. As Dr. Daybleed had said, a delay of a day or more in treatment would have amounted to more Cinder-inflicted flesh that would need to be carved away.

Father knows what else I might have lost if Count Erlwine had not come to my rescue.

"No, sir," she said, standing, stepping towards him, then dropping to her knees. She found his hand, with its long, elegant fingers, and she kissed it. "I owe you my life and will never forget what you've done for me."

"Come, come, Fair Daughter." He helped her to her feet and escorted her back to her chair. "What's important now is for you to eat a hearty meal, bolster your constitution, and make a full recovery."

He returned to his own seat at the end of the table, several chairs down from hers.

"Sir, do you remember yesterevening after you saved me, I mentioned another young lady traveling with me?"

"Of course."

"Her name is Amity Lancaster. She was wearing a dark-green dress and has red hair, a very winsome young woman. We lost track of one another when the Nilwere attacked two nights ago. I don't know if she was killed or if she managed to return to Canton or is still wandering in the forest, and—"

"Say no more of the matter, and set your mind at ease. I will have a search party comb the barrens for her." Count Erlwine nodded towards Smugrove, who had all this time been lurking near the entrance, but upon receiving this order from the Count, he bowed his decrepit person out of the room.

"Thank you, Count."

"Please: you may call me Litney."

She nodded, and their breakfast continued.

Why is it that until now I have never heard of Erlwine Manor, nor of a Count Erlwine? she wondered. She could not very well ask such an indelicate question of him, confronting the man about the reason for his obscurity. She took a bite of some buttered eggs.

Another approach, then.

"How many days' ride is it to Canton from here?"

He scrutinized her for a moment, then smiled. "Only... what? Three days' journey? No longer than you were on the road."

She blushed, realizing the silliness inherent in her question, hiding her embarrassment behind a bite of toast.

"I can understand why you would be surprised to find us out here in the middle of nowhere. I don't imagine many of your fellow villagers wander out into the barrens, and I never go out Canton way. Hemlock, certainly, but never to the north. We are a self-sustaining estate—with some minor exceptions."

"I see," she said, smiling. *And what of the People's Uprising and the Purging of Royalty? How did you, this place, survive, and not be reduced to ruins as in Canton's Castle Hill?* she thought, but again held her tongue. Though she had been born two score after the great massacre of royalty in the northern kingdoms, a number of the Canton folk were whispered to be distantly related to those who lost their lives during that period of political upheaval, and she understood the delicacy of the subject, where referring to someone as belonging to an aristocratic bloodline could constitute a veiled threat. But apparently, the purge had not been as thorough as the history books and Mr. Prisewick's lessons had led her to believe. Indeed, Smugrove had made no apology for his master's status, and the Count himself seemed unconcerned with the subject.

"What is to be the fate of Canton, sir? Was it a lie, then? What you said about my village?"

"Not exactly," he said, slicing a well-peppered ham steak and running it through a muck of egg yolk and cream sauce. "As promised, I sent a rider to the capital to inform the professionals of the situation in Canton. By this hour he should have arrived, and a contingent of physicians will be on their way to help. Changing horses, riding at top speed, they could arrive by Dochday coming."

"But Dr. Daybleed—he seemed to be dismissive of their understanding of the disease. Some disagreement about whether it might be magical in nature."

"No matter." He dismissed this with a wave of his hand, then chewed his steak with gusto. "Daybleed's age makes him skittish when it comes to the subject of magic. Besides, whether the disease is magical or not, the good doctor's treatment is nevertheless the most efficacious."

"And drastic too," she whispered, examining the diminished shape of her hand.

She had not meant for him to hear, but he did and replied gravely, "To be sure."

"I don't mean to be indiscreet, Count Erlwine, but as a member of the aristocracy, were you not trained in the magical arts?"

He smiled. "Many of your generation have forgotten such details from their history lessons."

Of my generation?

"I learned a few parlor tricks, of course, the requisite bits of dazzle suitable to one of my station—" he plucked a currant roll from one of the trays and poked his pinky finger into the side "—nothing too extraordinary, mind you, but amusing enough." Removing his pinky, he brought the hole to his mouth and blew into it.

At that instant, the soft, flaky roll puffed up, and all the currants beading its surface, as if they had become eyes, began to wink at Constance, who gasped with delight. Gingerly, the Count set the roll down on the table, and it began to make squealing sounds as it inched its way around the platters of food to Constance. Soon, the flaky slug creature had climbed onto her plate, and she lifted her hands from the table, unsure what to do.

"Go ahead," Count Erlwine said. "Have a bite."

With her good hand, Constance grabbed hold of the creature, but as soon as she touched it, there was a delicious tingling sensation in her fingertips, the eyes stopped winking at her from their crusty lids, and the squealing ceased. The roll deflated slightly, as if the breath of life had flowed out of it.

She brought it to her lips and took a bite, and it tasted delectable—buttery and sweet and bursting with spices. "Astounding," she said, hiding her mouth as she chewed.

The Count nodded with approval. "In our library," he continued, "we have a number of books that speak of the dispelling of curses, the curing of disease by means of magic, and they are no less drastic than the procedure you underwent, involving (just for example): the sacrifice of children, the trading of a mental faculty, the ingesting of a body part, the destruction of a warlock's bloodline. You see what I mean?" From his plate he selected a flaky, buttery pastry obscured beneath a mantle of powdered sugar, bit into it, and chocolate blood dribbled down his chin.

"Is the Cinder mentioned in any of your books? Do you think it's possible that it's a curse, not a disease?"

Wiping his mouth, he said, "I'm afraid not. The books I've read on magic are predominantly historical curiosities. Every curse must be unique, you see. Once it is analyzed and understood, it loses its power, becomes defunct. And a stolen curse will backfire on the caster. The author of one such tome, a Master Antony Vivamus, proposed that this was the reason behind the scarcity of magic in the climate leading up to the People's Uprising—a dearth of creativity in spellcasters, causing them all to transmogrify themselves into toads and whatnot in their attempts to steal the work of their predecessors. Ironically, this state of affairs may very well have been a result of a sense of complacency in the royal thaumaturges who desired nothing more beyond the throne itself."

She sipped her coffee, considering his words, this novel interpretation of the decline in royal magic. "I would be most curious to peruse such a book."

"And you are welcome to. During your stay here you are free to do as you wish during the daylight hours."

Constance set down her coffee cup, the china rattling delicately. "My stay here? What do you mean? I thought I should depart forthwith and begin the journey back to Canton to see my family."

Count Erlwine shook his head. "I advise against that at the moment. More importantly, Dr. Daybleed said he advises against travel during your recuperation. In the meantime, you are welcome to remain my guest. Dr. Daybleed can make his daily inspections to assure you are healing well and that the Cinder has been sufficiently excised. I can guarantee you a full table and a comfortable bed, not to mention steam baths and constitutionals in one of the many gardens on this estate and access to the library and other forms of entertainment. In short, you shall want for nothing." As he was speaking, Smugrove reappeared, or rather, Constance shifted and noticed the faded and tatty manservant standing at the ready in the corner of the room, his face an impassive mask.

"I thank you for this most generous offer and for your concern, but aside from the damage to my vanity this disfigurement has occasioned, I feel strong enough to return to Canton and to be with my mother and father. If my father is stricken with the illness by now, he will need me to care for both my mother and himself. I couldn't bear to sit around here allowing myself to be pampered in luxury while they suffered."

"The medical professionals will be of more help than you could—"

"I disagree," she said, heat creeping into her voice. "And father is so stubborn when it comes to taking advice from others. I need to be there for him, you can't detain me any longer."

"Detain? I object to the word."

"Forgive me. You understand what I mean though."

"Of course, but surely you have considered the possibility that removing you from Canton was your father's goal all along—"

"Yes, I know that's what he intended."

"—to see you safely away from the plague under the guise of making yourself useful, for surely a conscientious and dutiful woman such as yourself would only abandon her family under the delusion that she was being of assistance."

"Has my usefulness all been some delusion, then?" she snapped, reddening.

"That's not exactly what I intended to say."

She remembered herself, her status as guest, and thought she caught some glimmer of concern flash across the waxen countenance of Smugrove, far removed from the table as he was. "I apologize, Count Erlwine," she said. "I let my temper get the better of me. I have never felt more distressed and… off balance than I do at this moment. I should not have spoken in that tone."

He smiled. "No apology is necessary, Constance. On the contrary, your filial commitment I find both touching and honorable, and I wished only to express how your family would derive some happiness from the knowledge that you are safe and out of harm's way of the disease."

"I have felt so powerless these past few days."

"Rest assured your contribution to the fight against the Cinder has been a noble one, but you have completed your task. Now is the time to care for your own health. In several days' time, according to Dr. Daybleed's prognosis, you should be robust enough for travel, at which point I will personally see to your safe passage out of the barrens and back to Canton. In the meantime, I can send word to Canton on your behalf."

Breakfast was followed by a tour of the house. After having seen so much of the place in her journeys to and from her room, Constance wondered if such a tour was necessary, and yet the Count managed to confront her with new sights at every turn. To think that only a handful of people resided in this enclosed city of excess. Such thoughts brought Constance close to the sentiments surrounding the People's Uprising—the bitter injustice her forebears had felt towards the complacent aristocracy, their lives made even more plush and cushy by magic.

But these thoughts were brief, flitting things.

What most absorbed Constance's attention was her charming host. The Count possessed a carefree, loose manner, with the full zest of youth, striding ahead of her to call her attention to this portrait or that architectural curiosity. At moments such as these, she could better admire the bulk of his strong shoulders and chest pressing beneath his ruffled shirt, the angles of his jaw and chin, the aquiline nose, and most striking of all, the stormy gray of his eyes.

They passed through a great hall of scarlet tile and gilded woodwork, with large double doors along one wall. Here the Count paused and turned toward her.

"How about some music to distract you?"

"I don't—"

"No, don't protest. This way, please, Constance. I do insist."

He led her down the hall and opened the door to a parlor in which a collection of instruments—harps and guitars, violins and a pi-anoforte—were angled about among sofas and tables so finely carved that the woodwork resembled lace. Seated around the parlor was a bevy of individuals, dressed in finery as frivolous as the furniture: ladies in shimmering, ruffled dresses with bustles, gentlemen in top hats and coattails and skinny ties—stovepipes and piston rods, she remembered Amity calling them. And every last one of them wore the same faceless mask as Helwise.

Noticing her surprised countenance, Count Erlwine commented: "Automata, they are called. The Helwise model. All the rage in Hemlock. No doubt you noticed Dr. Daybleed's ferent box. The mechanisms employed in these Helwises are similar—like clocks inside; ingenious, daedal contrivances."

Responding to the sound of the Count's voice, the group of them, sixteen in all, turned their small heads towards the human pair. Despite being trussed up as males and females, they appeared to be molded from the same graceful feminine cast as the other Helwises.

"Forgive my shock, but I must have misunderstood Mr. Smugrove yestereven, who seemed to refer to Helwise as a person."

"Oh dear me, no," Count Erlwine laughed.

"He mentioned them suckling Mr. Thingkley."

"You must forgive him, for at his age his mind is starting to slip. After all, he served as manservant to my father and his father before him. Now, come. Do you play?" Count Erlwine asked her, guiding her onward to the pianoforte.

She shook her head, imagining for some unaccountable reason how this scene might have played out with Amity acting in her place. She would have no doubt offered the Count some witty repartee. *"I think what you meant to ask was can I play the entire oeuvre of Ponce di Ferriche. In which case the answer is: quite naturally."*

"Pity, that. You have a beautiful speaking voice and, I'm sure, a matching ear."

Constance smiled regrettably, and Count Erlwine took a seat at the instrument and rolled his fingers up the keys in a delightful musical flourish akin to a knuckle crack. She stood at the side of the instrument, hands folded, resting on the rim, watching as he launched into a piece that spoke to her of a brisk morning, some countryside adventure, both luminously bright and thrilling, the galloping rhythm of it stirring up her pulse. Though she much preferred watching how his energy channeled through his muscular body, how his hands capered up and down the keyboard, summoning up the complex, overlapping harmonies. For the sake of decorum, she instead studied the interior of the instrument where hammers danced over taut strings with a corresponding delicacy almost as fascinating to her as the man producing the music. Indeed, it was almost a window into the quick and intricate operations of the Count's mind.

The music stirred the Helwises into life, lifting them from their couches and puppeteering them in concert towards a dance floor at one end of the parlor, where they paired off and began to execute a quadrille, skirts shushing and feet tapping. The manner of their dance Constance found deeply unsettling, for the closer they came to human equivalency, the further they seemed from actually being able to attain it, running up against a fine line between fluid and herky-jerky that could not be traversed.

Out of the corner of her eye, she noticed Smugrove suddenly appear in front of a wall-engulfing painting of a lush countryside in which two young couples were picnicking together, teasing each other and carousing. In his hands was a tray upon which sat a steaming teapot and ceramic cups and mortar and pestle, which he carried to a nearby table. Constance made an effort to redirect her attention towards the music, which was now drawing to a close, judging from the intensity of the tremendous interweaving runs of the left and right hands.

When he lifted his fingers from the keys, she applauded as vigorously as she could without aggravating her damaged hand. The Helwises froze in their two lines, regarding each other with eyeless faces. As her applause concluded and she remembered the question he had posed to her before beginning—"Do you play?"—the charm of his performance dwindled somewhat, as she wondered if he had in fact intended a cruel jab at the recent loss of her fingers. Had she been a musician, the loss of her fingers would have been a tragic blow indeed, but perhaps, after all, he had simply forgotten about her recent disfigurement. Either way, Constance could not decide which of these two alternatives was more troubling.

The next piece was more forlorn than the first, all moonlight and shadow, smoke and rippling water, unlike any of the intricate, clock-work-like pieces Amity had ever played for her or the rowdy tunes pounded out at the Fairwater Saloon in the middle of the night. The automata paired off to perform a sarabande, turning and revolving about each other, legs bowed, ceramic arms curved. Several minutes into the piece, Smugrove cleared his throat, interrupting Count Erlwine's train of thought and causing his fingers to stumble. The manservant took two long, dried mushrooms from a dish, packed them into the mortar, and began to grind them with the pestle into a gray powder. Having recovered his composure, the Count continued to play, but the music soon tapered off inconclusively, and Constance could not be sure if the man's enthusiasm for playing had waned or if this was how the piece had been written to end. Nonetheless, she remembered to applaud, though she felt more flummoxed than pleased by the performance. The Helwises had ceased dancing, frozen in bows and curtsies, waiting perhaps for a musical coda to return them to their seats.

As the Count stood, she noticed the tears welling in his eyes.

"Are you well, Count?"

"Please forgive me, Constance. Times of plague are trying on all of us."

"It was… touching," she said, a hopeful note in her voice.

"You will understand soon enough," he remarked enigmatically and led her across to the table, into the purview of Smugrove, whose manservant gaze was trained beyond them, beyond the automata, beyond the walls of the parlor, beyond the manor itself, into some obscure yonder of future or past events.

An eerie quiet dominated the parlor now, with the music dispersed like smoke cleared through an open window. The scuffing of dancing feet halted, the floorboards no longer creaking. The tea was ready, aromatic with its earthy and meaty tones—indeed, each cup's steaming surface seemed to be layered in frothy gray soil. Constance did not care for mushroom-brewed tea, but when he asked her, "Will you take mush with me?" she nodded.

"I find it most satisfying after a large meal. Stimulates the digestion." Count Erlwine lifted the two delicate cups from the table by their fixed saucer bases and offered one to her. She accepted it.

Despite the well-crafted face and hands, the Count looked ursine to her, a foot or so taller than herself, over-developed muscles pressing through the fabric of his clothes; he could easily strike a threatening or imposing figure in the right circumstances, but not now, not with this encouraging, simple smile that lacked any hint of aggression or lechery.

Still, she could not shake a feeling of presentiment, as if she were one false step away from plummeting off a cliff—hadn't Mother said something similar about the forest path?—and what Constance wanted more than anything was to be away from Erlwine Manor, to be back in Canton with the weasels and the lechers. That world, with its muddy streets transected by planks, its greasy rats, its odors of night soil and thrush, its overflowing cuspidors and quick-draw duels—*that* at least was familiar to her, *that* was home.

Downing the tea in one gulp, she fought back a grimace. In fact, it tasted nothing at all like the mush she was used to. Perhaps Smugrove had used different mushrooms than her mother did, or there was a touch of mildew on them. She smiled up at the Count and found that he was studying her face.

"Forgive my boldness, but you"—he reached out, his skin brushing her hands as he collected the cup from her, just a split second, electrifying and all too brief, then he set the cups down on the table and turned back to her—"have a striking face, one that must be commemorated on canvas. Have you ever posed?"

"Of course not." She blushed, her heart fluttering, and she fought to stave off the foolish thoughts intent upon invading her mind.

Counts marry other nobility, not butchers' daughters.

Yet, the nobility have been eradicated, leaving the Count with no one of his status to love or wed or help carry on his bloodline.

No, Constance, do wake up. You are a dalliance, an interlude, nothing more. How easily impressed you are. Impressing silly girls is probably just a hobby of his. He's merely teasing you with something you could never hope to obtain. This is all some cruel, elaborate joke.

THEIR "PEREGRINATION," AS THE Count put it, continued through an endless circus of splendor. At one point, Constance found them ambling through a wondrous garden set amid the many interconnected buildings of the estate. From the upper tier of this garden she could appreciate the symmetrical, flowing shape of the paths, a kind of stylized flower bud design guiding the walker past explosions of color. As they descended to these paths, the temperature grew warm and balmy. Once they reached the lower path, the great house retreated from view, leaving them in a lush jungle full of the buzz and churr of insects she had only seen in picture dictionaries. She swore, as they walked, she could hear the crash of ocean waves in the distance, while vibrant avian fantasies streaked overhead, cackling and cawing.

The Count paused along the path, plucked a blossom from a bush, and held it out from his body. He stood for a minute or more, still as a statue, neither blinking nor (it seemed to Constance) breathing. After an awkward moment, Constance started to ask what he was doing—when the Count closed his hand into a fist, completely swallowing up the flower. As he brought the fist up to his lips, the sound of the jungle dropped away, and the waving of the large, waxy leaves of the flora slowed, as if everything had been plunged underwater. He whispered a couple of words, then opened his hand. Just like the currant roll from earlier that day, the flower was transformed, now animated, flapping its pearlescent petals as if it were a winged butterfly, the pistil and stamens twitching like antennae. The creature lifted off and circled and danced around them, dazzling as a shard of living sunlight.

Count Erlwine took Constance's hand, opened it, turned it palm up, and ran his fingers down hers, the touch of them sending a shiver of pleasure up her body. As if attracted by the electricity, the floral butterfly descended and settled into Constance's hand, its wings coming to rest, delicate as tissue.

Her body, which had been so tense over the past few weeks, was suddenly filled with lightness—and Constance, forgetting all her troubles, laughed with childlike joy. This further excited the flower, which hopped along her arm and up her shoulder in short, rapid bursts of flight, finally settling into her hair.

As they continued on, through bowers, over stone bridges, the manor reappeared so suddenly that it startled her, and the briskness of autumn fell upon them like a cloudburst. She realized she had been so warm that she had been sweating.

Standing at the entrance was Smugrove, who cricked into a deferential bow. "Count Erlwine, your presence is required elsewhere." Simultaneously a command and apology.

Erlwine nodded. "You will have to make do without me for a time," he said. "But I won't be long. Consider Erlwine Manor your home."

The Library

L EFT ALONE, CONSTANCE GAZED out a window in the hallway, overlooking the garden and idly petting her fragrant butterfly flower with one finger, all the while humming the more somber and reflective of the two pieces the Count had played for her earlier that morning. She held this pose for some minutes, mind a complete blank, no doubts or worries plaguing it, unaware that a new streak of gray had already appeared in her dark hair. Then, a detail in the garden suddenly came into focus: a suit of dented and begrimed armor watching her through its closed visor from within a shower of leaves beneath a golden maple. The presence of this apparition snapped her back into reality.

She backed away from the window and hurried down the sunlit hall, casting the occasional wary glance out the windows she passed. Soon the armor was obscured behind a hedge, and Constance sighed in relief. Her footsteps slowed to a stroll, and she ambled aimlessly for a few minutes, wondering about herself and that uncharacteristic spell of absentmind-edness she had fallen under. As she walked, the flower flitted about her head, sometimes settling into her loose hair, sometimes gracing her bosom with a corsage, scenting the air with its delightful bouquet.

Up ahead on her right, she found one of Erlwine Manor's few un-locked doors. Inside, a cavernous library stretched out before her eyes, lined with staggeringly high cliffs of books, some new, some dusted, some faded, some reduced to crumbled masses that she dared not touch or even breathe towards for fear of disbursing them like puffs of spores. Through a stained-glass skylight, sunlight filtered down, bathing the stacks in rose and berylline and amethyst hues, and in the upper reaches bats or some manner of bird had taken roost, for they flapped their dusty wings and fluttered from perch to perch, stirring up eddies of dust and desiccated leaves of paper that spun and swirled in the air.

She circled around a catwalk, and from here she could see down into the subterranean levels, the light much dimmer there. She paused for a moment, listening, sure she had just heard someone screaming—a faint, distant sound. What's more, she was certain that it had been the Count's voice. Smugrove's words came back to her about the phantom echoes of large buildings.

Yes, phantom echoes. Surely that was it.

As she explored the room, she scanned the titles of books or at least attempted to do so, for the spines were either sun-faded, obscured by films of black mold, or simply printed in some foreign language wholly incomprehensible to her. She selected a volume at random, flipped it open, and slammed it shut after a second of seeing a horde of tiny black insects skittering across the page. After shoving the book back in place, she started to move on, but then hesitated, taking the book out again and opening it once more. These were not insects moving about the pages, she found on closer inspection, but words scrawled in the spare orthography of some exotic language, looking very much like centipedes crawling in circles, scrambling over each other. Frowning, Constance closed the tome and returned it to the shelf, dusting a word off her hand and feeling more irritated than mystified: if words could move across a page, what use was it to the book, whose meaning would simply change from moment to moment?

What nonsense, she thought.

At breakfast, Constance had been struck with an idea of how to make herself useful to the situation in Canton—researching about the disease and, more specifically, whether or not it was indeed magical in nature—but as she stood here now, gazing at what must be hundreds of thousands of books, she realized that the task of finding the one particular tome of interest to her was well-nigh impossible.

Something brushed past her, and she startled, sneezing as a cloud of dust billowed out around her, then stared in bewilderment as she saw what had struck her: a book flapping its cover and pages, soaring out towards the drop, then drifting upwards as if on a breeze. Gawping in wonder, she realized that the volant creatures from earlier were all books flapping to and fro. There were more, she saw now, below her, flitting about from stack to stack, like disturbances of moths riled up by a gust of wind.

Of course, this only complicated matters further, for even if she could locate a catalog or some other key to the organizational system of the library, it would prove moot as the books seemed willing to disorganize themselves. Or maybe they were doing something else entirely. They could, for all she knew, be *perfecting* their organization. Then again, maybe it was simply the books' playtime, time to stretch themselves and exercise, to resist the effects of time, the stiffening of their spines, the aging of their bindings.

As these ideas were occurring to her, a book wheeled down from the heights, paper vans outstretched, skimmed across a nearby table, and settled with a graceful flap into her hands. She examined the volume, which was titled *Treatise on the Methods of Library Organization.*

How peculiar, she thought. *The exact topic I'd just been pondering.*

She carried the volume into one of the reading alcoves and sank into a chaise longue. Curious though she was to decipher the tome, she quickly grew bored of its long-winded author. More importantly though, she had devised an idea that might (if correct) prove more useful to her purposes than reading the entire one thousand pages of dense text she now held between her hands.

Her mind made up, the book launched out of her hands with a vigorous flapping of its mildewed pages and had soon vanished into the upper reaches of the library. She turned her mind back to the problem at hand, and within a minute another book swooped down, colliding with several other books in the process, and slammed in a billow of dust on the table before her. After an interminable fit of sneezing and waving her hands to clear the air, she picked it up and found it to be a much older text than the previous one, the paper inflexible and difficult to separate.

She did manage to pry it open to the title page (the spine and cover were hopelessly faded) and saw that it was as she had suspected—*A History of Magical Curses: Case Studies and Theory* by Master Giles Cloth—exactly what she had been wishing for.

She opened it at random to Chapter Thirty, subtitled "Belalisa and Dracon." She found this section to be a case study told in verse, a unique one, the verbose footnotes explained, because it involved a person intentionally cursing himself.

Under scorchling, wisteria-clad boughs,
Belalisa and Dracon said their vows,
When with sclints all agleam and bruming flumes,
The Oxelos away snilched Dracon's bloom.
For ages this knight did pursue his kill
O'er bonehollow and brill and slantyhill,

And then, alas, in quimmering morass

He spied the Oxelos slumbering fast.

Great axe in glove, he sludgelled west to east,

Gallantly beheading that diresome beast,

And freed the damsel from her stitched-skin cage.

A kiss, cooed lovewords, and then an embrace.

But the headless Oxelos as it swooned

Vomited bowel acid from its wound.

Bedrenched, the lady screamed, deliquescing—

Reduced to nought but a frothy gold ring.

Dracon frashingly swore an oath—in vain:

From her grimlot he would his wife reclaim.

And squeezing into that caustic belly,

Was soon no more than an armored jelly.

And evermore, in sunplay and moonrill,

O'er bonehollow and brill and slantyhill,

His spirit wanders pleaming with dolor,

To save that fair soul that exists no more.

Despite the horrific content and bizarre language, the story was illustrated beautifully in the style of the Old Southern School, the characters flat and stylized: a lady in a light, airy gray dress and the armored knight on bent knee, raising her beringed hand to his lips, oaks bearded with wisteria towering above them, the sky hazy with the famous sizzling humidity of the Southern Kingdoms, and the golden eyes of the Oxelos watching them from the darkness of a nearby swamp.

She flipped backwards to look through the previous chapters and was surprised to find that Chapter Twenty-Nine was missing from the order. Before the tale of Belalisa and Dracon was Chapter Twenty-Eight, and from what she could tell, Chapter Twenty-Nine was the only one missing from the book. Besides, the ease with which the book opened to Chapter Thirty suggested that pages had been removed from the text.

She skimmed through chapter after chapter, spending an hour or so in study, lost in case after case of curses and their resolutions (or lack thereof), but her mind kept returning to the problem of the missing chapter, which bothered her to no end.

She pried open the book to the table of contents, finding a listing of the chapters and their titles... starting with Chapter Fifty. Again, the previous page of contents had been ripped out. She flipped around some more as her mind worked over the problem, immersing herself in the histories of curses for a while longer, the flapping of paper wings and creaking spines fading into the background. As she read, other books floated down with delicate grace or harassed her to be perused. By the end of her studies, many stacks of volumes old and new had accumulated about her study alcove, in convenient human-sized towers.

A distant bell tolled the Hour of the Son, rousing her from her studies.

She started to rise, when another idea suggested itself to her, and she picked up Giles Cloth's *Magical Curses* once again, flipped open to the voluminous index and there, at last, found what she was searching for—a single word—and sure enough it referenced several pages in the missing chapter. More words came to mind, and she found that everything she had wanted to learn had vanished with the missing chapter.

But why? she thought.

"Mistress Constance?" Smugrove's voice came tinnily to her ears.

One of the horns in the communication pipes.

She slammed shut the volume on curses, and it swept itself away, intuiting that its usefulness to Constance had reached an end. As she extracted herself from the labyrinth of teetering stacks, each one quivered and collapsed, its components disbursing to the far corners of the library in a migratory swarm, evoking from her several more sneezes in the process.

Smugrove called out to her again, and she tracked down the sound of his voice to a booth set in the wall between the stacks, this one far more elaborate than the one in her tower, like an anatomical study of a brass creature's viscera. After some trouble she located the bell etched "Head Office" in an elegant script and spoke into it. "Mr. Smugrove? Hello?"

"Yes, dear, Mistress Constance. I thought you would have stayed put near the garden."

"Just thought I'd do a little exploring."

"Marvelous, absolutely tremendous, and I do certainly hope your time among the Count's books has been a fruitful and enlightening one."

"It has indeed."

"Marvelous, simply marvelous and tremendous. My intention in disturbing you is only to inform you that Count Erlwine will be taking his dinner al fresco and that he hopes that you would be keen to join him, as suiting your own convalescent requirements, of course."

"You mean would I like to dine with Count Erlwine outdoors?"

"That is my meaning, Mistress Constance, most perspicacious and percipient of you to decipher."

She wasn't sure, so subtly did the man flavor his speech, but she detected notes of acid in his voice and found herself recalling the Oxelos and the horrific fate of Belalisa.

"If that is what Count Erlwine wishes, then I will be happy to join him."

"Most excellent. I will enlighten and inform him of the matter."

"Umm, Mr. Smugrove?"

"Yes, Mistress Constance?"

"Well, I'm alone here and have no idea how to find the Count. It's a…" *Wilderness,* she nearly remarked but was saved by Smugrove's eagerness to interrupt, to anticipate her wants and needs.

"A larger and grander estate than most, yes. You are correct in that assessment, and am I correct in assuming that you would like an escort to your dinner?"

"Yes, please, Mr. Smugrove."

"I will dispatch Thingkley to you directly. Ten minutes should suffice."

"Thank you," she said, shuddering somewhat at the thought of meeting the strange little man again. "I wonder if it wouldn't be simpler to give me directions; I hate to be a bother to Mr. Thingkley."

"It will be his absolute pleasure to serve as your escort, I assure you, and given the time it would take me to relay to you the multitudinous lines of directions to reach your dinner, you would peradventure already have been delivered there by the humble personage in question."

"I see."

"*Most* perspicacious and percipient of you." Definite acid.

"Well. Goodbye, Mr. Smugrove."

"Good afternoon, Mistress Constance."

As she stepped out of the booth, another sound caught her attention. Like a whimper. She paused at the threshold of the glass communication booth, listening… She heard distant footsteps, the winged activity of the books, and—

"Calmed," whispered a voice behind her, rasping and light, so much so that Constance couldn't tell if it was masculine or feminine.

She reentered the booth and scanned the confusion of the brass bells and knobs and crystal-tipped levers.

"Be …" the voice came again. "Calmed."

Constance thought the sound was coming from one of the bells in the lower portion. She crouched down, examining the labels: Warehouse, Sunflower Tower, The Gallery, Drawing Room, Tertiary Hall, Great Attic... The names went on and on as one would expect given the incredible scope of this place, evoking images of the wonders (e.g., Melted Glass Tower), the bizarre (The Corkscrew Room), and the depths (Pit, Level Five).

"H-hello?" Constance said.

"Mother... be... calmed," the voice said. The sound appeared to be coming from a bell labeled Shamrock Room.

"Is there anything more, Mistress Constance?" Smugrove inquired from the bell farther up the panel, the Head Office bell.

Constance straightened, feeling the tightening of panic in her chest. She directed her mouth to the bell and said, "No," her voice croaking.

"Ah, how peculiar, you see I thought I had heard you speak."

"You... must have been mistaken, sir." Constance was unsure why she lied. It was the same instinctual reaction of brushing spiderwebs off one's face.

"Quite possibly it is my mistake, what with the peculiar echoes of Erlwine Manor in its advanced age and ponderous dimensions, compounded by the advanced age of my own humble personage. Might I suggest that it would be within your best interest to wait in the East Hall, so that the diminutive Mr. Thingkley does not have to ambulate farther than is necessary?"

"A fine idea," she said. "Goodbye again."

"Goodbye, Mistress Constance." Then came the groan and shuddering of metal inside the walls, followed by a loud *clunk!*

After that, silence from all avenues.

Including the Shamrock Room.

THINGKLEY WADDLED DOWN THE East Hall, minuscule compared to the grand columns and the rough, wind-swept countryside visible through the windows—like some detestable insect that had accidentally wandered into an immaculate home, where it was only a matter of time before a great hand slammed down and splattered its guts. Constance stood there awkwardly awaiting his arrival, first watching him, then turning towards the view so as not to be rude, then back towards Thingkley and wondering whether to advance towards him.

"Mr. Thingkley," she began, following along behind him once he had finally reached her. "How do you like living in Erlwine Manor?" Unsure what to say to him, she thought this question might prove a useful way to open him up, if there were a linguistic intelligence embedded in that skull, that is. Mr. Smugrove had indicated otherwise, but then... something did not sit right with her when it came to the old manservant. The change had been gradual since she first met him, but Constance suddenly realized that she did not wish to see him again, neither alone nor in the company of others.

Never again if it could be helped.

This was a sentiment she felt towards all of the strange inhabitants within Erlwine Manor, save the Count himself, towards whom she felt quite the opposite. Since leaving his side, even during her brief hour or so of study, she could not shake the man from her mind, his smile, the electricity of his touch; she needed to see him again, craved it, and felt a kind of embarrassing giddiness at the thought that he was waiting for her in some faraway plot of this rambling estate.

Thingkley muttered unintelligibly.

"Does that mean you like it?"

He repeated the sound.

They passed into a corridor of marble floors, the walls lined with paintings of every topic imaginable—the soot-colored slums of Hemlock, the dramatic cliffside shores of the Shamrock Sea, serene temple courtyards. Some of these paintings were of a massive scale, and many looked familiar to her. Perhaps she had seen some before in one history book or another. Indeed, while she could not recognize the work of any particular artist, they were of a similar style, maybe even the work of the same brush. A woman's voice whispered into her ear: *"La Bavure, the Blur—all the rage in Hemlock. Though I can't help feeling something is lost when compared to the works of the Clarity Period, pre-Purge."* Constance shivered, turning towards the sound, but finding no one there.

Struck as she had been yestereven with a sense of déjà vu, she left Mr. Thingkley's side and passed through a wide entry into a spacious hall of polished wood floors, the walls filled with more and more of these paintings. *The Gallery*, she thought, recalling one of the labels in the communication booth. She wandered from room to room, searching for the source of that voice but finding no one and soon growing disoriented and overwhelmed by the sheer number of portraits and landscapes, all painted in the same blurred, smoky style.

Then something froze her in her tracks. She noticed along one wall the very same painting that had decorated the music parlor where the Count had played for her earlier that morning, and she immediately understood that her familiarity with some of these paintings was because she had seen copies of them elsewhere in the manor. Here was a painting of a girl picking sunflowers, which also hung on the walls of her bedchamber in the Sunflower Tower. And over here was the Battle of Hemlock. And there hung in portrait orientation the interior of a locomotive car—now where had she seen that one?

She became aware of the distant pseudolinguistic protestations of Thingkley and the scuffling of his boots on the floor. She turned from the painting and sought out her escort, discovering him a couple of rooms over, huffing and puffing from the exertion.

"I'm sorry, Mr. Thingkley. I thought I heard someone speak. Now, I fear I've lost my way in the pursuit of that aural phantom. Can you lead us out?" she asked hopefully.

Thingkley scolded her with his thick, purple tongue.

T HEY LEFT THE MANOR and walked along a colonnade overlooking a hedge maze. Count Erlwine, who was smoking a pipe at a small glass patio table, arose upon seeing Constance emerge from the building, set his pipe on the edge of an ashtray, and strode over. He kissed her hand—here was a new first for the blushing Constance—then he linked arms with her and led her to the table. When he noticed her shivering in the brisk wind, he surprised her with her own cloak, now clean and perfumed with lavender, and took the liberty to drape it over her shoulders.

Mr. Thingkley had disappeared, she found, as soon as they had sat at the table, Count Erlwine making a fuss to pull out her chair, dusting it with a cambric handkerchief, and guiding her down.

"How did you find the library?" he asked, taking back up his pipe. "Smugrove let slip that you managed to find your way there."

Her instinct was to apologize, but she found his clear, encouraging eyes and simply spoke what was in her heart. "The enchantments never cease here. It was practically alive with books, and so many of them too—probably as many as in the Library of Hemlock—"

"More, I've been told."

"Very well—and the way they come and go as they please (or as the reader pleases, I suppose). The only bit of magic left in Canton is the statue of Duke Guillemet Cantone."

"Ah, yes."

"After they ex—" She stopped herself, face reddening.

"Go on and say it. Executed. I'm not offended."

"Yes," she said, recovering from the faux pas. "After they executed the Duke and burned his castle, they... removed the head of his statue and tossed it into the Main Street gutter. The story goes that the next day the head had reappeared resting atop Duke Cantone's shoulder, countenance serene, eyebrows arched, just as if nothing had happened. So they defaced it in other ways, lopping off legs and arms"—she did a quick imitation of the statue's ambiguous posture, in which he seemed to be testing for rain or waiting for a bird to alight on his palm, then slicing off the arm in question—"and yet every morning, the statue would appear to have been unharmed. Finally, they dragged the thing across town and dumped it into the Fairwater River, but sure enough, in the morning it was back in its original place—its rightful place, or so the statue must think. Strangest of all, there were no footprints or marks on the ground. It seemed to have just materialized there. And so, there it still stands, making everyone in town uncomfortable, for it is clearly an object of great power, not to mention a powerful reminder of the horrors of fifty years ago."

He laughed. "I have heard of similar enchantments. The Cantonites have my sympathies; being forced to look upon Duke Cantone's odious aspect is a grave offense to anyone's aesthetic sensibilities."

It was her turn to laugh. "Count Erlwine—"

"Litney."

"Yes. Right. Litney. Forgive an impertinent comment, but I wonder, for your sake, if it is wise to keep such a library and perform your lovely... tricks for your guests." As she uttered the word, the floral butterfly fluttered down and alit on her bandaged hand, flexing its papery wings.

He nodded. "Like the statue of Duke Cantone, a magical library is not easily transplanted. If you're worried for my safety, then worry no more. I won't trouble you with particulars, but Erlwine Manor is safe from the Antiroyalists and will never come to harm." He gave her a wry smile. "You're not an Antiroyalist, are you?"

She smiled. "Hardly. All I do in my spare time is read Eton Brimley novels, and in fact, most of my morning was occupied in the perusal of a text that has likely been banned by the State of Clairmont. It was penned by a Master Giles Cloth."

His gray eyes brightened. "I'm familiar with the scholar and his lucubrations."

"I regret to say that your copy of his *A History of Magical Curses* is damaged, a number of pages missing. An entire chapter, in fact."

"Well, I don't find this particularly surprising. Our library was constructed with a duty to educate and entertain humankind, and to that effect it will serve its purpose. However, enchanted books have a tendency to edit themselves, which I have found to be frustrating for my own research. You never can quite trust the information a magical book delivers to you …"

There was a momentary pause in the conversation while one of the Helwises brought out a decanter of wine and poured it into stained-glass chalices. Constance watched the creature discreetly, wondering if this was the same automaton that had retrieved her from her room earlier that day. She or it was dressed in the same white apron and black dress and wore the same extravagant wig. She nodded and thanked the Helwise, which bowed meekly in response. In that instant Constance glimpsed the numbers *388* along the jawline, though it was almost concealed by the voluminous curls of the wig, then she turned back to the table and pretended to study the gorgeous facets of the glass chalice as she continued the conversation with the Count.

"If I could guess, and I can and shall," the Count said, "I'd wager that that mischievous book in question edited out the topic you wished to investigate."

"Yes, not only did it remove one of its chapters, but it also tore out the page of the table of contents that referenced the missing part. However"—she licked her lips, watching the Helwise disappear back into the manor and wondering how many Helwises were crawling around the vast grounds—"it neglected one aspect of its edits: the index. And that omission was enough to tell me something that I had not before guessed at."

The Count, who had been swirling the burgundy wine in his glass, stopped suddenly, his expression rigid.

"Is there something wrong, Count… um, that is, Litney?"

"Not at all. Prithee proceed." He flashed her one of his encouraging smiles, but Constance noticed a crumb of consternation in his look.

"It's not much, but well, I think there is some connection between the Nilwere and the Cinder. And it seems that this book did not want me to apprehend that connection."

The Count continued to swirl the dark red liquid in his glass, stirring up the fine sediment at the bottom, and took a sip. "It's a fascinating theory, and I believe you may be correct. But their connection is likely only incidental. As a hunter of the Nilwere, I can tell you a good bit about them."

"Them? You mean there's more than one?" she asked, alarmed.

"Yes, you find them sprouting up like mushrooms after rain in the right conditions, and plague times are ideal circumstances for Nilwere formation: bodies piling on top of each other, their humors commingling. You may have noticed the passing sentimental mood I experienced when playing the piano today, about how plague times can be trying on us all. Well, now you can appreciate my feelings on the matter, why the disease itself, horrendous and tragic though it may be, is not the sole concern."

"Indeed." She felt both disappointed and disconcerted by the Count's explanation of Nilwere formation. When she had discovered the possible connection between the Cinder and the Nilwere in the library, she had thought (hoped) that the Nilwere may have caused the Cinder, and not the other way around. Hence her disappointment. On the other hand, if he was correct, there was a risk of a Nilwere forming in the center of her hometown, or was it the case that the creature that had followed her through the woods was composed of the corpses of her townsfolk? She recalled the day she had left town, how the bodies had been shifting over the mountain of decay, and shuddered.

She turned back to the Count and found herself gazing into his luminous gray eyes, like clouded skies with the sunshine just on the verge of shining through. His demeanor was apologetic, for he well knew this was not the explanation she had wanted to hear.

She started to speak, but just then the Helwise appeared again, a stiff-moving swan dressed as a scullery maid, wheeling out a silver serving cart that gleamed as it passed from the shadow of the arcade and into the slanted light of the autumn day. She uncovered it, sending gusts of steam and inviting aromas their way, and set to serving them in its cold, jerky manner.

"How many Helwises do you have working here?" she could not help asking.

"Better ask Smugrove. He keeps records of that sort of thing."

And yet, a couple of hours ago, Litney had warned her about the unreliability of Smugrove's memory.

"Uh, Constance, would you be so good as to say a Prayer of Gratitude?"

She was more than happy to comply.

The meal was less extravagant than breakfast, but still they did not lack for anything: there were minced pies, tongue in aspic, cornbread fried with sharp cheddar (which Constance particularly loved), pickled beets and cucumbers, a bowl of golden pears and red apples, and a soup of chard and lentils. The food had the effect of curtailing the conversation about the Nilwere and segued into an appraisal of their dinner, leading to comparisons with meals past, broadening to a general appreciation of the here and now, simple pleasures, the enjoyment of each other's company, comfortable, amiable chatter, flirtatious at times, peppered with small humorous observations. As she told him about life back in Canton, about her father and mother, her eyes wandered across the table, found the ashtray, with its piled construction of cinders. The sight fixed itself in her mind, unsettling her. When her eyes teared up, he took her undamaged hand in his and promised her that her family would be spared. She in turn promised that once the ordeal was over she would return to Erlwine Manor and bring him one of her mother's carvings. When her mother was well again, she would describe everything she had seen on her adventure, and her mother would carve for her Erlwine Manor and its cast of grotesque characters.

In the afternoon sunshine the Count seemed older, less energetic, and more melancholic than he had that morning, and when she jested about the touch of silver in his sideburns, he coughed and grew reserved, studying the final swig of wine in his glass. She was concerned that she had overstepped some boundary, unfortunate because although there was clearly a larger age gap between them than she had initially supposed, she found him all the more handsome for it, and Constance found herself remembering the many blushing encounters she had had with the silver-haired Sheriff Sykes when she would deliver his food orders to the jailhouse or to his apartment above the Fairwater Saloon.

"Yes," he said at last and downed his wine. Then his eyes sparkled. "Finished, are you?"

Constance nodded.

"How are you feeling?"

"Quite well." She managed to look up at him. "Quite... full of energy, in fact."

"Wonderful. I spoke with Dr. Daybleed, and he suggested fresh air and some light exercise would be beneficial to your convalescence. What would you say if I proposed a game?"

She dabbed her mouth with a lace-trimmed napkin and gave a nod of approval.

"Are you familiar with 'The Dromenon' from *The Book of the Family*?"

"Of course. It's the favorite of every schoolgirl." It was the story of Daughter Innocent, of the tenth generation of descendants, who tested the might and wit of her four suitors by designing a maze for them to pass through, complete with snares and a monster with a taste for human flesh.

"A most excellent story, I concur. And we are conveniently in the presence of a labyrinth."

Constance turned and gazed down at the hedge maze laid out below them. "How does one play this game?"

"It is a variation on the theme, but splendid fun. There are two players: the Monster, who begins at one end of the maze, and the Suitor, who must thread the maze and exit on the other side without getting caught."

"And which of us should be which?"

Count Erlwine smiled mysteriously, rose, and offered Constance his arm.

Love Games

T HEY STROLLED ALONG THE balustrade above the maze, which spanned a couple of acres, and all the while Constance examined the layout, looking for landmarks she might remember once she had descended into the thick of things. Though large, it was not too complex. Crucially, there appeared to be more than one solution to the maze. Aside from the curvy, zigzagging corridors, there were a handful of open gardens, each furnished with benches or fountains, statues or urn-shaped flower plots thick with silvergrass.

"This is your staircase, Fair Daughter." He smiled, bowing slightly, then left her to descend.

By the time she reached the bottom of the stairs, dwarfed by the tall hedges, he had already vanished behind the wall of green, which shivered in the brisk autumn wind. There was a brass horn rimed in verdigris positioned by the entrance, and after a minute or so she heard the Count speaking through it.

"At the ready, Constance?"

"Yes."

"Begin!"

She dashed inside, her cloak billowing out behind her.

She had thought she had memorized the layout, but after only several turns, she was lost, flitting in and out of the shadows of the hedges, passing through different gardens, which also failed to orient her. What had appeared trivial to her from a bird's-eye angle became a baffling puzzle. Each of the suitors in "The Dromenon" had employed different strategies to escape the maze. The first had walked with one hand against the left wall, but the maze was so vast that he ended up dying of dehydration before he found the exit. The second suitor had walked with one hand against the right wall, and after only a few turns had been sliced to pieces by a wall of swords. The third had left a trail of breadcrumbs, attracting the attention of the monster, which crushed him beneath one of its giant hooves. And the fourth... he'd simply waited for the monster to find him and swallow him whole, and when the monster exited the maze, he hacked his way out of its belly and won the hand of the princess. The last of these strategies didn't seem terribly useful at first blush, but what if the Count found her without realizing it?

As the idea occurred to her, she caught movement at the entrance to one of the gardens. She dashed over to a fountain and dropped down behind it, an advantageous angle for hiding if someone were to pass through the garden, which opened onto north, east, and west passages, but not to the south. She strained to hear anything over the babble of the water spilling out of the raven-headed gargoyle's mouth.

And what if he does catch me? What then?

Her excitement mounted at the thought, remembering the look of bridled passion in his eyes during their dinner, the way his gaze had bored into her at times. It was becoming easier and easier to hide away in this enchanted place, playing games while the disease consumed everyone she knew. Easier to forget, easier to let herself be led around by this handsome aristocrat, easier to be cared for, easier to turn inward, to focus on her own pleasures, her own needs, to cast off the world.

She heard footsteps, the grass crunching.

If he found me so quickly, he must be very intimate with the maze. Perhaps he's even played Dromenon with some other butcher's daughter before today.

The footsteps approached the fountain, hesitated there, his shadow appearing slanted in the afternoon sunshine, falling just to the left of the gargoyle's. The shadow seemed to consider east or west, merging with the gargoyle's shadow as it did so. Whether he went east or west didn't matter, for she knew her move.

The shadow at last retreated, heading westward. She waited a few seconds, peeked over the fountain rim and saw that he had gone, then crouched back down, waiting.

She waited several minutes before she again heard the crunch of grass beneath his footfalls, and this time there was no deliberation as they headed for the southern passage, whence they had originally come.

He must have threaded the maze all the way to the entrance, Constance reasoned, *and having not found any trace of me, he will head back towards the exit.* And then? If she were in the Count's place, she would then try an alternate route to the entrance. *If that was indeed his plan, he would lead me right past the exit.* At which point, she would win.

She dashed after him, on the balls of her feet, quiet as can be. At the entrance to the passage, she glanced this way and that, just catching sight of his black cape as he rounded a corner. She pursued him, skulking as quickly and quietly as she could manage, pausing at every juncture and peeking around the corner to make sure he was not doubling back on his path.

Soon, he had led her into a garden all ariot with colorful blooms, and she knew they had reached the center of the maze. She paused at the entrance, watching the Count as he loped towards the opposite passage, soon vanishing down another verdant hall. She sprinted after him and again paused at this passage, ears pricked for the sounds of his feet. She heard nothing at first, but then a whistling came to her ears: rambling, bouncy, unmistakably di Ferriche's "The Son's Waltz." As children, Amity had tried to teach Constance how to play it (without much success). There was something so cocksure how the Count gave himself away, but it was also contemplative and hesitant, sending a frisson of excitement down her spine. He was just on the other side of the hedge, moving slowly. She could picture him turning to look down this avenue and that, temporizing.

Biting her lip, Constance crept towards the break in the wall that would bring him within view. Unbeknownst to her, the flower butterfly lifted off from her hair and fluttered upward, rising above the shivering green wall.

The Count broke off whistling suddenly, and all was quiet. The lush branches of the arborvitae walls waved and rustled in the wind. Constance glanced through the entry between the hedges, finding a small topiary garden beyond.

A good sign, for if her memory served correctly, it was the garden closest to the exit.

She had made it, but where had the Count gone?

Ears pricked, she crept through the garden, then paused at the garden's exit, surveying what lay beyond. All the while, the butterfly circled high above her.

Suddenly, there came a rush of footsteps, and a little yip escaped Constance's lips as she first stepped one way, then decided on the other. A hand reached out from behind her and scooped around her waist.

She screamed with pleasure and excitement and turned on Count Erlwine, tried to slap him for his nerve, but he caught her hand, and now their bodies were pressed together, both of them gasping for air, hearts pounding. Then, at last, she noticed the butterfly, for it was now fluttering back down to her, its purpose accomplished.

She tried to shove him away. "You cheated! Your magical gift was a ruse!"

He held her all the tighter. "You cheated. Exploiting my knowledge of the maze."

"I had to even the odds."

"And I couldn't have you escape. Not yet."

He placed his hand on her lower back, leaned down, and kissed her, and everything seemed to slow around them and freeze. The hedges paused mid-sway, the wind died down, the chirping of birds became drawn out. Her maimed hand, throbbing with pain, was placed on his chest, and she felt for the first time how taut his body was, like a piece of carved wood. He tasted of pipe tobacco, traces of cherry and vanilla blossoming with every exploration of their tongues.

I will not, she told herself.

I will not give myself to this entitled man, to this man who has every-thing, I will not give him anything more. She thought this as she unlaced her corset, she thought this as she guided his hand inside.

CONSTANCE WAS UNSURE HOW much time had passed.

She had been napping lightly in his arms, warm in the delicious afterglow of their lovemaking, when Count Erlwine's hand suddenly grabbed a fistful of her hair and his body tensed beneath her, then he began to quiver and shake. Wincing in pain, she struggled to free his hand from its grip on her. At last his fingers fanned out rigidly, and she slipped free and turned to him. His mouth was foaming, his normally serene face was seized up, every crease exaggerated, new ones forming, lips pulled back and teeth bared like some wolf—and a thought (later embarrassing) came to her: *lycanthropy, he's a werewolf.* Indeed, he seemed to be visibly transforming before her eyes into some horrific creature.

Still, she did not leave him but held all the tighter to his shuddering body, repeating, "Litney, Litney, Litney," as if to invoke a spirit or appease a demigod. She smelled urine and saw the spreading wet heat down the side of his leg; the foam was now pouring out of his mouth and onto his chest, and Constance directed his head so that it flowed out unheeded onto the grass. It had grown pink and smelled of blood.

She was wild-eyed with panic, clinging to him, calling out for help, catching some glimmer of a future where Count Erlwine dies in her arms and, attempting to seek help, she grows lost in the infinite wilderness of the great house, starves to death, only to be discovered many years later by Smugrove or Thingkley or one of the Helwises: a dusty skeleton in a rotted, bug-eaten dress, hair a brittle, cobwebbed frizz.

Then, just as abruptly as it had begun, the attack ended, and Count Erlwine grew still. His choked gurgling, the thumping of his boot on the ground, these sounds ceased, leaving them with the gathering wind, howling over the thousands of eaves and stone chimneys and gables of the manor. It was freezing, she realized, and they were only half-dressed.

Count Erlwine's eyes struggled open. The orbs rolled back down from red-cracked white to those clear gray irises. The pupils constricted. She watched him focus on her, brushed a sodden curl from his forehead, cleaned the frothy blood from his mouth with her sleeve, then leaned down and kissed him on the temple and breathed in the smell of him.

"Litney, what's happened? You frightened me so," she whispered.

He had not transformed into some horrific creature, but the attack had left him breathless and older somehow. Did she imagine the gray on his temples or had they been like that before? Yes. She had joked about them at dinner. *But this patch of white on the top? The wrinkles at the corner of his mouth? The creases in his neck? Is this the Cinder? Have I infected him?*

"It was nothing. An attack... of nerves is all. They do strike from time to time. Never, I'm sorry to say, at the proper moments."

It was difficult in the fresh outdoor air to ascertain, but she thought that his *odor* had changed too. What had once been an attractive musk, an alluring, virile smell now contained an unpleasant note in it, repellent even.

Maybe he soiled himself in more than one way. Only that, nothing more. Do have pity on the poor soul.

As if to give support to her thoughts, he said, "I'm afraid... at such times I'm rendered as helpless as a babe."

"Please. Don't speak of it. Really. I-I was afraid you were dying or... or..."

Or transforming.

"In time," he grunted. "I will be back in full form, the vigor of youth."

"Please do not strain yourself so."

"I must... be cleaned. It is an embarrassing moment to spend with one as lovely as you."

"I don't mind. I've never been very squeamish. Just rest a moment."

Nodding, he closed his eyes, his face pale, filmed with sweat, his large hand clammy in hers. There was something sunken and defeated about him, as if he had sacrificed a spark of his vitality, as if he were decomposing right before her eyes.

EVEN AFTER HIS SPIRITS had revived, Count Erlwine was still unsteady on his feet, so Constance assisted him up the stairs and back to the house, though she dreaded returning there. Wondrous though it was, every time she had left its doors today, first for the garden constitutional, and then for their dinner, she had felt a burden lifted from her shoulders. In the countless array of windows, glossed over with the reflected gray of the sky, like larger versions of the Count's eyes, she imagined the strange servants standing in a row, watching as they struggled up the stairs and across the patio: Thingkley, Smugrove, Dr. Daybleed, the innumerable Helwises.

It was at that moment, glancing up at the sheer face of the great house, that Constance began to suspect that the two of them were wrapped up in an immense plot, one that she could almost formulate, but which at this moment lay just beyond her ken. Yet she could sense its complex structure as a psychic must glimpse the future, obscure and smoky though the image may be. She detected its sharp edges, but not the bulk of it, nor the complexity.

She squeezed Count Erlwine's hand and felt him squeeze hers back, but neither of them spoke. A pall shrouded his face. Frigid rain had begun spattering the walk, awaking a deep mineral smell.

They had barely reached the shelter of a cloister before the downpour commenced, masking all the world. Count Erlwine held both her hands in his, and they looked first to the rain, then into each other's eyes. Every other color faded between the poles of his clear gray, almost silver, eyes, and Constance's sparkling emerald. All grew hushed and empty, a bubble outside of time.

"Constance, I must leave you now," Count Erlwine said. Though the attack had aged him considerably, somehow the bond of love that had sprung up between them fixed her to the spot, palliated his every flaw, and endeared them to her. She adored the careworn brow, the patches of white, the somewhat slack lips, the crow's feet around his mouth and eyes.

"Please don't. I... I have a dreadful presentiment, Litney. Take me from this place. We'll ride out in the rain, to Canton, to Hemlock, I don't care where, as long as we're together. I can't pass another night here."

He shook his head. "I've ruined things. That is, my condition has."

"Your condition... tell me, tell me what's wrong, tell me what has happened. What is happening to us? Please, Litney, please."

"It is the same old tale, Constance. Rest assured we will see each other again soon. For now, I leave you in the capable hands of Mr. Smugrove."

Constance had failed to notice the man standing near them, who had emerged from some doorway or shadow or dungeon or netherworld. He stood wrinkled and ancient and grim, a creature of sticks and brine-cured skins, a reminder of their ultimate fates, and Constance did not wish to, could not bring herself to turn and acknowledge the manservant.

"Remember the time we spent together," Count Erlwine said. "Remember all of it up until the end."

She shook her head. "No, no, no. I want to stay with you. Please."

"Yestereven, after I hunted the Nilwere down, I don't remember much more than the pain, Constance. Nights, they're painful times for me. I can't have you bear witness to my suffering. It wouldn't be fair to you."

"Smugrove mentioned something along those lines—"

"No doubt he did, but ..."

"But what? You're ill, Litney. Surely, Dr. Daybleed can help you—or perhaps you can seek out help in the city."

He laughed grimly. "No, no. I'm afraid not."

"What then? What is it?"

"I have been very fortunate to be able to spend this day with you, Good Mother." Mother? His attack must have rattled his mind too. "I live for the daylight, but it fades apace. Life is very wonderful, and very strange," he remarked, squeezing her good hand once more, then rushed away, his wet cloak clinging to his body.

She stood watching him disappear down the long breezeway.

"It is time, Mistress Constance, if I may be so bold as to suggest it, for afternoon tea," Smugrove said. He had crept up even closer. She could hear the simper in his voice.

"Thank you, Mr. Smugrove, but I don't fancy tea just now," she said, turning towards him. He was not in fact smiling, which bothered her more than she could say. His wrinkled mouth looked as if it had been stitched onto his face. "I would like a change of clothes."

"As you wish. I will escort you to Sunflower Tower so you can freshen up before—supper." The pause that came before the word *supper* made her wonder if he had been about to say something else.

Peculiar how she had fallen so easily into the role of a lady, this butcher's daughter who a handful of days ago had been doing figures behind the counter at her father's shop. How many times had "Mistress Constance" been drilled into her since her arrival?

When will this strange dream end? she wondered. *When will I wake and find that I am still wandering Forest Road?*

The Hour of the Mother

ONCE SHE ACKNOWLEDGED THE pain, the cramps in her belly, she realized the discomfort had been gathering there for some time, a heaviness in her, a sluggishness of her limbs. The pain heightened her sensitivity to everything: the rustle of her dress and the chafing of Smugrove's suit and the creaking of his limbs, the man's mildewy odor and puffs of peppermint, the tortuous route to Sunflower Tower.

They had reached some lushly carpeted hallway, and at that moment Constance noted that the pain was not the only thing plaguing her: she felt bloated, the whalebone of her corset biting into her sides. Hoping that the one was causing the other, she discreetly loosened the laces when Smugrove was looking elsewhere, and waited to see what effect it would have on the pain.

If anything, the pain intensified.

Maybe I just need to relieve myself. That might assuage the pain.

Dear Mother, how much longer will this journey last?

She recognized none of the halls through which they passed nor the stairs up which they climbed, and though Smugrove pointed out objects and rooms of interest, mint-flavored facts about construction and history, the information slipped across her mind like oil over water. *Father, Mother, Son, Daughter,* she thought over and over again, a prayer, a mantra, a solace. Maybe the cyclic prayer would ease her suffering, but at least it would distract her from the man's incessant, perfumed chatter.

Finally, though, she could stand it no more. "Mr. Smugrove, excuse me," she said, interrupting his meditations on why they had chosen crimson carpet for this particular hallway. "Perhaps we could just walk in silence."

"I hope you don't mind my inquiring if everything is very much well with you, Mistress Constance." The sweet peppermint breath was cloying, nauseating.

"Perhaps it was something I ate. It's my stomach."

"Oh dear, dear me, most unfortunate, most unfortunate—"

Must you repeat every damnable word? she thought unkindly at him.

"—we are nearly there, and once we have arrived I will have the doctor sent up."

"No, please no." She couldn't bear the sight of Dr. Daybleed in this queasy state. The memory of his scarred face hidden behind that painted canvas veil ratcheted up the pain a notch, and she felt the first urge to be sick. Though she fought it, she knew it would not be long, that within minutes whatever was inside her would force its way out.

"Come to mention it, Mistress Constance, your visage, your normally lovely countenance, doesn't look exactly tip-top, ship shape—a little color lost, perhaps, a shade more wan than before, a shade less rubicund."

"Please, sir," she gasped, stifling another urge to vomit. The excesses of Erlwine Manor were eating away at her mind—flashes of portraits she had seen, the faces of the servants and the Count himself, they assaulted her inner eye, each image toppled by the next in a sickening phantasmagoria of things and foods and rooms, like a Nilwere assembled out of disturbing memories instead of cadavers.

"Oh dear me, yes, yes, I will take your request to heart and strive for the strictest degree of silence, not a word more from this point on, except for the most essential of linguistical utterances."

She groaned but kept her mouth shut, for she was bursting, and the pain was something unprecedented, a writhing inside her, not exactly stationary and focused, but expanding, as if she had swallowed a live mink and it was now clawing its way out of her through whatever exit it could find. She looked down and was shocked to find that her belly had swollen to the size of a pumpkin so large that it had snapped the whalebone of her corset.

She was sick suddenly, a hot, acidic rush. She shut her teary eyes so as not to see the mess—for her entire head seemed to be expelling fluids at this moment.

Mr. Smugrove was commenting unhelpfully, though Constance couldn't make out a word of what he said. Then a mummified hand was trying to help her up, but she pushed it away, sensing she would be sick again.

When at last the final bit of dinner had vacated her and her pain was alleviated only a small degree, she allowed him to help her stand. She mumbled an apology and at last opened her eyes to keep from tripping on the stairs. Soon, they were ascending the spiral of Sunflower Tower, and she noticed her belly was still swollen—everything about her body felt different, stiff and pudgy, the bones wrong somehow. She no longer felt sick to her stomach, but the pain was returning, and with it a surprising heaviness, as if lead weights had been inserted into her body during the last half hour.

"Here we are, then, arrived at your domicile," Smugrove said. Cheerily. *What in the Father's name are you so fucking cheery about?* she wanted to scream at him. "I will leave you now. Given your current state, it might be wise that you take your supper in your chambers, and that you make it a light one, just a nosh perhaps, and I will thus accordingly instruct one of the Helwises to bring up a service."

Constance nodded, fumbling with the latch, in a daze.

"Ah, it's locked, remember?" He produced the key and opened the door.

"Thank you, Kind Father."

"You're most welcome. I know you do not want company at the present time, but Dr. Daybleed will be up later in the night to check upon your health. I'm afraid I must insist, given the serious operation you underwent yestereven."

She nodded reluctantly.

"Anything else you care for? A bath, perhaps, might do wonders."

"Yes. A bath. A bath may help." The edges of the world had grown blurry. It was as if the dream were finally fading, and behind it all this time had been lurking this mass of pain.

"Excellent. It will be a few moments, a few moments only. Please do have a lie-down, and I'll see that the tub is prepared for you."

She obeyed. Everything was hazy now, as if she had crawled into one of those Bavure paintings in the gallery downstairs, and the pain came crashing down upon her and retreating in relentless waves. She collapsed onto the bed and heard through the muffling cotton wall the sounds of Smugrove prattling and prating as he crept around the apartment, the clanking of something by the head of the bed—the chamber pot, she hoped. The room was dark, but for one candle sputtering on the bedside table. She tried to focus on the rain lashing against the windowpanes, relaxing in its way, even if the wind rocked the tower disconcertingly, even if the thunder made everything shiver and tremble.

She rolled over onto her side, aimed for the chamber pot, and was ill again. When she opened her eyes, she found that the rug had begun to disintegrate, its golden geometric patterns fading. She reached out for the candle, and her hand brushed against something brittle.

A brown leaf.

Beyond the table, she found the wall brimming with dead foliage. She picked up the candle, guided it towards the floor, and saw that the rug and chamber pot had vanished, leaving behind an overgrown dirt road. Without warning, the pain began to retreat, mercifully, and she stood and cast the candlelight about the room. In the shadowy edges the room was still visible, but as soon as the light touched it, forest became exposed. She turned a full circle, the room vanishing beneath the candle's illumination.

After all that had happened to her, the old refrain held true: she was still wandering Forest Road.

The appearance of the road, the trees towering above her, the fading light filtering down through the canopy, the churring of a nightjar, the crackle of leaves stirred by the wind, these sights and sounds washed over her with untold relief. It had all been nothing more than a tortuous nightmare. There had never been a Nilwere or a strange mansion in the wilderness filled with a dashing Count and ghoulish servants. Of course not. *What tripe!* as her father would say.

The woods ended up ahead, and in the distance, she could make out the rushing of the Fairwater River: she was close to reaching Canton.

"Thank the Father," she said, lumbering forward. Her body was still swollen and her hand maimed, dissonant facts that her mind nevertheless ignored. And when the forest ended and the farmlands unfurled before her, towards the tidy collection of frame houses, false-front businesses, and warehouses that was Canton at sunset, she forgot all else and waddled towards home as quickly as she could manage.

As she passed the Canton town limit sign—*KEEP OUT, CINDER*—she heard the temple bell tolling the Hour of the Mother. A new sign had appeared here in the past few days—*BEWARE PROFITEERS*—and beside the sign was the head of Charity Hobbs mounted on a stake, foul and almost unrecognizable beneath a thick, rippling veil of flies.

Constance was still holding the candle, protecting the flame with her hand from the cold wind. As she passed down Main Street, she saw only a few windows lit. The shops and saloon were all closed down, and she did not encounter a soul before finally reaching Dunn's Fine Meats and Fancy Sausages. She grew at once ecstatic and fearful when she saw the gaslight burning in the window upstairs. Before she knew it, she had burst through the backdoor and was clambering up the stairs.

In the empty kitchen, there was a large black bloodstain beneath the table, a shard of snail shell glimmering in its gummy center, but she had no time to process this. She passed down the narrow hallway, glancing first into her tiny bedroom, then the family room—both empty. The only source of light streamed into the hall from her parents' bedroom. She stopped at the threshold, mustering up her courage.

"Father?" she said, peering into the room.

"Connie? Is that you? Am I going mad?" Thurgood glanced up from where he had been sitting at the bedside, head in one of his hands. The man was gaunt and pale, back bowed, white hair standing out in his mutton chops. "You disobedient fool of a child, why have you returned? There is nothing to be done here."

She heard the crack of a pistol in the distance. Thurgood read the surprised concern in her eyes. "That would be Mayor Lancaster. Must have been a hitch in the hanging." He turned his attention back to the bed, where the thing that had once been her mother lay. Constance could only see the cadaverous face, everything else covered by a counterpane depicting highlights of the Season of the Mother—Reaping Time, the Harvest Dance, the Pumpkin Festival. The head was shriveled and gray, appearing to be caked in ash, bald save for a scraggly white tuft at the top. Pus was seeping through the cracks in her face and pate, drying quickly in the air, forming into more ashen ridges. Her eyes milky and totally bereft of color, the form beneath the quilt was so diminished that for a moment Constance was under the impression that there was nothing beneath it, that her father had gone mad and placed his wife's head atop a pillow.

And the bloodstain birthmark... was erased. The Cinder had equalized Rachel Dunn's flesh, showing her as she might have looked without it, though aged to the point of being ancient. Never in her life had Constance wished more to see the birthmark again than she did now, the birthmark that had been the subject of so much gossip and mockery, the birthmark that had probably helped craft her mother into the soft-spoken, humble woman that she was.

In the quiet, Constance heard the wheezing of breath and saw that her mother was trying to speak.

"Come here," Thurgood said. "Come say goodbye to your mother."

Another gunshot echoed across town. Far off. She could tell now that it had come from Castle Hill, the execution grounds.

She approached slowly, hearing every familiar creak and groan of the floorboards. She set the candle down by the gas lamp. Her father relinquished his chair to her and guided her down. While he was too distracted, it seemed, to notice the drastic physical changes she had undergone, she did notice his right hand, now nothing more than a bandaged stump.

She remembered the bloodstain in the kitchen and had to suppress the scene that sprang into her imagination.

"Oh, Father," she said.

"Never you mind. Sit."

She obeyed, and as she settled down she realized that the intense pain she had been suffering from before waking and finding herself on Forest Road was still with her, buried deep, but not deep enough. Almost too faint to hear, it called out to her like someone buried alive in a shallow grave.

She reached forward and set her hand on the counterpane, positioned over her mother's arm, but she felt nothing there. By now she had likely lost her feet and hands—even if by some miracle Constance could cure her at this very instant and tell her all that she'd dreamed about, her mother would not be able to carve a little figurine of Mr. Thingkley or the Helwises; she would never carve again. The head wheezed, and Constance leaned in close and caught a whiff of something repulsive, but she forced herself not to recoil, not to show any signs of disgust. Her body was shaking with the effort.

Father, help me. Mother, help me.

The head turned towards her ever so slightly, the milky eyes looking askance. "Con... nie." The voice was a death rattle, wholly unfamiliar.

"I'm so sorry, Mother. I'm so sorry I left and abandoned you and Father. I tried to come back. I... I—" Tears streamed down her face, her voice quavering.

"You've br... ought... us... some... thing." Gritty-looking saliva oozed down out of the corner of her mouth from the effort of speech.

"What?" *The candle?* she thought stupidly.

She turned towards it, found it flickering like mad, the pearls of wax streaking down the sides, melting in sped-up time.

Oh Family, what is happening to me?

Then suddenly the candle had regrown, the flame no longer fierce and blazing.

Something touched her belly. It was her mother's... hand, reaching out from under the counterpane, and yet it was not hers. In fact, there were several hands reaching out from beneath the quilt, caressing her belly, poking it, testing it. They were all porcelain with jointed digits, just like Old Lady Yorin's.

"You... are... the Daughter's... ghost... reborn... a m-mother."

Constance shook her head confusedly.

She heard water being poured in the corner of the room, saw on the desk against the far wall a tray covered with a silver cloche that was much too opulent for the Dunn household. And there had never been a desk in her parents' bedroom... A dark figure was creeping through the shadows of the room, its skirt swishing, ignored by her father and mother.

"Mother, you must hold on longer. You must hold on. Doctors are coming. The Count said so."

The head smiled.

"You lost... your way... wandered too deep."

Constance nodded. "But I'm back now, Mother. I'm here." As she spoke the words, tears coursed down her cheeks, but she let them flow.

"I'm sorry," the head croaked. "I always... feared... you would carry... my bloodstain. I pray... our grandson... won't... be marked... with blood. Forgive... me... Connie."

Suddenly, the pain surged up through Constance's body, and she groaned, her vision fraying confusedly. Hands stood her up and were soon pulling her dress up and over her head, removing her unlaced and split corset and chemise, pulling down her drawers and stockings.

She was naked, standing in the center of the room, not her parents' room, but the room at the top of Sunflower Tower. Her body was humongous, her breasts sore and heavy, her mind reeling with disorientation. She would have fallen over had someone not caught her and led her behind the vanity and to the griffin tub. Cold hands (so many hands) helped her inside. The water was warm as saliva, murky and thick, with a chemical pungency to it, deeply unsettling, like a pool of insect slime. Fragments of the poem about Belalisa and Dracon and the Oxelos bobbed to the surface of her confused and clouded mind. *"O'er bonehollow and brill and slantyhill, Vomited bowel acid onto Dracon's fair moonrill."*

Am I being digested? she thought, sinking down, concealing her naked body in the opaque liquid.

"I'm going to be sick again," she told one of the sets of hands. Her voice sounded muffled. The air had suddenly condensed into millions and millions of cotton balls. It would feel glorious, if not for the throbbing pain. "Please, the chamber pot, I'm going to be sick."

The figure rushed away. It was indeed one of the Helwises, for she could hear its twitchy footsteps against the carpet.

A chamber pot was presented to her, and she filled it with another hot rush of acid, then sank back into the tub.

A wave of pain struck her again, and she grunted and moaned. She had the vague notion that if she produced the correct sound, it would harmonize with and alleviate the pain. The cold, smooth hands were clamped on her shoulders, fixing her in place. Massive as she had grown, her belly was the hump of a whale breaching the surf, the protruding bellybutton its spout. She laid her hands on the island of flesh and could feel, could see, it moving, undulating with a life of its own. Something was inside her—*oh, please, mercy*—kicking and clawing at her insides, pushing this way and that, mad to escape.

It's impossible, she thought. *I'm with child. Dear Mother, Merciful Mother, I'm with child, how could this be?*

A fresh wave of torment washed over her, drowned her, and she screamed out, and the Helwise's grip tightened on her shoulder. She could smell the thing's body odor—old cooking oil and sweat. Sweat... why would an automaton sweat?

The pain receded, but Constance felt that whatever it was inside of her had dropped down lower into her body, squeezing her in all manner of strange places, pressing out the contents of her bladder and rectum, which now bubbled up obscenely to the surface of the water. She had heard of such things happening during a birth, having been warned once in a conspiratorial whisper by the village midwife never to eat the day of a birth (as if the timing of the event were as predictable as the tolling of the temple bell), and Constance, in all her naïveté, had sworn to herself that the scene of her imaginary child's birth would be a pristine one.

But here it was, pushing down through her birth canal, this magical child.

"Push," the Helwise whispered in a resonant and serene voice, a voice like the plucking of harp strings.

The next wave of pain struck, and Constance, obeying the Helwise, as well as the dictates of her feminine instinct, pushed, fighting, straining to free this bulk of affliction caught inside her. She realized dimly, as the pain reached its peak, as she screamed out obscenities and squeezed Helwise's smooth, skinny arm so tightly that the porcelain surface cracked, that this was not a magical child, but some kind of imp, a demon that had fashioned itself from her clay, a fiend that intended to ruin her in order to live. It was splitting open her insides and would take with it her heart from her still-quivering, dying body.

The face of Thingkley flashed darkly in the back of her mind, and she screamed again with the effort to rid herself of the obstruction.

Then the babe freed itself from her vagina with a sucking sound, and a head bobbed to the surface of the water, Constance's belly deflating almost instantaneously.

It was not a demon that she saw but a child, a beautiful, screaming babe, purple and delicate and confused. Her heart aching with concern, she reached for it, but Helwise held her back, pinning her arms down.

Another Helwise, this one dressed identically, had appeared, wielding a kris, its wavy blade nicked and black with age.

"N-no!" she stammered, struggling against the Helwise positioned behind her, whose skinny arms possessed an uncanny, vise-like strength. At the sight of the knife, all doubts and fears about the nature of this child vanished. She only knew it was hers—and she would fight for and protect it at all costs.

The knife-wielding Helwise plunged a hand into the water, thrashed around, and fixed onto something, bringing it to the surface—the umbilical cord, Constance saw, gasping with relief. The babe was cut free with a flick of the kris, but the Helwise did not pluck it from the waters, struggling though it was, screaming for its mother.

"Air, air, it needs air!" Constance screamed as the placenta slid free of her body, bobbing to the surface, and as if in response to her pleas, the walls of the tower began to rumble and quake. The vanity was knocked over; the blurry painting of the girl with the sunflowers fell to the floor. The liquid, befouled with urine and blood and feces, bubbled and splashed and frothed, and the tub spread itself wide, opening up along its seams, like giant brass fingers uncoupling, revealing a tunnel of flesh beyond, folded and slick and pulsing, releasing an odor high and rank, making a horrific gurgling sound as the liquid began to rush out and down this fleshy tunnel, the child drifting towards the opposite end of the tub, arms wriggling.

"Stop it!" Constance screamed. "My baby! My baby! You monsters! Damn you!"

The Helwise behind her was clenching her shoulders impassively, while the one opposite her stood, a single drop of blood beading the tip of the kris.

"My child, Blessed Son, you're mine!" Constance shouted as she kicked out and tried to pincer the babe with her swollen knees, but its body was too slick, popping out between her legs and slipping down into the darkness. Then the brass fingers interdigitated, fitting neatly back together and leaving Constance sobbing in a shallow pool of filth.

The Smell of Blood

THE TWO HELWISES CLEANED her as Constance replayed in her mind the transformation of the bathtub into... well, she was unsure what it was she had just witnessed. Though the image was burned into her mind, she could make no sense of the event. The two maids worked in perfect silence, manipulating Constance's naked, limp body as if readying a corpse for the grave, and Constance stared at the inner seams of the tub, remembering how they had opened up and gulped down the baby.

Gulped it down into where? The walls of the manor? The *belly* of the manor?

The pain had left her feeling burned down, a walking, human-shaped cinder pile, disintegrating speck by speck. Questions ate at her, questions of this bizarre place she had stumbled upon, a cackling parade of questions, gleeful at the inscrutable shadows that concealed their answers and the fear and paranoia they stirred up inside her.

The desire, the necessity, to leave Erlwine Manor, the decision that she must accomplish this no matter what the cost, came upon her suddenly, as the Helwises lifted her from the tub and guided her towards the bed. The sacrificial dagger had been set back into the pocket of one of the

Helwises' aprons, where it lay awaiting the fulfillment of its purpose, awaiting the next drop of blood to taste.

Now that they have used my body to extract some sort of fairy child from my womb, are they cleansing me only to drive the blade through my heart? Or is there something even crueler planned? Constance wondered from the bed, as she watched the creatures going about their seemingly mundane chores.

"I want wine," she said to them, her voice was cold and demanding, almost defiant, daring them to deny her this kindness after what she had just been through. One automaton looked to the other, perhaps revealing a hierarchy among them.

The other Helwise nodded.

The more humble of the two crossed the room while the other turned back towards the wardrobe and selected a suitable nightgown for Constance. Absorbed with perusing the fine, shimmering fabric, it failed to notice the naked woman steal out of bed, dash on the balls of her feet towards the other end of the room, and slam from behind the Helwise who had just picked up the glass decanter.

The decanter dropped, rebounded off the table, and shattered, sending wine and glass spilling across the room, and the creature's arms pinwheeled as it fell forward face-first onto the crystal knob above one of the brass horns. There was a sickening wet crack, and the creature's willowy form went slack.

Constance glanced back towards the other one, who was staring at the scene with what seemed to be surprise, a frilly, pearl nightgown held in its delicate hands; then Constance looked down at the table and saw a pool of blood spreading outward.

Constance gasped. "Blood? But... but—"

The other lurched forward, dropping the nightgown. Constance lunged towards the door and tried the latch, but of course it was locked, and when she turned back towards the center of the room, the Helwise was upon her, its beautiful ceramic hands seizing her throat and strangling her with its preternatural strength, the blank mask cocked at an angle, completely silent.

Struggling for air, Constance attempted to wrench free from the hands, but the automaton stayed with her. She turned and slammed the thing up against the door, then into the writing desk, and when she lost her footing, the two of them spilled onto the floor in a tangle, but nothing she could do eased that terrible, draining pressure. Her vision began to grow fuzzy, her face livid, purple lips opening and closing uselessly. Before darkness settled over her, her hand felt something cold and solid on the wet carpet. Constance grabbed it and stabbed upward at the creature's head.

There was a juicy rip, and the Helwise's hands loosened at once, blood burbling down the front of its dress and apron and splashing onto Constance. Gasping for air with a rattling croak, Constance arched her back and turned onto her side, into the puddle of wine and broken glass. The Helwise, a long jag of crystal lancing up through the seam between its jaw and mask, fell forward onto the girl, and the two lay there for a few seconds before a blood-slick Constance slipped free and stood, still wheezing, surveying the mess with a dazed, disbelieving look.

"Blood," she whispered, looking down at her crimson-drenched body. "How?"

What brought her around was the voice emanating from one of the brass horns, muffled by the body of the Helwise slouching over it.

Mr. Smugrove. She could almost smell the peppermint on his breath.

"Helwise, is everything going smoothly there? I thought I heard a bit of a commotion, a bit of a hubbub, some most disturbing crashes and thuds. Has Mistress Constance delivered yet?"

Constance padded over, mindful of the glass shards and the squelching, wine-sodden rug, then leaned towards the horn, her heart pounding, ears pulsing and ringing. She bent down, inserting her head between the dead Helwise and the desk. She remembered the voice that had whispered to her during the birth and doing her best to imitate that cool, placid tone, cooed into the horn, "Yes."

There was a pause, then Smugrove said, "Very well. Have the Mistress's room spick-and-span for Dr. Daybleed; he's anxious to see to her and will arrive anon."

Constance swallowed. "Very well."

"And Helwise, something seems to be occluding the crystal, I do believe. Have that cleaned, if you would be so good."

She looked up at the lifeless creature, whose face had been impaled on the crystal knob above the horn into which she was speaking, blood oozing down its shaft.

CONSTANCE WIPED DOWN HER body, dressed hastily, and pilfered through Helwise's apron, finding in the pockets the skeleton key and knife. She unlocked the door and descended the tower stairs in darkness, dashed across the moonlit glass tunnel, and then paused in the dark, lavish hallway beyond. Though she'd come this way several times, she was still uncertain which path to take, which way led out of the immense labyrinth that was Erlwine Manor.

To escape, she needed a guide. It was the tale of "The Dromenon" all over again.

Along one side of the hall was a balustrade and a grand staircase curving down to a confusing intersection of hallways, which she knew now lay plunged in complete shadow. Pausing atop the stairs, she heard footsteps below and quickly ducked behind an arras, peeking out around the edge and watching for activity.

Before long, a glowing green mist appeared below, growing thicker and brighter by the second, pale as rotting flesh. It seeped out like smoke from an orifice on the top of Dr. Daybleed's ferent box, Constance saw, when that insectile man finally rounded one of the corners. As he started to mount the stairs, there came a susurrus at her ear, and she saw the shimmer of the floral butterfly's wings as it flittered off, but this time Constance was too quick for it. She shot out her hand and snatched it back to her before the creature could give her position away. In doing so she accidentally crushed the thing, for when she opened her hand, the creature was reduced to a wad of rumpled petals and nothing more.

She heard the footsteps pause at the top of the stairs, and Constance slid back from the edge of the arras deeper into the darkness. Her sudden movement must have stirred up a billow in the tapestry, for the phosphorescent gas seeped around the edges, and soon, like a snail's eyestalk, the ferent box appeared several feet from her head, puffing out that glowing smoke. Constance crept back farther, moving as silently and slowly as possible, till she reached the other end of the tapestry, and, pulling the kris from her pocket, she skulked back towards the doctor, who was crouched down at the base of the arras.

He was, she saw, as she drew near, examining the crumpled floral butterfly.

When Dr. Daybleed dropped the dead flower and arose, she moved in right behind him and slid the knife beneath his painted veil, pressing the blade against the floes of his scar-thick throat.

Pale green smoke still puffing out of one of its orifices, the ferent box emitted a burst of static, as if it were clearing its throat. "What is it that you want, Mistress Constance?"

"You're taking me out of this damnable place." Her nose wrinkled at the smell of formaldehyde.

"Ahh yes, I understand."

"Walk."

"As you wish."

It was difficult, given the disparity in their heights, to keep the knife held up to his throat, but with her free, bandaged hand, she pressed down on his shoulder, keeping him slightly stooped as they moved in tandem.

"Of what you said to me," she whispered as they descended the stairs, "how much of it was a lie? How much of it was truth?"

"Forgive me, Mistress Constance, but due to some idiosyncrasies of the ferent box's inner workings, there is frequent crosstalk between the sensorial inputs, and as a result the sound of your voice distorts the visual field, effectively blinding me when you speak."

"Answer the question. The Cinder. Begin with that."

Dr. Daybleed stumbled down a step but caught himself on the banister. Constance was quick to move the blade back into place. "Truly, Mistress Constance, it is like a smoke waterfall from a chemistry demonstration in my student days, the way your voice cascades and occludes everything."

"Speak, Bastard Son!" she hissed, pushing him onward.

"And the knife blade. It is difficult to speak with it pressed to my throat. I am a man of mercy, a healer. I am unarmed now, nor have I had the inclination to carry a firearm since my soldiering days."

Constance, ignoring his request, pressed the blade more firmly against the scarred flesh. "You lie. The box speaks for you. Now, tell me, the Cinder. Start with the Cinder—"

"Have you inspected your bandaged hand, Mistress Constance? That is to say, have you unwrapped it and examined the amputation sites?" As he spoke, his ferent box rose slightly, hovering around his waistline.

By that time, they had reached the bottom of the stairs, and Dr. Daybleed paused. "Walk," she said.

"Which way?"

"Lead us out of here."

"As you wish. Now, your hand, have you examined it?"

"No, I—"

"Well, perhaps you should," the box said, popping and crackling.

A drop of blood collected on one of the waves of the blade as she dug its edge deeper into the flabby, scarred flesh of his throat.

"Why? So you can get the better of me when I let my guard down?" Anonymous doorways slid past them as they moved, illuminated by the pale green gas, which seemed to touch and crawl along the floor and walls, feeling out the passage for them.

"I am a doctor, dedicated to the practice of saving lives, easing suffering; getting the upper hand with you is the furthest thing from my mind at this point, Mistress Constance." The ferent box inched higher, reaching his navel.

"Stop calling me that!"

"What? You mean 'Mistress Constance'? Does it bother you?"

"I don't understand any of this, don't understand you, what you've been doing to me, what you want from me, what this place is. And that child... where did it come from?"

"Please. I can and will explain everything to you. But first tell me how your hand feels."

"It pains me, Doctor, and yet ..."

"Perhaps it doesn't agonize you as much as it should, as the stumps of an amputation should agonize one the day following the procedure."

"No," she whispered. "No, it doesn't."

"And for good reason."

"Because of the Cinder?"

"Precisely, Mistress Constance. We did not stymie the spread in time, and your health is imperative to Count Erlwine. We must cut away more flesh. The entire hand must go. Every mistress that can be reused is precious—"

"Every mistress? What?"

"For the Count must continue to live, you see, and he needs you to do so."

"Then he's... a vampyr?"

The doctor's box chuckled a dry, burning-paper chuckle. "No, Mistress Constance, the master is not of the undead. Not ... exactly."

"And the Cinder... it *is* a curse."

"Yes, but forget that for now. Your hand should take precedence in your mind—your priorities have grown inverted in your excitement. I promise you that no harm will come to you.

"Now," he went on as they turned the corner and proceeded down another inscrutable hallway, "would it surprise you to know that I knew you were hiding behind that tapestry back near Sunflower Tower?"

"What?"

"The Count's servant tried to alert me, I saw, but you put a stop to that. Even so, I smelled it on you before I reached the top of the stairs."

"You smelled the flower?"

"Sadly no, for this tool has difficulty with most odors," he said, lifting the box even higher, so that it was just below her arm. "The ferent box's olfaction sensors are to a nose what a *La Bavure* painting is to a daguerreotype, but however granular and imprecise its functionality is, one scent always manages to shine through in its full robustness: blood. And you reek of it, Mistress Constance. I can smell it all over you, gumming up your hair, smeared all over your face and neck, trickling down between your legs and into your shoes. I gather that you learned some interesting facts about the Helwises, is that not so?"

In the green glow of the ferent box's smoke, she noticed on her left-hand side the entrance to the art gallery filled with all those duplicate paintings. Dr. Daybleed stopped again and breathed. Or the box breathed. Maybe Dr. Daybleed was actually inside the box. Maybe the appended device was this scarred body, and the box was him.

"Why did you take me here?" Constance asked, confused, and relaxed the knife with the intention of getting a better grip on the thing—but in that instant, a door slid open on the top of the ferent box and a tiny porcelain hand slithered out and jabbed a needle into her wrist.

Her vision swam, and she collapsed.

Thingkley's Plaything

S HE HEARD VOICES, MUFFLED and distant. Unable to move or speak or even think straight, her grogginess was like a prison, a claustrophobic cage into which she'd been stuffed.

Poison. A thick, sloppy thought sluicing down through her.

Her mind started to fade, the cage of grogginess shrinking around her, but then she heard a steady creaking sound, and all at once the walls of the cage, which might have crushed her to death, began to dissolve.

Her eyes fluttered open. At first it seemed too dim to see in here—wherever *here* was—but then a coffered ceiling unraveled before her eyes out of the darkness, the delicate filigreed design illuminated by the pale light of a candle several feet from her, a fragile thing half burned down.

She struggled to move but found her arms and legs bound, a strap pinning her down against a wooden surface so tightly she couldn't breathe except very shallow, unsatisfying breaths, nor could she wriggle her hands or feet without the ropes sawing her skin. As her eyes adjusted to the light, she saw heaped in the corner of the room a mound of mildewed clothing, mostly dresses and undergarments, which were piled up to the low ceiling. The moldy, peeling wallpaper encircling the room depicted characters from nursery rhymes—Egghead and Strawman and

Little Miss Rosebloom—soiled and nearly unrecognizable. There was a playhouse in the corner opposite the mound of clothes, with little stitch-eyed dolls peering out of the windows at Constance. Tops and trains and wooden blocks and farm animals lay scattered about on a low table beside the playhouse. Farther back from her, a neatly made child's bed was situated with a portrait of an effeminate young man hanging above it, done in the same blurry style that proliferated throughout the manor.

The voice came to her again: Dr. Daybleed's crackling parody of speech.

She craned her head back and saw upside down the doctor towering over Thingkley, who was seated on a rocking horse, creaking back and forth.

"...must see to the others," the doctor was saying. "Doubt this one will deliver willingly again without redoubling our efforts..." When he noticed Constance watching them, he straightened and said, "I regret, Mistress Constance, that I cannot stay for the procedure, but I have other matters to attend to at the present time. Besides, Thingkley here is most skilled with his hands and can care for your every need, perhaps even introduce you to some treatments that you may not have been aware that you required."

The rocking horse grew still.

"Lemme gah." Her words were inchoate—a child's first attempt to speak.

"Do not fret, Mistress, for I will return and check up on your progress. For now, I bid thee adieu." The doctor nodded curtly to her, the movement exaggerated by his lanky form. She saw that his throat had been bandaged, which gave her a confusing wash of pleasure at having harmed him and a twinge of regret at not having carried through with the deed.

He ducked out of the room through a small door, abandoning her to little Thingkley, who continued to rock on his horse, his beady eyes watching her from his protuberant moonscape head.

Her blood turning to ice, Constance cried out for the doctor to return, for Count Erlwine or Smugrove, and insensibly for her father or mother or Sheriff Sykes or anyone that could hear her cries. She continued for many minutes, her voice hoarsening, Thingkley watching her all the while, a figure of perversity rocking on his little wooden horse, wearing his little trousers and his little waistcoat, and finally Constance's voice petered out to a whimper. At last, Thingkley dismounted and waddled towards the sniffling woman and was soon standing at her side, rummaging in his jacket pocket.

Constance wanted to look away but could not. She had to see what strange manner of cruelty he would produce.

It turned out to be a wilted corsage—the butterfly she had crushed.

Her brow furrowed as he placed it to her nose, then grunted at her. Constance turned away, but his hand, much stronger than she would have guessed, gripped her forehead and forced her back towards him and stuffed the corsage against her nose. Again he grunted, and after futilely attempting to resist his grip, she inhaled it deeply, trembling. Under any other circumstance the odor might not have offended her, but now all she could think of was the scum left at the bottom of a flower vase after several weeks—and she snarled at him.

He cocked his head at this new expression from Constance and emitted a hiccuping rasp, novel life animating his bizarre face, the crinkling of his skin seeming to reveal an underlying ribcage of his skull. Then he smelled the corsage himself, deeply, sensually, his damp and beady eyes rolling back in their sockets.

He returned the flower to his pocket, then his hand reached in fits and starts towards her arm, and when it at last touched her, her entire body shuddered, goosebumps breaking out, as if to steel itself against a polar chill. He ran the leathery, warty pad of his hand over her bare arms, slowly, very slowly, up and down, up and down, long tufts of wart hair whispering against her skin, his eyes intent on the work, foam collecting at the corners of his mouth. Then, noticing the tears welling in her eyes, he pulled out a handkerchief and dabbed at them and grunted something unintelligible, whether well-meaning or disturbing Constance could not begin to say. Her face was a tragicomic mask, her power of speech caught in her throat like an accursed chanteuse robbed of her one true gift. Thingkley tucked the handkerchief back in his pocket and returned to her arms, then he seemed to lose control and pressed his proboscis-like nose into her armpit through the dark-red, rough linsey-woolsey of her dress. His body tensed, he nuzzled there, suffocating with pleasure, for an interminable, frozen minute, then wrenched himself free and staggered out of view, completely overcome and drunk on her scent.

The danger of her situation had blown away every trace of grogginess. She heard him waddling around the chamber and saw him at the play table, pushing the train back and forth on its squeaky wheels. It seemed to Constance as if he was in no rush. Perhaps he was enjoying drawing out this scene. She shook and kicked and railed against the bindings, the pinching and biting leather, her wrists and ankles wet with blood. They were not sloppily done; Constance was not the first one to be tied down to this table, a plaything offered to Thingkley. If only she could free up one limb, she could defend herself against him when he returned. Just one free hand, even the mutilated one would do.

From far off, she thought she also heard something rattling and clanging, as if a machine were grinding away within the walls of the great house. Oddly, it struck her as a familiar sound, but her frantic mind could not imagine anything beyond the confines of Thingkley's chamber, beyond what was to come.

Mr. Thingkley grunted and seemed to be speaking to himself, using the limited range of sounds he was capable of—guttural things, growls and yaps, like dogs fighting over an old cut of meat in the alley behind the butcher shop—managing a deranged conversation of sorts as he played an obscene game with his dolls and animals.

When he returned to her, he was holding a pair of embroidery scissors, the rings of which barely accommodated his knobby digits. He climbed onto a stool, and, still speaking to her with his stiff purple tongue, he worked at the hem of her dress and her drawers, cutting up the length of her body, making sure to catch her chemise too, and when at last he reached the neckline, he folded all the fabric carefully across her body, exposing her nakedness, her blood-smeared stomach, her baby-ready breasts.

He seemed lost in thought, staring down at the triangular mound of soft, brown hair, and in the ensuing quiet, Constance heard the clanging, louder now than before, and she suddenly felt a skin-crawling portent—*It must be some device Thingkley is having prepared for the next step in his little game. Maybe next to this nursery is a chamber of horrors full of all manner of torture devices.*

You miserable fucking blackguard! she wanted to scream at him, but she restrained herself. Angering the creature would accomplish nothing for her, not with her hands bound.

There must be another way.

The creature lowered himself between her legs and smelled deeply of her, just as he had done before with her armpit and the crumpled flower. She squirmed against the feel of his nose pressing into her crotch, tried to snap her trembling legs shut, but his grip was too strong, her legs too tightly bound. Then he stood up straight again, his eyes closed with a look of contentment, his nose glistening and slimy with blood and mucus.

"P-please," she said to him. It took a herculean effort on her part, but after she spoke, after the word hung there between the two of them, Thingkley, looming over her, acknowledged her with a shift of light in his black-glass eyes. "Please, Mr. Thuh-Thingkley. L-l-let me free. I just want to go home. I want my father. Please, please. Good Son. Good, Good Son, I beg you."

The crescent-moon face smiled at her, exposing behind the thin lips a row of canines that seemed ready to shear off more than just her clothes, drool collecting on the tips and dropping freely onto her naked skin, each drop a twinge of acid.

"Please, please. You can come with me. You... can live with us. Yes, that's right. You—you like how I smell? You like that? Every night I would let you... I-I would let you smell me in that way... just for saving me... for being a chevalier."

He grunted and brought up the scissors, spreading and closing the blades meaningfully, and he locked eyes with her and lowered them to her breast, positioning the metal around her nipple.

"No... please. Dear Mother... no."

A sudden knock resounded through the room, and the scissors fumbled out of Thingkley's hands. He turned his attention beyond her, towards the door of his nursery. Constance realized from the curious crinkling of the sides of his face that he was confused, surprised even. He barked out a curse at the door.

The knock repeated, more than a knock: a boom echoing through the room, jarring to Constance's nerves.

Mr. Thingkley stomped on the wooden table to which Constance was bound, spittle flying as he garbled out another curse—it was akin to watching a spoiled child throw a tantrum when the nanny interrupts their playtime.

Another boom.

The table shook this time, and bits of plaster rained down on them.

At last, Mr. Thingkley descended from the stool and waddled over, grumbling.

Constance craned her head and twisted her body as much as possible, ignoring the sting in her ankles and wrists, and watched as the little man unlatched the door and pulled it open.

He stood in the entrance, gazing up at the darkness beyond.

There was sudden movement, a *thunk*—and all was still.

She blinked, trying to make sense of what she had just seen, when she heard the fast dribble of blood on the carpet and noticed at last the wedge of axe blade jutting out of Thingkley's back. Then, with a wrenching sound, the axe was yanked free, blood splattering so far across the room that it speckled Constance's forehead and chest. Half of Thingkley's head and torso slid forward, while the half still holding the door open remained upright. For a brief instant, she viewed Mr. Thingkley in cross-section—the mass of gray sponge that was his brain, the Byzantine interlacing of nerves and vessels, the opened chambers of his heart and the thinness of his ribs—a medical-school curiosity, a study of a rare (possibly unique) specimen.

Then came a sound like the pouring out of a slop bucket as his entire body collapsed into the threshold, and something stirred in the darkness beyond the door, squeaking and shiny in the faint candlelight. Constance blanched at the sight, not knowing if she should be grateful or worried at the change of guard, for it was the grubby suit of armor that stomped and clanged across the chamber, bloodied axe dragging behind it.

For a long moment nothing happened. Bits of Mr. Thingkley's viscera continued to slide out of his split corpse, and Constance breathed shallowly, her heart racing.

Then, the armor continued its forward lurch, its hinges squealing, the clank of its sollerets muffled by the carpet. It came to her side and dropped the axe, unsheathed its rusty sword with some difficulty, and cast it over her body like a dowsing rod, passing over her belly, over her heart, her throat, and at last bringing it down to slice her right hand free of its binding with a few saws of the still-sharp blade. Next, it sliced through the one across her torso, and with these loosened, Constance twisted away from the knight and unbound her left hand, then sat up and undid her leg bindings as well.

She scrambled off the table, covering herself with the tattered clothes, a blood-stained and feral animal. The lopsided suit of armor secured its sword back in its sheath and stood there with one crushed gauntlet outstretched, palm up. No eyes gazed out at her from inside the misshapen helmet, but she could nevertheless feel the thing watching her.

"Thank you," she managed to say. Speech, she found, was difficult, her mouth's movements imprecise from the poison. "I am... indebted to you."

Her gratitude was met with silence. The suit of armor held its pose, and she was at first reminded of the statue of Duke Guillemet Cantone.

"What... do you want?" she said.

When this failed to elicit a response, she continued: "You saved me from something... too horrific to imagine." The image of the scissors snipping off her nipple flashed in her mind. She was screaming, blood spurting from the wound, and Thingkley's grotesque mouth suckled the bloody fount in a sanguineous parody of breastfeeding. She shook the image from her as she would a swarm of blue bottle flies from a festering wound.

Constance studied the suit of armor, perused every etched curve of plating, noted the clods of dirt sprouting little flowers, as if she were reading some dense poem, admiring the exquisite detail of the interlocking steel like carefully paired couplets.

Then she noticed beyond the knight, the corpse on the ground—Thingkley had changed. Though split in two and leaking fluids, his distinctive moon face was now... attractive, sensitive, unmistakably human, the once-truncated body longer now, better proportioned. The hands, their smooth, olive skin, they looked delicate, almost feminine. Her eyes found again the portrait hanging over the bed, Thingkley's portrait.

"What's happened to him?" she asked the apparition, not expecting an answer—and not receiving one.

She turned back to her savior, standing statue-still before her, arm outstretched.

Suddenly, the assemblage of armored plates groaned down to one knee, and Constance glanced around in confusion, at a loss as to what was happening. Then, all at once, the image sprang into her mind—the illustration from "Belalisa and Dracon" in the book she'd encountered in the library earlier today.

"You've been cursed." It was not a question. "So had he been," she added, turning back towards Mr. Thingkley's bifurcated corpse, its innards still steaming.

She turned back towards the armor—*Dracon*, she corrected herself. "You need my help, don't you? You need to be freed from the curse."

Silence.

She took a step towards the armor. Even her approach received no response, but she understood what she must do, how she must repay this knight for his service. She must complete the tableau, the illustration she'd seen in the book of the knight kneeling before his lady beneath the wisteria-framed bower. She placed her damaged hand in his battered gauntlet and allowed him to bring it to his faceplate—as if to his lips. A deep rumbling began in the floor and worked quickly up the walls of the windowless nursery, up through Constance's bones, her teeth rattling alarmingly. The toys on Mr. Thingkley's play table gyrated around and toppled over. A hot wind as glittery and scintillated as mote-filled sunshine surged through the room, transforming everything it touched. Weeds and flowers sprang from the carpet, the peeling wallpaper turned to wisteria, and the coffered ceiling was transformed into the thick branches of a massive oak. She could hear the chirping of crickets, could feel the cloying humidity spreading itself across her skin and the sunlight beating down on her hair, could smell the sun-baked soil beneath her feet. In large flakes the rust and dirt shook free from the armor, uncovering the dazzle of metal beneath, and all the dents popped back into shape, the twisted bits jerkily untwisting themselves. Then the shell of armor that was Dracon shuddered, a bright light blasting out between the chinks in the plate mail, neither bright nor hot, but a cool and creamy light that filled Constance with a sense of euphoria for the fleeting moment it surged over her.

It felt to her like gratitude.

The Next Mistress

I N THE DESK DRAWER from which Thingkley had retrieved his embroidery scissors, she gathered up enough pins to temporarily hold her clothes back in place. Her cloak she found bunched up atop the pile of clothing, and in an interior pocket (apparently overlooked by the doctor and Thingkley) was the skeleton key she had stolen from the Helwises. Beside the clothes pile was a mound of shoes, and here, too, she located her brogans.

Fully dressed, she stepped back through the "Belalisa and Dracon" tableau, which remained woven into the corner of Thingkley's nursery, a pocket of hot and fresh air, a grove of trees and blooming flowers extending into and beyond the walls. Tucked into the a hollow of a spade-leafed tree, Constance discovered a trunk full of knickknacks that Mr. Thingkley must have stolen from his other victims, and among them, on top of the pile in fact, were the knife and hatchet that had gone missing from her bag. She stuck both into her sash belt, then surveyed the room for ideas about her next step. She found an extra candle and added some more light, for the sunlight in the tableau did not illuminate beyond the limited bubble of magic. Atop his sewing desk, Thingkley had laid out a small meal with bread and cheese, cold bacon and an apple and a stein of beer. In the jacket slung over the back of the chair, she found matches and a holdout revolver, which she pocketed in her cloak.

She crammed the bread and cheese and chewy bacon into her mouth and guzzled the beer, spilling some onto her dress, and devoured the apple, core and all. Despite the discomfort in nearly every corner of her body, she was ravenous, and the beer was especially pleasing to her.

I could down a million more steins, she thought, *and curl up in the southern sunshine and sleep for an eon.*

As she ate, she noticed her left hand, whose wrap had been removed at some point after the doctor had poisoned her: the entire thing was gray and flaking. The nail of her thumb had fallen off and the others looked loose. The twinge in her right hand and her toes told her that the accursed disease had taken root elsewhere in her body. Her hair drooping down over her shoulders was predominantly gray.

Maybe amputation will help me. Or am I doomed? Damned? Cursed? Possessed?

Well, so be it, she thought.

Curiously, the disease did not bother her as much as it might have several days ago. Just as the disease muted the pain, maybe it also gnawed away at her instinct to live. In any case, she would only have witnessed so much of the disintegration of her body before it would steal her mind from her, and her memories, including the horrors that had befallen her in this Family-forsaken place.

So be it.

The Cinder would be a mercy, but before that happened, she had work to do—she had to purge this house of horrors, complete the work of her forebears, rid the world of the last vestiges of aristocracy, not to mention sorcery. Even more importantly, though, was the new, uncomfortable throbbing in her chest, which could not be denied.

Love for the child, her own babe. Imp or no, she had to find it before the disease took her mind. She needed to hold it and comfort it and find a home for it, someone to raise it. It must, at this very instant, be screaming for its mother, for Constance, to come and nurse it.

Her eyes strayed towards all those garments heaped in the corner of the room.

How many have come before me?

The doctor had said something curious before he had left—"See to the others", "Check on the others", or "Look after the others"—she could not recall the exact phrasing but understood that there were more "Mistresses" in the manor still living, more like her, and the urgency of what she must do struck her like a dousing of cold well water.

C ANDLE HELD BEFORE HER, she ducked out of Thingkley's room and found herself in a dank cave. The room she had just exited was in fact a small house constructed at the end of a wide tunnel with mildew growing along its interior in patterns like maps of the netherworld. She was careful to shield the candle flame, for there was a breeze coursing through this tunnel, a breeze which she used as a guide, moving with care across the jagged and slime-slick floors. All manner of pale, milky-eyed critters darted and hopped and slithered about her feet. Here and there were patches of a glowing blue fungus.

After many yards and turns, the passageway spilled out into a cavern whose size she could not judge with the beggarly light of the candle. Several steps in, the ground dropped off suddenly, her foot hanging above it, very near to carrying her down into nothingness. She backed away from the eroded cliff edge, breathing hard but managing to shield the candle flame from her ragged breath, nursing it back to life by clearing the puddle of wax. To her left, a precarious wooden walkway skirted around the wall. She crept along this creaking platform, every pop and groan of the rotting wood echoing in the void, and she paused several times, waiting for the echoes to die, to be sure that there was not something else moving out there in the darkness, piggybacking on the sound of her footfalls to mask its approach.

The platform began to climb, turning up and up, the decaying wooden stairs and posts infested with translucent, many-legged creatures that skittered away from the light, giving Constance a sense that the darkness was moving around her, shifting uncomfortably to accommodate her presence.

Up and up and up she climbed. Such a climb, there would have been no way Thingkley could have made it past the first landing. There must have been some other way, some path she missed, and yet she had seen no doors along the way, no intersections. She began to doubt if she were even heading back to the great house, but then the stairs terminated at the twentieth landing or so, and over the lip of the final step dangled a hand shining glossily in the candlelight. For over a minute, Constance watched it from below for any indication of life before satisfying herself that whatever it was attached to was dead.

The Helwise was lying in a twisted heap on the edge of the abyss, very near to slipping off into the darkness. Constance crouched down, turned the stiff form over, to find this one dressed in a bustle and a gorgeously elaborate blue dress—*as furbelowed as a wedding cake*—its blank mien cracked and leaking blood, and one of its legs missing. Hesitantly, her curiosity getting the better of her, Constance peeled off the wig and found beneath it a pale, scrofulous scalp and patchy gray hair enmeshed with panels of ceramic with clever little handles that could be opened to access the brain.

Shuddering, she recoiled, and in that instant one of the creature's hands flexed, snatching ahold of Constance's ankle.

Constance gasped, the influx of air extinguishing the candle flame.

Darkness flooded over them, and, as if crushed beneath its weight, she fell towards the cave wall, onto her rump, kicking herself free of the creature's grip. In doing so, the candle fell from her hands, clinking on the stone.

The Helwise's dress rustled in the darkness like an animal wriggling out of a leaf pile, its ceramic fingers scrabbling at Constance's legs; the thing seemed mad to latch onto her.

Constance slid back along the wall, then fell backwards onto more stairs, stone stairs.

She scrambled up them, bashing shins, banging her head and damaged hand. How many minutes she scrambled up through the dark passage she could not say, but when she stopped, she could still hear the swishing of the layers upon layers of the dress's fabric as the creature inched up after her, scratching its ceramic fingers along the wet stone.

She continued on as the stairs turned and spiraled up and up, completely blind, feeling along the narrow, tilted walls, so narrow she could not fully extend her arms without touching both sides.

The next time she stopped, all she could hear was the *plink plink plink* of dripping water. She climbed more slowly now, still hunched over, not trusting her balance, afraid she might tumble down the same way the automaton had.

Soon she was walking on smooth tile, and the air was cooler and drier, her footsteps echoing. She bumped into what she first took to be a wall, but later realized must be a column, a fluted one, and as she circled this column, she heard distant footsteps and the rustling of a skirt.

She froze, ears pricked, wondering if this were a phantom of her mind's creation or maybe another Helwise coming for her or—

There was a faint light in the distance, bobbing and dancing, and stirring up the shadows, which swayed to its rhythm. Though very dim, it was enough to illuminate her penumbrous surroundings, and all at once she realized she was in the front hall of the manor, the forest of bone-white columns she had passed through last night before meeting Smugrove.

Constance crept forward, pulling out Thingkley's pistol, and was overcome with a dizzying sense of déjà vu—Erlwine Manor seemed to breed déjà vu—for here she was again creeping through a dark forest, filled with dread, gun drawn, stalked by a nameless horror.

Maybe I should call out to them. Whoever they *are.*

She held her tongue and flitted from shadow to shadow, as the light floated parallel to her in the distance like a will-o'-the-wisp. Paired with the swishing of a skirt, the footsteps were undeniably feminine—light and quick—and sometimes they would hesitate and the lamp would rise up, then fall back down, or it would be obstructed by the person's body.

Then Constance noticed the warm firelight streaming out of a doorway, and the figure hastened towards it, giving her the briefest glimpse of a brown dress and dark hair before she disappeared into the room. Constance could not make out anything more of the lantern bearer, but because she was beginning to fathom the procession of events in Erlwine Manor, she could guess at the manner of person she was trailing—and where they were headed and what was in store for them.

Constance crept towards the doorway and paused right at the threshold, still occluded from view, waiting and listening.

She heard voices.

"Welcome, Fair Daughter. We have been expecting you." It was Smugrove. "A supper has been prepared at the master's behest. We hope you find it to your liking."

"How considerate of you," the woman said in a stuffy, fatigued, and vaguely familiar voice. "I cannot express my gratitude enough, but I will endeavor to make the attempt: Thank you, Kind Father."

"The pleasure is ours, most humbly, I do assure you."

"And just as I cannot hope to thank you enough, I must make repeated apology for my disheveled and sodden appearance and weakened state. I've been wandering for days on the road without provender or a bath, and I—" The woman caught her breath as Constance heard the sound of a service cart wheeling into the room. From the exaggerated shadows that writhed on the walls, Constance could recognize one of the poofy-coiffed silhouettes of a Helwise twitching towards the table. Then came the clatter of cutlery and dishes placed on the table, and the woman offered a gracious, but still uncertain, "thank you" as the cart was wheeled away.

"You were saying, Mistress," Smugrove nudged.

"Yes, regarding the atrocious state of my habiliments, I do apologize—"

"And for that there is no need to apologize, I assure you, I most sincerely do."

"But, Kind Father, there is a much more pressing matter that needs addressing this very moment before I break bread. First, I must alert you to a creature haunting the woods near this mansion. Myself, my pupil, and our driver were attacked on the road three days ago. I was seized by it but managed serendipitously to escape. However, when I returned to the scene of the attack, I could find no trace of my pupil, meaning she must have survived and has likely been wandering in the wilds ever since."

"I see, Mistress, most shocking, most shocking indeed."

"Mistress? You keep addressing me as such, and I must object, for I harbor no pretensions at being a mistress to you nor to anyone else. I assure you, Kind Father, I am nothing more than a humble governess, and it would be more befitting for you to address me as Ms. Jones or any of the Familial forms of address. The kind soul that brought me here has assured me that a search will be conducted for my pupil, a spirited and dear, dear girl, whom for all her quirks I have come to love and view as a bosom companion. Her name is Amity Lancaster."

The woman's words were like puppet strings, tugging Constance out of the shadows and into the light of the room, slowly, her gun raised. And before she knew what had happened she was standing in the middle of the dining room by the time Ms. Temperance Jones had finished her tale and Smugrove was in the process of insisting that she sate her hunger before worrying a minute more about the state of her dear, dear pupil, whom, he assured her, would be searched for and whisked back to Erlwine Manor with as much alacrity and celerity as possible.

But then Smugrove registered the look of horror that had suddenly come over Temperance's face, and his gaze followed hers to the other side of the table.

"Mis... tress Constance?" Smugrove stammered, as if he could not place her.

Constance glimpsed the gray-haired, bloody apparition staring back at her from the many reflective surfaces of the dining room, her roughly stitched-up dress, the blood-smeared arms and battered face, the chunks of gore that had somehow gotten tangled up in her stringy, befouled hair.

Of course, the governess looked no better. Her bonnet and shawl gone, her amber dress caked in mud, her lustrous bushel of black hair now a bird's nest of twigs and leaves. Still, by some miracle the woman showed no signs of the Cinder.

"Ms. Dunn? Ms. Constance Dunn! Dear Father, what's happened to you, child?"

Pistol trained on Mr. Smugrove, Constance glanced from him to Temperance and back, stumbling through an abridged retelling of what had befallen her. "I've been imprisoned here, they amputated my fingers... have used my body in unspeakable ways... this one and his ilk, all of them dark actors, dark hands in the dark arts... exploiters of the people... profaners of the Family."

Temperance's eyes narrowed with concern, her sooty, intelligent face turning back towards Smugrove, regarding him now with a pinched look of suspicion and shock and outrage. "Is what this young woman says true? Speak."

But Constance would not let him speak, interrupting the man as his wrinkled lips unstitched themselves to deliver their line. "And it's not only me they have violated and abused. There have been others, many more I suspect, and there will be more if we don't stop them. You apprehend, Ms. Jones, that you were next. You were next in line. This"—she gestured towards her blood-drenched appearance—"is what you were to become."

"Mistress Constance," Mr. Smugrove pronounced, summoning up a thespian-sized clutch of indignation, "I object most wholeheartedly, most wholeheartedly indeed, to these vile and besmirching traducements. Mistress Temperance," he pleaded to the new victim, his tone of voice shifting from outrage to concern, "you must hear, must attend to, both sides of this account."

"I told you not to call me that, sir." Her voice was ice.

"Ah, yes, I, erm, what our dear Mistress Constance—"

"Don't call my friend that either," she snapped.

"What this Fair Daughter is striving to communicate to you is true, but only partially so, yes, with only crumbs of truth scattered about in a confusing maze of deceptions." The prolix Mr. Smugrove twiddled his fingers as he fought to regain his footing. "For you can see for yourself that the poor darling creature has been afflicted with the Cinder and amputation was indeed required, but I'm afraid and most doleful, most saddened indeed, to report and relate to you that the disease must have... wormed its way beyond the body and into her brain."

"Enough!" Constance's scream rang out through the dining room, rattling the crystal chandelier and window panes and echoing in the great front hall. "I've been fed lies since the beginning, so many lies my head is still spinning with them, but I can guarantee he means you ill, means to hoodwink you and use you." She began to sidle forward, keeping in her sights the manservant, who was recoiling from her.

Temperance stood and coolly drew a gleaming derringer from her soiled, wilted flower of a sleeve. It was no doubt the same firearm that had so shocked Amity in her own story.

"The Nilwere," Constance continued. She was close to him now, only a few yards away, and he was turning away from her in fear, his left hand clawing behind him at a painting of the opulent interior of a train car. "It began with the Nilwere, Ms. Jones. I, too, was abducted by it, but I don't believe I was ever actually saved from it."

A gun appeared in Smugrove's right hand out of nowhere, a much heftier model than the mere token firearms the two ladies wielded. As soon as it appeared it had fired, striking glass and setting off a gorgeously musical chain reaction of shattering. Amidst this glockenspiel chorus the shot was echoed by two other, higher-pitched explosions. At the same time three clouds of acrid smoke billowed toward each other like a ghost party preparing for a quadrille.

Constance strode forward into the smoky confusion, drawing her hatchet and poising to strike the killing blow—but the manservant had vanished in the blinding burst of fire and smoke. Eyes stinging, she stared at the space before her in confusion, a creeping sensation spreading across her skin. A cold wind surged into the room, an invisible and idle finger swirling the smoke, playing still more of that curious music with the broken glass of the shattered window.

Constance turned toward Temperance. The governess, her face bloodless, trembled from the cold or the shock of what she had witnessed—or the small black hole in her throat where Smugrove's bullet had pierced her. Beyond her, the once-immaculate décor was spattered red from the explosive exit of the bullet. The woman listed sideways, dropping her derringer, and tried to catch hold of the table. Instead, she caught onto the tablecloth and dragged it down with her as she fell forward onto the tiled floor.

Dishes spilled, glasses overturned, candelabra toppled.

Constance rushed to her and knelt down beside her. Temperance's breathing was labored, coming in quick, little gasps, and she seemed to want to speak, but only blood bubbled onto her lips. When the fits of breath finally ceased, Constance kissed her forehead, then with a Cinder-flaking finger drew an invisible Circle of the Family where her lips had touched.

The crackle of flame recalled her from this ceremony: one of the toppled candelabra had set the tablecloth ablaze, recooking the meal prepared for tonight's new Mistress of Erlwine Manor.

Very well, she thought. *Let it all burn.*

Maybe it was in fact the Cinder mucking up her mind at this point, as Mr. Smugrove had suggested, even if he had intended a calumny. Maybe it was the Cinder making her think that the destruction of everything was necessary, was preferable, was good. In the end of *The Book of the Family*, the Mother had burned down the world in order to recreate a less sinful one, and the rebels of the People's Uprising had donned masks depicting her likeness as a symbol of that divine cataclysm. It was only fitting, then, that on the night Constance had become a mother, she would also become a destroyer.

She retrieved Temperance's gun, but its last bullet had been fired. Four shots remained in the one Constance had filched from Thingkley.

She turned to leave through the door Smugrove had led her through yesternight, when something checked her movement. She saw the splash of blood on the wall beside the painting before which the manservant had vanished and remembered the breakfast with Count Erlwine and their repose in the parlor afterwards—the Helwises, Smugrove, they had all passed through hidden swivel doors, hadn't they?

Perhaps that was how Mr. Smugrove had escaped so quickly. Yet she could make out no seams in the wall, no buttons, no pedals, no levers. Nothing to indicate a hidden passage.

She almost turned to leave again, when something curious happened. A single drop of blood, which had been hanging at the lip of the upper frame, broke free and coursed down the surface of the painting. Yet after a second, it vanished, and the surface of the painting shimmered and rippled. Constance stepped up and dabbed the spot where the bead of blood had disappeared—and her finger passed into the painting as if through the surface of a pool of water.

She pulled it back into the room, inspected it. The finger, one of the few still unafflicted, was intact and tingling. She tried again, dipping her entire hand inside. At first it felt as if her hand was passing through a pile of raked leaves, but then the leaves flitted away from her skin and she could see in the painting her hand suspended there in the train car right beside all the other smartly dressed passengers, seated, looking out windows or conversing with one another or reading penny sheets or novels. Constance kept pushing until her entire arm had entered the painting, where it felt curiously warm, befitting the summery scene.

Then she plunged inside.

La Bavure

THE TRAIN CAR ROCKED from side to side, a faint wind gusting through the open windows, disbursing the summer heat with pastel streaks. The central aisle was lushly carpeted, with face-to-face seats tasseled along their fringes and carved woodwork arching over each row. Though it was eerily quiet inside, after a moment she could discern the whisper of passengers, a bell faintly clanging, and the far-off chugging of the machine. Beyond the train car foreground, the countryside was a frozen smear of bright summer day, the clouds smudging a pale blue sky. At her feet she saw the drops of Smugrove's blood seeping into the texture of the carpet—not actual carpet, but canvas cleverly made up with paint. As she... flickered down the aisle, a blurry flipbook figure, she glanced at each of the passengers' faces, revolver in her right hand, hatchet in her belt. Up close, the well-dressed passengers, who from outside of the painting had looked very detailed, wore blurred mockeries of human visages, and while indistinct and indecipherable conversation flowed from their lips, they moved not an inch, nor did they cast their pigmented eyes askance to survey this new passenger blinking past them.

Halfway down the car, as she bypassed the vague cloud that from a distance was the ticket collector, she saw a bloody shoe print staining the carpet. Even farther down another shoe print indicated her prey's progress, leading to the car door at the end. Except it wasn't a door at all, but a painting with an identical frame to the one she had just now passed through. When she saw the scene framed within, several strands of the mysterious events over the past day began to come together.

Her body passed through—again, as if she were plunging into a pile of leaves, scratching her skin, rustling against her ears, and when the sensation abated she found herself standing in The Gallery.

It was dark, save for a wash of moonlight slanting through a distant chamber. She listened, scanning her surroundings, and heard far off the echoes of unsteady footfalls, labored breathing.

She turned back towards the painting and noticed the brass plate screwed to the frame, which read "Glass Dining Room" in cursive.

The painting itself was not identical to the one she had entered in the dining room but, rather, its inverse. Now that she noticed what to look for, she could see the minuscule window into the Glass Dining Room at the end of the train car, saw the tiny roaring flames within this frame as if she were watching a house burn from a distant mountainside. Then the flames crawled into the painting, indistinct in the appropriate *La Bavure* style. She took a step back, watching as the fire slowly consumed the car and its oblivious passengers absorbed with their quotidian activities.

She turned back to the hall and, lightly as she could step, approached the nearest room. Mid-stride, she swerved, changing route, as she spotted the black streak left by a blood-filled shoe. She reached the threshold to the next room and scrutinized the shadowy corners for the manservant, when a burst of light exploded behind her with the whoosh and crackle of flames. Startled, she whirled around. But it was not the explosion from a gun. Rather, black smoke was pouring from the train car painting, flames licking up the walls like hungry serpentine tongues.

"Mistress Constance!" a voice called out. "Prithee, do not dally; there are wonders yet to show you in Erlwine Manor."

Constance followed the sound of the voice and the trail of blood towards the threshold to another chamber, the orange glow behind her continuing to grow all the while. She crept along the wall, sidling towards the next entryway. The brass labels of the portraits shone in the growing firelight—Library, Dance Hall, Music Parlor—each painting a strand of silk spun out from this heart of the rambling, behemoth spider's web that was Erlwine Manor.

At the doorway she peeked into the next room, scanning every corner before entering, satisfied that the man was not poised to ambush her. As she followed his dragging footprints, she listened for the sound of footsteps or ragged breathing, but now she could hear nothing except for the flames as they ate indiscriminately of art and structure. The trail was fading, the blood fainter, thinner, more sporadic, and in the next chamber the firelight was so dim, she had trouble seeing anything at all. But at last she spied the last vestiges of crimson, a mere sprinkling of it leading up to one of the pictures on the far wall.

The label read, "Head Office."

No doubt he was planning some trick in there.

A bloody handprint told how the man had hoisted himself into the frame, passing into the scene of some anonymous lamplit street at gloaming, drizzle falling on a carriage as it rode up a cobblestone avenue. On a hilltop in the distance, a palace was ablaze with gaslight. As she climbed into the frame, the rustling brush of paper on her skin, another explosion came behind her, this one a gun.

She plunged forward into the painting, losing her grip on her pistol, which in the muted sound of the painted world seemed to have clattered down hundreds of feet away on the wet-looking, yet completely dry, stones of the street. As she reached for it, a searing pain shot up through her side. She screamed out, her voice distant, sliced up, but her clutching fingers pulled the papery pistol back into her grip, and she turned as the leering face of Smugrove loomed up into the frame she had just fallen through.

She fired and a black streak rifted out of the gun, connecting to the image of The Gallery, within which Smugrove's head vanished from view. Along this rift, the interior world of the painting was scorched and bubbled up, puffs of smoke like spilled gray paint bleeding out and discoloring the cobalt, misty rain that was suspended above Constance. She struggled to her feet and heaved herself back into The Gallery, where Smugrove was screaming and whirling, hands clutching his leaking face. He collided with the wall and rebounded off, smearing brain matter across the glossy white surface. A large flap of flesh and skull had gone missing from the back of his head. She fired at him again, missing twice, then pulled the hatchet from her belt, studying how he wheeled, anticipating where to strike. She strode forward and delivered the blow through his decrepit, bony hands and into his face.

The axe blade wedged in.

The once antic manservant swayed on his feet, calmed suddenly, as if she had just now administered a soporific and not a death blow. Then, his fingers detached and pattered to the floor with a stream of hot blood. He teetered and fell onto the blade with a sickening crack.

She noticed the man's revolver lying on the stone floor, plucked it up, wincing, and dropped it into her cloak pocket. Behind her, the painting of the city street was crackling with flames, and the light of the spreading fire from the far chambers now was glowing alarmingly hot on the threshold, thick black smoke swirling in along the ceiling like ink drops in a glass of water.

Groaning and favoring her wounded side, which was slick with blood and burned as if a firebrand had been inserted beneath her skin, she turned the curiously weightless man over with her foot, fixed her heel on his throat and began working the hatchet free from his face. As she did so, the process of decomposition and dehydration took place within the span of seconds, the skin marbling and turning blue, then gray. The eyes caved in as if the tiny hands of his homunculus yanked them into the man's skull, then moldered and dissolved. The lips thinned and cracked and blackened as they stretched back along the gum lines. At last, the remaining black leather of flesh pulled taut and split along the bone, growing dusty and flaky as ancient papyrus. The blade at last yanked free of his shriveled melon of a skull, nothing but a puff of dust bursting into the air.

S HE LOOTED FROM HIS withered body a set of keys, several hard peppermint candies (which sent a wash of nausea over her when she touched them), a flask of whisky, and what appeared to be a jeweler's eyepiece. She took a deep pull of the flask, eyes closed, listening to the roar and cracking of flames echoing through the hall. As for the mysterious eyepiece, when she placed it to her eye, the world shattered into millions of glinting slivers. She examined the opposite end, finding it to be convex and faceted.

"A kaleidoscope?" she murmured.

Leaving the candies behind, she stuffed everything else in her pockets and started to hobble back the way she had come, sweating from the waves of heat that wafted continually through the space, grunting from the effort of keeping her body functioning. She was heading back through The Gallery, looking for a piece of art that stirred recognition, when something stopped her in her tracks: a small, square landscape painting of a smooth sea with still, green waters blushed with rose, the sky the color of a light mushroom broth, a single schooner at rest in the distance, its sails slack. The vivid colors of the sea were what first attracted Constance's attention, but as she neared it, and the fires in the adjacent room flared up, the name leapt out at her: Shamrock Room.

She remembered the voice that had spoken to her at the library communication terminal: *"Be... calmed."*

Not "be calmed," she realized suddenly. Becalmed. A ship becalmed at sea. The Shamrock Sea.

It took several abortive attempts to hoist herself up into the frame, her side flaring up with each attempt, but at last she crawled through and stepped down onto the soft, crinkly water. On this side of the painting, her own pain was blessedly dulled, and she breathed a sigh of relief. In here, she could almost smell the brine in the air, could almost feel the water sloshing into her shoes.

But no. It's empty, she thought. *It's only my imagination.*

Yet when she looked down at her feet, which flickered over the surface of the water just as they had over the carpet in the train car, she could discern the gray sleekness of sharks below the surface. Despite the fires blazing behind her, the leaking gunshot wound, the uncertainty of what lay ahead, she felt this small, painted sea to be a perfect place. Serene and wondrous. She wished she could lie down on the water and gaze up at the gentle whorls of dun in the sky, but she trudged on over the surface of the water, like some phantom haunting the waves beneath which she had drowned, towards the schooner.

Then the frame appeared, pressing out of the hull of the ship, and with a pang of regret she slid one leg through the rustling threshold and stepped into Shamrock Room.

It took a moment for her eyes to adjust to the darkness. The embers of a fire glowed at the hearth in the corner, and nearby an old woman sat in a rolling chair, staring out at the rain-beaded panes of the diagonal muntin windows. Flies buzzed at Constance's ears, nipping her flesh and careening towards her eyes and mouth. A plate of cold, untouched food lay on a side table.

The woman did not notice when Constance crawled out of the painting and lowered herself with a stifled cry to the carpet, nor did she make any movement when Constance said, "Good Mother?"

With her lower right leg and left foot removed, the woman looked insubstantial, as if she were in the process of vanishing; Constance felt a pang in her heart, remembering how her own mother had looked in the uncannily real vision she had experienced during her sudden pregnancy. She approached and laid a blood-stained hand on the woman's bony shoulder—that was all there was on the right side of her body—and while it had been bandaged, the skin around the wrappings was already crinkled with Cinder. She leaned down and peered at the face, which was a landscape of wrinkles of a dusty gray, cracked and ancient as weathered stone. The woman's delicate retroussé nose was half rotted off, leaving a disturbing tunnel into her head, a convenient byway for the pestilent flies. Even through this diseased topography, Constance saw that the woman's features had once been fine—eyes of limpid, dreamy blue, a neck swan-like and elegant.

"Good Mother? If you can hear me, please give me some indication."

She waited. In the distance, a child cried, and the sound was a hand reaching into her chest and squeezing her heart, the same sound she had heard hours ago, the same she had heard yesternight.

"I've come to liberate you from this damnable house. Smugrove and Thingkley are dead—killed." Among the beldame's white frizz, she saw a few strands of fire, the color she had lost. "The place is burning as I speak, so we must be expeditious. Can you blink?"

The woman did—though full seconds passed in the process.

"Excellent. If you want to come with me, blink twice in succession."

The old woman did so, with a little more alacrity than before. Then her lips quivered minutely.

"What is it? Do you wish to speak?"

Breath passed over her lips. Constance knelt before her with another groan.

The woman attempted to speak again.

"It's okay," Constance said, stroking the woman's arm. "You can speak to me. I won't hurt you. I'm your friend. I have no tricks." The words felt strange coming out, covered as she was with the blood of so many others, like some abattoir dominatrix.

Her words, her kind smile, her soothing touch, they stirred a sound out of the wretched creature.

"C-C-C..." The stutter came in a series of disturbing inhalations.

"Yes?"

"Con... nie."

Constance's face turned from anxious to perplexed. She sat back on her haunches, wincing at the pain, studying the figure before her. Distant lightning crackled, illuminating her face, its purple hues smoothing over all the wrinkles and coloring her hair, returning to her the ghost of youth—no, not youth, but health. This was still a young woman, after all, a young woman horribly disfigured by disease and surgery.

"Amity?"

The decrepit girl repeated Constance's name, the flaking gray papier-mâché claw of her left hand stretching out towards her. Tears streamed down her grooved face—rain trickling over dried estuaries. Constance pressed Amity's hand to her breast, squeezing it reassuringly.

"It's going to be alright, Amity. I know something of the horrors you've been through, but our time is short. Erlwine Manor burns. We must flee now."

The mayor's daughter smiled her mischievous smile, flashing those vulpine teeth. She had not yet lost them. Another glare caught her face, wiping away the disease, but the source of this light came not from the window but the painting of the becalmed schooner. The sea was glazed over with slow-morphing flames drowning the waters in a slow tide.

"The... l-l-little one—it's him."

"You mean Thingkley?"

"S-s-sending... flames now. Instead of his h-horrible visage. The little one—he lives on th-the sh-sh-ship. He tr-traverses the waters. As if they were glass. As if they were grass, glass, as if they were as if they were—a-a-a-and he is secretly half bird. Have you not n-noticed his ibis-beak nose?" Amity was trembling, stammering out drivel, and Constance held her, stroked the brittle, wiry hair and wrinkled skin.

"No, Amity. Mr. Thingkley is dead. And we will die along with him if we don't leave this infernal place."

"Escape is i-i-impossible, impassable, improbable, unimaginable. They're all w-watching us, you see, you, you see, you see. The little one watches from the ship. It's not a painting, silly Connie. It's a world. Listen. Do you hear his music? It crackles like fire, which m-means he's angry at me." The more she spoke, the more fluent she grew, as if she were shaking off the ash that had settled over her mind and tongue. "The old one—he watches through the crystal eyes and listens through the brass ears—"

"What? The old one? You mean Smugrove?"

"Really, Ms. Constance Dunn! You must listen more carefully." A flash of the young woman's former self shone through, a brainsick version of Constance's old friend. "*Pennyroyal Peppermint never was a proper gent, nothing more than a ghost, a skeleton, a spectral host, a banshee phantom poltergeist, and aside from that not very nice,*" she listed in her singsong way with the three remaining fingers of her only hand. "Why, the old one is Erlwine Manor itself—with brass ears and crystal eyes and a rumbling tummy. It's a clock actually. We're inside one great clock and we are the hands, the many hands, of a complicated brand of time that mere mortals cannot comprehend and that's why they took my hand because I could only be one hand oh and I see you poor thing they have begun on you too, have begun to take it from you to turn you into a piece of the clockwork but never mind all that, Constance, you see I have a very important announcement to make, wouldn't you like to know what it is, I know you would, don't be coy, *Coy Little Connie stole a sweet from Mommy* ..."

But Constance had stopped listening.

"Crystal eyes," she repeated, recalling what Smugrove had said: "*Something's occluding the crystal; can't see anything.*"

Constance shook off Amity's hand as her old friend continued to improvise a new rhyme, then pushed the squeaky chair towards the room's communication terminal—the knot of metal veins with that shimmering convex crystal set in its heart. "The very same shape." She pulled the eyepiece out of her pocket and held it up to the growing firelight. "But concave."

She fitted the convex and concave pieces of crystal together—they locked in place as if magnetically attracted—then she peered into it.

The Book of the Family

Thick smoke spewed out of open doorways, clogging the passages with impenetrable, churning black walls. Her eyes and nose stung, and she was coughing and gasping from the exertion and pain in her side, but she rushed on, pushing Amity in the rolling chair.

Constance had in some curious way become twinned, split into a duality of the physical and mental. For while she seeped blood and sweat and grunted and panted, the vision she had seen in the crystal had not decayed from her mind but had frozen itself into her memory with a cool vividness that felt preternatural. It was like the projected image from one of the magic lantern shows she'd seen at the Lancaster household, everything lit intensely and perfectly, but on a much grander scale. She seemed to be holding Erlwine Manor in her hands, and it was a massive piece of fruit with its skin peeled back, so that she could see into every room at once, not simply from the top, but the sides and at angles as well—could descry the empty chambers dusty and webbed, could tease apart the burning skein of corridors, could enumerate the tiny amputated horrors laid out in their beds, which would make Amity seem whole by comparison, or those partly reassembled into the Helwises they were destined to become—but most of all she could see *them*.

Them.

Together. In the heart of the house.

And while the fires blazed and this piece of Constance's mind retreated into the vast maze, Amity served as her demented tour guide, her diminutive body rocking and jerking with the violent lurches of the chair, as the harried Constance rammed it up stairs and flung it around corners.

"Down that passage we have the Games Room. Have you paid it a visit yet, Connie? If you could make a quick stop I would be ever so appreciative, for I think it possible that I lost my hand there when we were having a try at skittles. It's probably sitting on the coffee table. Yes, I'm certain of it."

They transected the Music Parlor, where the Helwises, their frozen limbs gnarled and expressive in the climax of dance, watched the immense portrait of the picnic, in which the picnickers were now burning in a landscape of ash and ember and skies of glowing charcoal.

"What a marvelous work of art, don't you think, Constance? The Count showed it to me during a concert yesterday. Did you know that Count Erlwine plays? And not too terribly. I could have instructed him in sensitivity if not for my hand—which, by the way, you have yet to find for me—but in any case, sensitivity cannot really be taught, only admired. Don't you find it to be so? Especially when it comes to nocturnes, mastery of which I've always said requires three parts sensitivity and one part practice. You're taking me to him, are you not? As it should be. We'll be there in a trice, I believe, then I can share my news with the both of you. And what tremendous news, absolutely tremendous!"

They soon emerged into the hall of red tiles and gilded wainscoting, and here Constance's steps slowed, mindful of the echo they made, for the place was crammed full with a society of Helwises dressed in all manner of raiment—ball gowns and aprons, livery and pinafore—some among them aflame, casually, philosophically. They stood there motionless, directing their eyeless faces towards the double doors farther down the hall. Constance wheeled Amity through the throng of ceramic-limbed, swan-like women, careful not to brush against any of them, conscious of the way the chair squeaked in the silence. The smell of smoke and roasting flesh permeated the air.

As they reached the doors, the clock struck the Hour of the Father, the four knells of the bell resounding deeply in the hall.

She grabbed hold of the latch.

It was cold to the touch.

In the quiet of the hallway, the fire a distant roar, she could make out the sounds of the crying child that had haunted this manor since her arrival—or was it hers? Doubt flooded into her heart, weakened her resolve to face what she knew she must. A sudden urge came over her, compelling her to turn back, to dedicate herself to extinguishing the fire and restoring the great house to peace.

Surely it was not too late; surely with the help of all these Helwises, all these mannequin mistresses, they could save the place; and Constance could return to Sunflower Tower, to the embracing comfort of that immense bed; and in the morning she could breakfast with Count Erlwine, then spend the day in talk and play and lovemaking; and she could suckle the babe and rock it to sleep in her arms. With Thingkley and Smugrove dead, and Dr. Daybleed... well, she had not spied him through the crystal eye, but now that those other unsavory elements were removed from Erlwine Manor, it would be such a more palatable palace—the magical, enchanting dream castle of any girl with even the tiniest drop of romanticism burning in her veins: Hers and His Ever After.

And Theirs.

The shuffling, faceless army of brutalized girls too bewitched to act.

And Amity?

Constance looked down at her friend and was overcome with affection and pity for her. Her stomach curdled, the spell in her mind breaking with a decisive snap. Though the gabbling thing couldn't say how she had been followed by the Nilwere the night of the migrant massacre, how she had she fled the camp, been rescued like a fairy-tale princess, and brought here, Constance knew in her heart that, just as Temperance Jones had been meant to replace her, Constance Dunn had replaced Amity Lancaster. If she remained here, her destiny was to become another neglected Amity, withering in some remote cranny of the mansion like a vine in winter.

She shut her eyes, mind reeling so with the unreality of everything that she had to grip tightly to the rolling chair's push handles to prop her up.

"Dear Father, give me strength. Guide me out of these inhospitable woods."

Amity's deformed hand reached back and found hers, and she remembered the portentous dream she'd had during the ride to Erlwine Manor, the feel of their mutilated hands holding each other. "Constance, please, I won't tell you my news, so stop pestering me for it."

Constance plucked Smugrove's keyring from her pocket and tried several different keys till one responded with a satisfying *click*.

A N OPULENT BEDCHAMBER OCCUPIED the foreground, the picture of what Constance would have expected of a man of the Count's status—the mantle above a roaring hearth decorated with a rifle, mounted heads, and other barbaric tokens of the hunt; lush carpets spread in a pell-mell patchwork; wing-backed chairs arranged before the fire beside a tableful of glass decanters of liquids as alluring as melted gemstones; and of course the ironically extravagant four-poster bed for the gentleman who never sleeps—but beyond this scene of wealth and comfort, as if some leviathan had chomped down and ripped free the back of the room, a grand cavern towered up, composed not of stone, but rather of corded flesh and webs of bone and lianas of pulsing blood vessels tangled together in perfect symmetry.

Then, Constance noticed the child, her newborn grown into a toddler, who was held in the embrace of a branching, fleshy mass that protruded out of the floor on the other side of the hearth. The child was cradled in one of its boughs, cushioned by lumps of fatty tissue and suckling on one of many nippled tumors that beaded its surface. The wholesome sweetness of milk overpowered even the smell of the burning wood and another familiar and foul undertone.

Count Erlwine, who had been contemplating the hearth fire from the comfort of one of the chairs, turned towards the door to regard Constance and Amity with a mix of resignation and pride. He had in the time since they had made love in the garden maze metamorphosed into an ancient man, white-haired and shaggy and liver-spotted, flesh saggy and crinkled, his jowls drooping down over the collar of his shirt. She might not have recognized him had it not been for his outfit, that and the clear gray eyes unclouded by the advances of age, which still burned with as much passion for her as they had before.

"Do you see him, Constance?" Amity said, breaking the silence. "My baby. It's my child. I'm a mother. You're shocked speechless by my news, are you not?"

"No, Dear Mother," the Count said, rising from his chair with difficulty. "The babe is not yours, though your love for him shall be that of a grandame's. Indeed, your child stands here before you"—he laid a gnarled hand on his sunken chest—"on death's door, but I do forgive you your error, for we are but identical links in the endless chain."

Amity shook her head vehemently. "But I've dreamt of him. I've waited for this moment to hold him. Those devilish Helwises robbed me of the chance."

"The Helwises... yes." He turned towards Constance, and she saw now the firelight-tinted tears streaming down his wrinkled face; he seemed to be bleeding fire. "My faithful, loving servants. Though numerous, each one is dear to me, and for the death of each one I weep, I weep, Constance, for this sin you have committed against our family, our forebears. Is this how I'm repaid for my hospitality, for welcoming you into the great circle that is the Erlwine Family? I expected from you the meekness and gratitude of a daughter, the wisdom and the boundless love of a mother, not the impertinence and bloodlust of a son!" His voice rose to a yell, spittle flying from his slackening lips. The effort clearly pained him, for the anger recoiled back inside as soon as it had flashed its teeth. "I have saved many, known many, given the gift, the ultimate gift of motherhood to so very many. Life, love, family. What more could you have desired?"

He sighed. "You have only glimpsed a brief arc of the wondrous machinations of our achievements. Oh, that you could see more, live the cycle without being ground down beneath it. I have found that what had once struck me as perverse is in fact an encapsulation of beauty, of life itself, of meaning."

During this speech, Constance heard the rustling of wigs and skirts as the stoic Helwises filed calmly into the room behind them, like painted-in shadows or dim recollections of persons, and there they stood dumb and quiescent, basking in the presence of the Count.

"I have found little beauty in your house, Count Erlwine," Constance said, her voice cold.

He shook his head and stripped off his cloak, setting it on the chair by the fireplace. The cloak was wet—he'd been out riding in the rain, she realized. Of course. He rescued Temperance Jones from the storm. A busy, busy man.

"It is simply the price of great magic—a devising of my personal magician, Mr. Smugrove—"

"Now deceased."

"Now deceased," the Count echoed, licking his lips with an inarticulate tongue. "Yes, I felt his parting, our bond of blood. We fled to this bastion long before the People's Uprising, hundreds of years ago, at the first signs of the Cinder when it appeared in Abbey Creek, one of the hamlets in my demesne. Its first victim was my paramour, you see, a young woman named Helwise, a baker's daughter, whom I encountered one market day and soon had become my sole reason for visiting that town. I decided that in order to prevent infection, we would cut ourselves off from the outside world. Smugrove used my blood for the spell—they always require something unpleasant, these charms: blood, excised flesh. Even for something as harmless as a love potion." He smiled meaningfully at Constance.

Constance, who had slowly been stepping towards the little one, caught what the Count said and remembered Smugrove preparing their mushroom tea earlier that day. "You mean the mush? That was a potion?"

He nodded. "Made from the ground-up cinders of your fingers. The effects of one dose are not lasting, unfortunately. But by the second or third, love becomes unconditional. Behold the perfect devotion of the Helwises"—he made an expansive gesture to the hundred or so mistresses that had squeezed into the room—"all of the lovers and mothers that have survived. Bit by bit carved away, served their potions, until all that remained were the very cores of their being—the capacity for love and parturition. They've drunk the charmed liquid so many times, they have become utterly devoted to me, too devoted to consider fleeing. For it isn't every night I can bring a maid or two back to the manor. It is perhaps less desirable when the flesh is not genuine, but it is a matter of survival. Survival of both myself and Erlwine Manor."

Constance turned from him in disgust, and her eyes landed on the child. Despite the revolting cradle of pulsing flesh, her instinctual love won out, and she approached.

"But I get sidetracked," Count Erlwine said, oblivious to Constance's reaction, addressing himself at times to the fire, at times to Amity, at times to his mute mistresses. "The enchantment on this land was a different story—with a mix of my blood and the earth, Mr. Smugrove managed to fold all our lands into a self-contained knot. And yet it was too late; the disease had already found a foothold. We needed more drastic measures—immunity. Before we could attempt another spell, the majority of the servants were dead or infected, my mother, and finally even my wife, Lady Erlwine. Several days before her death, she confessed that the Cinder was in fact her own creation, a curse laid upon me and my demesne. You see, she had been following me when I set out on my amorous adventures with the baker's daughter and wanted to make both of us suffer for the humiliation we put her through, and to inflict such horror on us, she had sacrificed her sanity. Facing these dire circumstances, the four of us—myself, Smugrove, Dr. Daybleed, and my manservant Mr. Thingkley—devised the spell with a line from each of us, and a drop of blood drawn from a kris:

"As I was in youth,

Timeless as my trade,

Ne'er beyond death's door,

Born anew each day.

"You have seen the peculiar results of the spell. Thingkley shrank into a monstrosity of a child. Dr. Daybleed, meanwhile, became fused with the tools of his trade, creating the oddity that you have come to know. A most unfortunate metaphor for him to have chosen, we all agreed."

The Count rambled on, but Constance had stopped hearing his speech, watching the contented child suckle. His skin was so pink and healthy. Such a perfect, robust creation, the Father and Mother could not have done better Themselves.

"Smugrove, only a man of a strapping thirty years at the time, withered to the very threshold of death, and there the aging process froze. And as for me... well, you've seen for yourself. I think in my heart I wished for the return of Helwise and my wife and mother to my side—and those wishes became entangled in the magic like string into a loom. Over time the curses have bled into one another, bred together if you will, creating something truly wondrous to behold."

Careful to unclasp each pearl button, he removed his shirt, exposing his warty chest and sagging melting-wax flesh. "My wife, Lady Erlwine, was the first to carry my seed, though by that time she was completely mad and afflicted with the disease she had created. The irony, of course, is that our tinkering with this place and our lives, has created a permanent

Cinder—shifting across the countryside and reaching out to far-flung kingdoms as the bounds of my demesne shifted throughout the years. It pains me, what I've done, and yet I cannot stop. The drive to live is much more powerful than any sense of guilt or wrongdoing could ever be. It's so powerful, so inexorable, it continues even as flesh begins to rot.

"But now my time has come, and I must relinquish my place for the next Count Erlwine. Take care of him."

He removed his trousers, standing naked and shriveled before them, his body riddled with clusters of tumorous growths, then he hobbled towards the wall on his bowed legs, the massive growths of his thighs jiggling and knocking together. At the sight of their aged, naked babe, the Helwises surged forward to seize him, embrace him, perhaps smother him with love.

But they were too slow. The wall swallowed him up, opening like a wooden-toothed mouth and snatching him into the velvety darkness beyond. And the mindless creatures clawed at the wood, moaning and sighing and calling his name in their serene voices.

Entranced by the child, Constance only barely registered what had happened, only barely registered the throbbing pain in her side screaming for her attention, as if she were being swallowed up by the mystery of maternity. Their eyes, son's and mother's, met, and she reached out an ashen hand and felt the child's small, perfect hand squeeze hers.

The wet nurse monstrosity, which towered over Constance, released the child into her arms and sank into the floor where, once it had fully gone, the splayed wooden boards folded back together like a closing fist. The child buried its face into Constance's hair and whispered with surprising eloquence, "Mother," and her senses were filled with the wholesome scent of his clean skin and hair.

The wound in her side forgotten, Constance squeezed her son, eyes brimming with tears.

"My son, my son. Mother is here for you. Mother is here for her beautiful boy."

She kissed her child and cooed and sighed with the same melancholic contentment that the Helwises were emitting for their decrepit Count. A warmth washed through her body as intense and all-consuming as the raging flames of romantic love; it was the warmth of life and growth and belonging, of unconditional love and harmony, but edged also with fear, anxiety for the child's health, and also the acceptance of one's own death, of losing one's place in the world. Though Constance could not articulate the sensation well, it made her feel complete or cured of some former, unknown blindness, as if a new sensation had sprouted up amongst the rest, nudging aside her senses of touch and sight and smell.

She carried the child over to Amity and said, "Look, Amity. Meet your... your grandson. Right?" If Amity had come the day before her, then the Count Erlwine Constance had fallen in love with was in fact Amity's son... and yet they were all the same Count Erlwine—her mind was fuzzy from blood loss and trying to make sense of this whirlwind of life and death.

Amity shook her brittle head, her gray lips trembling. "No, no, no. He's my child. I remember him perfectly. Every hair on his perfect head. It's the very same child I gave birth to yesterday. Give him to me. Please, Connie. Don't deny a mother her child. Give him to me."

Constance backed away from the woman, her once-upon-a-time companion, the companion that had turned her back while her father, the mayor, had had his prurient way with her... She fought to control the complicated emotions surging through her. "We must leave here, Amity, before it's too late."

The sealed portal where Count Erlwine had vanished suddenly burst into flames, engulfing a large portion of the Helwises. Smoke was creeping in from the doors behind them, drifting up into the cavern ceiling. There was no time to argue about who was what to whom. They were a family now; that much was clear. Constance sat the child in Amity's lap, the latter filled with joy and even a little self-righteous triumph, then Constance wheeled them towards the edge of the room, past where the wooden floor and carpets ended and the taut bony flesh of the cavern began. Amity cooed at the child and giggled, holding him as tightly and protectively with her one good arm as Constance would have with her two.

She stopped at the cliff's edge, where a knobby spine descended through a ribbed tunnel, almost like a staircase, down into darkness, out of which the reek of death rose, thick, almost palpable. She recognized the stench, recognized the faint rattling that was reverberating up through the tunnel. She grabbed a gas lamp from Count Erlwine's bedside and hung it from one of the handles of the chair. Then, spotting the very same rifle the Count had used to bring down the Nilwere hanging over the fireplace, she pulled that down too. Slinging the leather strap over her shoulder, she returned to the chair, then tipping it back, she wheeled them down into the depths of the cavern.

Above, the inferno roared, casting its own light down through the spiraling passage, the stark shadows twisting and writhing and capering.

The stench grew worse by degrees, the rattling and clicking growing louder, and when at last they reached the bodies one hundred or so yards below, any doubts in Constance's mind about what she would find were washed away, for here the cloaca of Erlwine Manor excreted the many slimy corpses of Count Erlwine, where they bled together in massive heaps of rotting flesh. The light was so poor with this lamp, the conflagration not quite touching the darkness here, that only a couple of the hillocks of the dead stood out before their eyes. The bodies blended together, like pools of wax from separate candles, into the Nilweres that would reanimate at their proper time and search the countryside for the new loves of Count Erlwine—that is, for the child in Amity's lap. One such hillock was shifting, inching across the cavern floor, its many skulls, tiny by comparison, chomping and clacking their teeth in a furious locust-like buzz. She saw all those milky eyes staring at them out of the dark, pale as salamander eggs, and even now she felt their love for her, their putrefying yen—or imagined she did.

Behind them came the shuffle and clatter of footfalls of every type of shoe imaginable; a drove of bewigged and singed Helwises tottered out of the coiling intestinal tunnel they had descended, and soon were staggering towards the undulating, necrotic sea.

Constance unslung the rifle from her shoulder, stepped forward over the bony, flesh-webbed ground, and took aim. But before she could fire, a gun went off with a flash and puff of smoke, and Constance screamed in anguish, her own weapon falling from her hands. Groaning as she regained her footing, she saw with an admixture of horror and confusion a penny-sized hole in the side of her cloak, reached in, and clutched where the bullet had shredded her bicep.

What—

Eyes wide and darting with confusion, she turned and her gaze settled on the now-smoking revolver Constance had plucked from Smugrove's corpse. Her oldest friend in the world was clutching it in a ruined hand.

But how—why?

Amity must have filched it from her cloak when they had embraced. As if to vent Constance's shock at this betrayal, the child was sobbing, beside himself, face buried in his grandame's neck.

"They're all mine, silly Connie, you goose. My brood of beautiful children, and I will not permit you to harm a single hair on their perfect heads," Amity said. When she pulled the trigger again, Constance flinched, but the hollow click told them that she had already used up her one chance. Her deformed hand was shaking the revolver at the butcher's daughter. Beyond them a fire suddenly flared up, spewing out of the walls and raining down onto the corpses and their mindless lovers and mothers. A look of horror overtook Amity's ancient face, and she screamed, her shrill voice echoing throughout the dark. She pushed the child aside and fell out of the chair, onto the ground, then began to wriggle and claw her way towards the thousand corpses of Count Erlwine.

Memories began to flicker up in her mind as Constance watched, bewildered. The two girls sitting side by side at the piano in the sunlit parlor, impossibly bright, Amity manipulating Constance's uncoordinated fingers to play "The Son's Waltz." Then there was Amity standing up for Constance on a cold autumn morning when Jacob Downing had insulted her. They were beneath the cozy warmth of a counterpane the night before the Winter Solstice Party, whispering about their futures, how handsome and respected their husbands would be. "We'll marry brothers," Amity had said, teeth flashing with excitement, "and feast together every Houseday night."

The recollections flared and blackened and vanished as the deformed ghost of her friend was swallowed up by the writhing mountain of corpses.

Grunting, Constance raised the rifle, but try as she did, determined as she was, she could not bring herself to pull the trigger. Maybe it was the vestiges of the potion or maybe there was simply no point in the act, for the fire seemed content to do the deed itself.

So as not to disturb him, Constance stifled her grunts and pushed on, indefatigable and uncomplaining, wheeling the chair through the cavern and smiling down at the reposing child. He had grown much since the moment when she had found him in the Count's chamber. Whereas once it had graced his ankles, the hem of his nightgown now drew up past his thighs. As she admired the boy's long black hair and his perfectly formed legs and smooth skin, her heart leapt into her throat, overcome with a pride and love powerful enough and ravenous enough to consume her. He was the most flawless creature she had ever laid eyes on, and he was hers. She had done this, made this, contributed this piece of beauty to the world. This was worthy of praise and rejoicing.

At some point a change in the topography around them had begun to occur, and suddenly she was treading through the narrow tunnel of a proper cave, flesh having yielded to stone, and she began to question if she had not imagined that nightmarish cavern before with its dead bodies and mutilated women.

Then the tunnel ended.

And with it came a pale light.

The morning was dark and gray, and ash was raining down, fuzzing every surface with massive cinder flakes, making mock structures of nature. It brought to her mind the delicate mille-feuille from Beatrice's Pastries back in Canton. Constance cast her eyes about, searching for the house, but could see nothing in this ash fall, just layers of gray folding and unfolding into the distance, making shadow forms of every tree, every stone. The world was quiet and windless, with that muffled hush of the first snow, the soft blanketing of everything, nature saying, "shush."

She walked on as the day began to brighten, and mother and son had soon turned into ashen creatures.

Brogans crunching the cinder, her labored breath, the peaceful breathing of the child—aside from these peaceful sounds, one of the wheels squeaked plaintively, disturbing Constance's mind, reminding her that something was not quite settled here, that an unpleasant epilogue was still to come.

She wished it would not squeak so. She wished ash were not covering the world. She wished to experience a beautiful morning with her child.

Happily, happily, happily ...

She came to a stop, her blood- and ash-caked face streaked with sweat.

Aside from the light susurrus of the cinder settling over the world, she could just make out the gentle sound of water lapping against the lakeshore.

The manor has burned. The fuel of the Nilwere destroyed. This... this cinder storm, it is the curse burning away. We are safe. It is done.

And yet, try as she did to ignore it, she felt the growing numbness in her limbs, in her toes, and knew that her affliction stayed with her, despite the burning of the Nilwere nest. The pain of her wounds had not grown worse with exertion. It waned even now. And if she could clear away the ash from her vision and study her good hand or her toes or her hair, would she not find troubling signs? Would she not see the lost nails and the drapes of silver her umber hair had become?

She gripped the sweat-slick handles of the rolling chair and looked off towards the rosy pinprick of the sun that had appeared on the horizon like a seeping wound staining a bandage.

Constance sat down on a rock, crushing the castle of ash that had built up there, and watched the child as he dozed in the chair. She watched him and imagined their life together: she an eccentric cripple, he a handsome and kind boy utterly devoted to his mother. He would protect her from the cruelty she might face out in the world alone, for wherever they went she would be the equivalent of the Old Lady Yorin of the locale—or even her own mother—the Handless Beldame or some name much worse, much crueler. She imagined him a grown boy, strong like his father, striking down a gawker for his insolence, and she heard herself scolding him for his actions but all the while harboring a secret pride for his respect and love for his mother, his willingness to fight for her honor.

"What will I name you?" she asked him. "Litney Erlwine, after your father?" Constance stared at the falling ash. "No, something fresh," she decided, as if in defiance of the ruined world, the unnerving silence. "To break the cycle."

To break the cycle. The cycle. The cycle.

Many minutes passed and many possible futures were constructed and destroyed in her mind before the boy's eyes finally fluttered open. She could not be certain, watching him awaken, whether he had actually been asleep at all or whether he had been feigning, waiting for this moment to pretend to awaken. His yawn and morning stretch were lusty, his smile frumpy, but his eyes shone with perfect lucidity.

"Good morning, Mother."

"Good morning, Son."

"Why have we stopped?"

"Your mother is tired. Your mother is resting. Your mother is …" Constance trailed off, frozen for a half a minute or so, staring off into the distance, then her mind seemed to snap back into reality. "Did you sleep well?"

"Yes, but I had a strange and frightful dream."

"Tell me all about it. Tell Mother all about it." She could not stop saying the word *mother*. It felt so good and natural on her lips, and yet a part of her wanted it to stop, never wanted to hear the word again.

"There was a fantastic castle built over a cave full of monsters, monsters that spread disease across the land, but you saved me from them, you destroyed the monsters, you made the world safe again."

"I did not save you, child."

"Mother, are you crying?"

"No. No. I'm not crying. Mother isn't crying."

Stop saying "mother." Stop saying it.

There was a striking look of intelligence in the child's eyes as he scanned his surroundings more carefully. "I'm hungry, Mother. Won't you feed me?"

Constance rose to her feet.

"I have nothing for you, child. Not a drop."

She looked down at the ground, shaking her head, trying to weed out the thought that just sprouted up in her mind.

No, no, no, she thought. *Not this.*

The child caught the dark look in her eye. "Constance, don't." It was no longer a child's voice, but an eerie blend of the child's sweet alto with the resounding bass of yesterday's lover.

Yesterday. It was only yesterday.

Tears coursing down her gray face, she stifled the scream that wanted to escape. Instead, she stepped towards her son, pulling the knife from her belt.

Epilogue

Cinder Day

ON THE EVE OF Cinder Day, Constance trudged up the rocky acclivity of Castle Hill to the site of the cemetery, ambled along the rows of stone markers, reading each one, and left a bouquet of yellow and orange mums on her mother's grave. Despite her silver hair, she was still very much a young woman, lovely but somber in her puffy black dress and cloak.

As she recited the "Dear Mother," the first fat drops of rain fell. Her missing fingers had been throbbing all day, portending the storm that was now descending upon them. She paused to open her umbrella and pull her cloak tight against the blustery weather. Her prayer finished, she continued to walk along the stones to the very last two markers of that row, two graves—one named and empty, one unnamed and full—neatly complementing each other. At the first, Amity Lancaster's empty grave, she placed more flowers and said another prayer. At the last, the blank stone marking the body of the child she had wheeled into Canton the day the plague had been eradicated, she left a single flower, and stared down at it in silence for a long time.

At last, she made herself smile, insincere as it felt this time of year, and turned back towards Canton, pausing before descending, surveying the town, relishing the view, the look of the orange sunset clouds over the Fairwater River. After the ravages of the Cinder, Canton had recovered, growing by several hundred people—new neighborhoods (whose layouts Constance had yet to master) now occupied the old baseball fields, and the players had moved their operations across the bridge to what was now being called South Canton, where more and more shops and houses had been cropping up like rashes of dandelion.

She caught sight of a bone-pale form at the base of Castle Hill, and as she started her descent, she realized it was a person: Mrs. Yorin in the buff, her black arm with its prosthetic porcelain hand held towards the sky. She was shivering in the cold, her mouth frothing. Constance slipped out of her cloak and wrapped it around the old woman and held her close beneath the umbrella as she led her back into town.

By the time they reached Main Street, the road was already slick with mud, and the two made their way along the boardwalk. Constance had found that while Mrs. Yorin could not move of her own volition during her episodes, she could be guided to do so through speech and assistance, but their progress was slow, up and down stairs and over narrow planks as they passed in front of the knickknackatory and general store and barber shop. Every door they passed had been painted with slashes of fresh red paint, marking now, in a curious reversal from three years prior, how many souls still lived within.

When they at last reached the jailhouse, she found Deputy Kelly (the one-eyed exterminator who had fallen into Sheriff Sykes's good graces during the Cinder period) playing a game of patience at the desk with a deck of bent and frayed cards.

He rose unsteadily upon seeing Constance enter with Mrs. Yorin. The raven bone with which he had pierced his forehead glinted in the lamplight, a luck charm that had cost him a pretty penny from Charity Hobbs, but which had seen him safely through the plague time. "Evening, Mrs. Sykes."

"Evening, Deputy."

He hobbled over and opened the holding cell, and the two guided the old lady inside, and with some effort Constance laid her down on the cot.

"Damned toes are aching," Deputy Kelly remarked as he seated himself back at his desk.

"I imagine most everyone in town is suffering from similar complaints. I'll send Benjamin over with some eel and corn stew—I find that helps on these stormy days."

"Merciful Father, the butcher's daughter is in league with the fishmonger!"

She smiled conspiratorially. "Our little secret."

"Wouldn't dream of telling old Mayor Thurgood his Connie's gone over to the other side. Much obliged to you, Fair Daughter."

"Good evening to you, Wise Father."

He stood again and tipped his hat, and she urged him down. It pained Deputy Kelly to stand—but nevertheless, he always stood for Constance Sykes.

She continued down Main Street, now lit by gas lamps, and crossed a bridge of wooden planks beneath the pattering rain to Broad and finally home—a two-story house Sheriff Benjamin Sykes had built after the end of the Cinder outbreak, to offer as a betrothal gift to Constance. She had had doubts at first, for her father, the newly elected mayor of Canton following Increase Lancaster's execution, spent less time at the shop than before, but Benjamin fully supported her decision to continue to run the business, saying that as a bachelor who had lived his entire life in a room over the Fairwater Saloon, he could take care of most things himself. He wanted for company, was all, but only her company.

The man himself was seated at the kitchen table, reading the penny sheet and drinking fresh coffee, pipe in hand. In his mid-thirties, he was a good fifteen years older than Constance—but both of them looked many years older than they might have had the Cinder not struck. His face was careworn, hair a glossy silver he kept slicked back with a tin of Avalon Superior Hair Pomade that smelled of sandalwood and leather. Like most Cantonites who had lived through the Cinder, his fingers didn't add up to ten.

"Mrs. Yorin's in the jailhouse," Constance remarked. "I promised Pious you'd take some stew over for the two of them. I'll just warm it before you leave."

Benjamin grunted his approval, cleared his throat, and folded over the sheet. "Was over in South Canton today. Little dispute over some pigs."

"It wasn't that Pleasant Tremaine again—"

"The very same. A thousand vexations. At it with the Otterhams now. Anyhow, while I was over there sorting out the mess, I happened upon a huckster's cart. Strange fellow. Wore a veil painted to look like a face beneath the highest top hat you've ever come across—"

"Stovepipes they're calling them," Constance commented.

"Stovepipes it is, then. At any rate, he had this curious contraption attached to his hand, not quite sure how to describe it. A box, very clever looking. The box spoke for him, in fact. Sounded a bit like a phonograph. Never seen anything like it. Bought a couple items off him." He lowered the penny sheet, and she saw lying on the table a hand pale as ivory. "The fingers move, you see, though I'm not sure how; I certainly couldn't follow the highfalutin explanation of the salesman in question. Thought Mrs. Yorin's hand was one of a kind, but I suppose I'll be revising that notion. It would make a mighty fine present for your father on Cinder Day."

She picked up the hand and examined it. It was smooth as the ivory handle of Benjamin's revolver, the fingers hinged together to allow movement. Looking into the base, she saw what resembled the interior of a piano, strung with metal cords and intricate wooden flaps.

"Why, how thoughtful of you, Ben. We'll try it, but there's no telling with Father. I can't imagine he'll part with his hook very easily."

When she had returned to Canton and found her mother dead and father with his hand amputated, Constance had registered no surprise, as if she had foreseen this. During the days she had wandered Forest Road, her mind had plunged into a strange dream that she now only half-remembered. Something about... well, she could not quite put a finger on it: royalty and knights and magic. Childish nonsense. Schoolgirl fantasies. It was the Cinder working on her mind, playing its little antics with her. People speculated that the party of girls and Mr. Emmanuel Solemn had been attacked by a longclaw—one of the shaggy bears roaming the woods that normally left humans alone but now and again suffered a spell of madness and would kill everything in sight. Indeed, days after her return, the body of Mr. Solemn was discovered mutilated and headless in the forest. Count Lento Daring had hobbled back into Canton several days after Constance's return, a festering wound in his side that did not, thankfully, turn fatal, but which did lend further credence to the longclaw theory. No trace of the horse or rockaway carriage was ever found again. Or of Amity Lancaster and her governess. Had Faith or Abe Sallyforth still lived, they might have proposed a different theory.

Constance's father, Canton's favorite contrarian, thought otherwise, but, like Constance, he could not articulate his beliefs about what had happened to his daughter and the others. One day, a year after the Cinder had passed, Constance had brought him several sausage rolls and an apple for his dinner in the renovated Lancaster House (now the Canton Town Hall). He had been upstairs in the mayor's office, the long-ago bedroom of Amity Lancaster, a corner room that looked out onto Main Street and the town square.

As she was preparing to leave, he stopped her. "I never told you about your"—he waved his hook around—"your mother's passing."

"Father, please, you don't have to—"

"Nonsense, girl. I do indeed. It's been on my mind this past year. Now sit and listen to what I have to say." She did so and watched as he filled his pipe. Without involving the hook, he clamped his lips firmly around the bit, stuffed it with tobacco with his left hand, and lit it with a match struck off his boot heel. "The morning of the day she passed, I realized my hand was turning, and that if I didn't do something about it, my mind would turn too—same as it had with your mother. So I... handled the problem." Restless, he stood, turned, and walked to the leaded-glass window, gazing out towards the statue of Duke Guillemet Cantone. Constance studied his broad back and tall, slightly stooped figure, waiting for him to continue. Where Mayor Lancaster always appeared in a waistcoat and cravat, her father was wearing unassuming russet-colored trousers, black suspenders, and a white shirt, which, though clean, still retained the brownish stains of his profession, as if to remind all of Canton of his predecessor's execution.

"But it seemed I was too late," he continued, puffing out smoke, "that I hadn't caught the disease in time. You see, that evening, right before your mother breathed her last, I had a dream or vision of some kind. I was sitting at her bedside, and everything had just quieted down after the parade of them carting the mayor out to Castle Hill, when I heard the backstairs door open. I could tell from the sound who it was in an instant"—he snapped his fingers—"and then came footsteps up the stairs. You've got a determination in your step, Connie, everywhere you go. I warrant I could listen to ten thousand different people walking up the stairs and pick your footsteps out amongst the rest every time. Well anyway, next thing I knew, I heard you calling out for us, and there you were. A ghost, I thought. Your mother said the same words in fact. I didn't know what to make of it. You looked"—he hefted up his own belly, then spoke through his teeth around the bit of the pipe—"with child, you were so swollen up, and your hand was bandaged. I thought maybe I was glimpsing the future, like a fortune teller does, but more likely I had gone mad from the Cinder. I sat you down by your mother, you said your goodbyes, and then you vanished. It was like snuffing out a candle flame: one moment there, and the next, not. Not even a drift of smoke left behind."

Her father went quiet, turned back towards her, and resumed his seat behind his desk. He looked very old to her—his hair had gone completely white during the plague, and while he kept it short, it always managed to look disorderly. His appetite also was not as lusty as it once had been. They were both left-handed, so Thurgood had not needed to learn to cut with a new hand, but even so, the sound of him at work had changed: slower now, quieter, almost thoughtful. He didn't bicker amicably with the customers the way he once had; in fact, he hardly ever spoke at the shop. He stayed in the backroom all day and emerged for closing time. But two days every week, like today, he spent in the office of the mayor.

"The next day, when ash was raining from the sky, when you returned, you were missing those two fingers, the same ones that had been bandaged in my vision, and you had that child with you." That child, the nameless one, whom Constance had discovered with his throat cut. "And I remember what your mother had said to you, her last words, fearing that our grandchild would be stained with blood, as if her birthmark were prophetic somehow. At first, I thought what she said was non-sense—her mind was lost at that point—but then when you came home, I started to have doubts ...”

Constance reflexively splayed out her hand on the desk, the ring and little fingers gone. She looked down at her hand and said, “I remember. I dreamt the same thing. When I was wandering Forest Road, I mean. I dreamt I was with child and so much more than that, but I clearly remember at one point having returned to Canton and finding you and Mother.”

Thurgood reached across the desk and laid his large hand over hers. “When you returned, I began to doubt that it had been some aberration caused by the disease. The minutes you were here with us, you were as real as could be. I could feel your shoulder. I could smell your hair. I could hear you catching your breath. I could almost feel your heart pounding. I have no words for what happened that night. Maybe we both dreamed the same thing at the same time.” He smiled sadly at her.

In the ensuing silence, they could hear the clop of hooves and the squeak of wagon wheels in the street below. Finally, he seemed to blink away the sentimentality that had stolen over him. “Now get on back to the shop before you cost us a customer.”

“I GOT SOMETHING FOR you as well,” Benjamin said, pulling something from the pocket of his jacket and setting it down on the table. Though she did not remember perusing it three years ago, an unsettling wash of recognition came over her: *A History of Magical Curses: Case Studies and Theory* by Master Giles Cloth.

"The salesman was insistent about me taking this. I wasn't so sure at first. For one thing, I can't be sure if it's a banned book, but the man said it would be perfect for you... Constance?"

Her eyes wide, face drained of color, she teetered forward and caught herself on the edge of the table. Benjamin stood and rushed over to her and held her arms.

"What's happened? Connie? Are you well, darling?"

She shook her head, her hands finding their way into his. The touch of his hands on hers brought her back to the present, the fear vanishing.

"Nothing, Ben. I'm fine... really. Uh, thank you. It's a lovely gift. As ancient-looking as you." She smiled uncertainly, and though he laughed at the joke, the unease didn't leave his blue eyes.

BY THE TIME SHE fixed up a basket for Benjamin to bring to work, it was pouring rain. He gave her a peck on the lips, then the Sheriff in his derby and cloak stomped off, grumbling his pet phrase into the dark, "A thousand vexations." Constance prepared dough for the morning's biscuits, after which she would finish *The Trials of Rhea Swan,* the thickest of Eton Brimley's novels, or maybe dip into the book Benjamin had just—

Something slammed onto the floor in the parlor. Wiping her hands on her apron, she crossed into the next room and saw that the book had fallen off the side table. She bent over to pick it up. It had opened to

Chapter Twenty-Nine, whose pages, from the look of the binding, had been sewn into the text very recently.

The chapter was titled "The Nilwere."

She sat down in the rocking chair her husband had made for her, increased the aperture of the lamp, and began to read:

The thing in the woods found her—

She had only read those first seven words when the kitchen door creaked open, followed by heavy boots on the groaning wood floor. Water dripping from a wet cloak.

Benjamin must have forgotten something. His tobacco pouch, no doubt. The silly thing.

A gangly, dark form appeared at the parlor threshold and stopped there. Out of the corner of her eye, she could see there was something off about her husband's lanky shape; it was unbalanced somehow.

She turned—and froze.

A voice crackled out of the creature's ferent box. "Mistress Constance, I fear you may have forgotten us. There are, you see, interesting curses to be made of memories."

As he spoke, the densely packed words of the book swarmed over the page, crawling onto Constance's hands in thick streams and entwining her arms like fast-growing vines. She screamed and tried to shut the book, but some force held it open; the surge of language out of the page—it was like trying to shut a floodgate. They had bound her completely and were coiling up her neck and streaming into her ears and eyes, tiny skittering word-insects. She tumbled forward out of the chair, rolled over, and managed to fling the book from her, and it crashed in a billow of dust against the far wall, falling to the floor with a thud and shutting itself.

In an instant, the words had dissolved from her body and face—she was swatting the air at nothing—and the thin, towering apparition of

Dr. Daybleed no longer darkened the parlor entrance. The air in the room felt changed, brighter, warmer.

She eyed the book apprehensively, not daring to touch it or even approach it.

She waited until Cinder Day dawned, when the weather cleared, and patches of pale sky began to shine through the torn shroud of storm.

All around town, Cantonites were dipping their hands into the cold hearths and rubbing cinders over their faces and clothes, waiting for the Hour of the Daughter to strike, at which point they would flock to the town square to begin the celebration.

But not Constance.

She slipped out before the Sheriff returned home from the night shift, a hatchet stuck in her sash belt, a revolver in her pocket.

Holiday or no, there was still work to be done.

Acknowledgments

Thank you to Dongfang Boiteau and Andrew Cady for offering feedback on early versions of *The Nilwere*. Many thanks also are due to Susan Russell and Olivia Dean at Grendel Press for their assistance in bringing this book to full, breathing life, and to Reese Dallas Bice for the beautiful cover art.

About the Author

Tim Boiteau

Tim Boiteau is an award-winning writer of dark, mind-bending fiction. His short stories can be found in Daily Science Fiction, Deep Magic, and The Colored Lens, among other places. He lives in Michigan with his wife and son.